BLACK
NARCISSUS

BLACK NARCISSUS

A NOVEL

RUMER GODDEN

OPEN ROAD

INTEGRATED MEDIA

NEW YORK

Copyright © 1979 by Rumer Godden

"Black Narcissus" series artwork © 2020 FX. All Rights Reserved.

ISBN: 978-1-5040-6637-2

This edition published in 2020 by Open Road Integrated Media, Inc.
180 Maiden Lane
New York, NY 10038
www.openroadmedia.com

BLACK NARCISSUS

1

The Sisters left Darjeeling in the last week of October. They had come to settle in the General's Palace at Mopu, which was now to be known as the Convent of St Faith.

Last year it had been called St Saviour's School, but, when the Brotherhood left after only staying five months, it lapsed into the Palace again. The natives had never called it anything else; they had hardly noticed the Brothers except, when they met them out walking, to wonder how they grew such beards on their faces; their own chins were quite hairless, though they had long pigtails, and they thought the Brothers must be very senseless to grow hair down their fronts instead of down their backs where it was needed to shield them from the sun. There had been only two pupils in the school; one was the General's nephew and the other the son of his cook.

The General had sent two men to show the Sisters the way and Father Roberts had lent them his interpreter clerk. Father Roberts seemed very anxious about them altogether.

'What is he afraid of?' asked Sister Blanche. 'I think these hills are lovely.'

'He thinks we may be lonely.'

'Lonely! When we're all together? How could we be?' But outside the town, they did seem a very small cavalcade as they rode away to the hills.

They rode on Bhotiya ponies that were small and thick-set like barbs, and sat swaying in their saddles, their veils tucked under them. They looked very tall in their veils and topees, the animals very small, and the grooms laughed out loud and said: 'These are women like the snows, tall and white, overtopping everything.'

One man said: 'I think they're like a row of teeth. I can't see any difference between them and they'll eat into the countryside and want to know everything and alter everything. I was peon at the Baptist Mission and I know.'

'Oh no, they won't,' said a very young groom. 'I know all about them. These are real Jesus Christ ladies like the Convent ladies here. They only teach the women and children and that doesn't matter, does it?'

Sister Clodagh rode on in front with the clerk. It was easy to see that she had been on a horse before, and the others watched her enviously as she sat, upright and easy, bending her head to talk to the clerk, sometimes half turning round to see if they were all following. They rode one after the other along the path, but Sister Blanche's pony kept hurrying to push to the front and Sister Ruth screamed every time it came near her. She was terribly nervous; when her pony flicked an ear at a fly she thought it was going to bolt, and when it tucked its hoof up neatly over a stone, she cried out that it was going to kick; the grooms walked negligently along at the back, laughing and talking, their blankets over their shoulders. Hers was a bow-legged small man in a black fur hat, and when she called out to him he smiled at her, but stayed exactly where he was.

Behind the grooms were the porters, whom they had over-taken already, fifty or sixty of them, some carrying enormous loads; they were gradually left behind and the ponies and the laughing grooms went down and down, into the forest between the hills.

They spent the night in the Rest House at Goontu, a market village above the forest. There was a long market ground of beaten earth with booths standing empty for the next market day and hens like bantams wandering under their planked boards. The Rest House was a whitewashed bungalow with a red tin roof; as they came up to it, they heard the squawking of chickens being killed for their supper and the caretaker came up to salaam them with the chopper in his hand. There was a temple at Goontu and the bells rang persistently from sunset until the middle of the night; the clerk told the Sisters that they would hear them at Mopu.

'Are we nearly there then?' asked Sister Blanche.

'We have to go up there,' said the clerk, pointing to the hill that shut off the north sky above them, 'and down a little; up again, higher and higher, and then down, down, down.'

They stood in front of the Rest House, looking at the silent great hill they had to cross.

On the afternoon of the second day they rode through the last stretch of forest; they were aching and sore and stiff. All day they had been climbing up so steeply that they were slipping over their ponies' tails, or going down at such an angle that they could almost have fallen between their ears. Now Sister Blanche's pony walked in its place and the grooms had stopped their laughing; they hung on to the ponies' tails and had tied leaves round their foreheads to catch the sweat.

The nuns' heads nodded above the ponies, they rode in a shade of green dark sleep; the ponies' hooves sounded monotonously on the stones, their tails hung in the grooms' hands, too tired to twitch at the flies.

Then round the bend, almost on top of them, swept a party of horsemen; suddenly they were in a sea of manes and rearing heads and clatter and shouting; legs brushed theirs rudely and their ponies were buffeted and kicked. Sister Ruth screamed and a horse began a wild high-pitched neighing. At last the grooms separated the ponies and helped the nuns down from their saddles, and the pandemonium died down. Sister Ruth looked as if she might faint; she stared at the horses, her green eyes bright with fright, and her little groom stood beside her, patting his pony's neck, telling her not to be afraid. They all called reassuringly to her, but Sister Clodagh said briskly: 'Come along, Sister. It's over now. You weren't in any danger, you know; that pony's as steady as a donkey.'

'How she loves to exaggerate,' thought Sister Clodagh as she watched the horses, which were different from any she had seen. They had swept up the path, and now the men could not get them to stand; they had galloped up the hill and still they swung and dodged as they tried to hold them. They were only ponies like the Bhotiyas, white and nursery dappled, but their nostrils were wider, their necks thicker, their tails more sweepingly curved; they were eager and powerful as they moved. 'They are stallions, you see,' said the clerk. 'The General has sent them to welcome you.'

'They might have done it more tenderly,' said Sister Clodagh. She had been in front and met their full force.

'They did not mean to do it so fast,' said the clerk. 'These horses gallop uphill. They are saying,' he added ingratiatingly, 'the men are saying, that the Lady-Sahib sits her horse like a man.'

The General had sent tea and, as he knew very well how to please and excite Europeans, he had told his men to serve it in handleless wine cups made of soapstone.

Sister Ruth was positive they were jade. 'Mutton-fat jade,' she said. She always knew everything.

They sat on their saddles, which the men had taken off their ponies and put for them on the grass, drinking the General's tea and trying to eat his cakes, which were very elaborate and very dry. They were tired, and the shade of the forest was greener and more pleasant than anything their eyes had seen for months; and, because outside the weather was sunny, the hill butterflies with wings like sulphur were flying through the forest, and, where the yellow ones flew, the white ones followed. They seemed more beautiful than flowers to the nuns as they looked after them through the leaves; each sat with her thoughts round her like a cloak, and after a while no one spoke; they were too tired.

Sister Briony sat on her saddle with her knees apart, her elbows on her knees; she was eating a cake with her handkerchief spread on her chest to catch the crumbs. She wondered pleasantly about the baggage and the porters who had straggled in so late the night before, poor things, and about their new quarters, and particularly that Sister Clodagh had said that there were plenty of cupboards. Sister Briony had been châtelaine at many convents from Wanstead to Lahore, and she could have told you every detail of every cupboard in them and how many keys they each had.

One of the most important things in her life was her keys. Waking, her life was bound by them, and sleeping, her thoughts were dogged by them, and she had always the comfortable feeling of their weight by her side. She was never quite sure of them, though, and if you saw Sister Briony's lips silently moving while her fingers were busy at her girdle, you were never quite sure if she was saying her prayers or counting her keys.

She was glad she was going with Sister Clodagh, quite apart from the cupboards. 'If there's one person I do admire,' said Sister Briony often, 'it's Sister Clodagh. I have, really I have, a great admiration for her.' She was the oldest Sister, but Sister Clodagh had passed her long ago; she could remember the brilliant little Clodagh, who had come all the way from Ireland, in her last years at school.

Sister Blanche was talking again. She was a chatterbox and dimples chased round her mouth like the butterflies through the wood; she was still pretty, though her face was beginning to fade and she was not as plump as she had been, but the girls' name for her, Sister Honey, still suited her and they came to her like flies round a honey pot. Everyone was fond of sentimental Sister Honey.

'Why Sister Blanche?' Sister Clodagh had asked when she was given her list of names.

'Sister Honey?' said Mother Dorothea, the Mother Provincial. 'I think you'll need Sister Honey. She's popular. You'll need to be popular.'

Sister Clodagh said nothing to that, there was nothing to say, but she asked: 'Why Sister Ruth?'

No one wanted Sister Ruth. She was an uncomfortable person. She was young and oddly noticeable, with high cheekbones and a narrow forehead and eyes that were green and brilliant with lashes that were so light and fine that they hardly showed; they gave her a peculiarly intent look and her teeth stuck out a little which enhanced it. She had a way of talking that was quick and flickering, and she seemed to hang upon your words, waiting for the moment when she could interrupt and talk again herself. She had come to them with a reputation for cleverness, but in the Order they had many teachers, some of them with high qualifications like Sister Clodagh herself, and Sister Ruth found she was given only a junior teacher's work and she resented it.

'She's a problem,' said Reverend Mother. 'I'm afraid she'll be a problem for you. Of course, she hasn't been well, and I think in a cooler climate and with a smaller community she'll be better, especially as she'll have to take responsibility. That's what she needs. That's my chief reason for sending her. Give her responsibility, Sister, she badly wants importance.'

'That's what I feel too,' Sister Clodagh had answered. 'She always wants to be important and to make herself felt.' It seemed to her that there was an undesirable quality in Sister Ruth, something that showed in all her work, clever though it undeniably was. It was even in the dolls she had dressed for the Fête, that made the others look like clothes-pegs; she remembered the poise and smugness, the complete take-in of those dolls, and said: 'Is it a good thing to let her feel important? I feel she should learn . . .'

'She's more easily led than driven,' Reverend Mother cut her short. 'Be careful of her. Spare her some of your own importance—if you can.'

Sister Clodagh was startled. Reverend Mother was looking at her; her face was such a network of lines that it was hard to make out her expression, but for a moment Sister Clodagh thought that she was looking at her as if she were displeased with her and at the same time was sorry for her. *Sorry* for her.

Mother Dorothea was eighty-one and as dry and unexpected as snuff; her bones were small and exposed like a bat's, and she weighed no more than a child of ten, but there was no one in the Order more feared and respected. Sister

Clodagh had a tall and supple figure and her face was smooth and serene, with beautiful grey eyes. She had white hands and almond-shaped nails and a voice that was cold and sweet. She had just been made the youngest Sister Superior in the Order.

She asked: 'Mother, are you sorry that I've been appointed to take charge at St Faith's?'

Mother Dorothea laid a hideous old hand on her arm. 'Yes,' she said. 'I don't think you're ready for it and I think you'll be too lonely.'

'Why should I be lonely? It will be the same for me as for the others.'

'If I thought that, I shouldn't worry so much, but I'm afraid you won't let it be.'

'I don't understand.'

'What's good enough for us,' said Mother Dorothea, 'isn't quite good enough for you, is it?'

That was nasty. Mother Dorothea had said some very nasty things. 'Remember, a community isn't a class of girls. The Sisters won't be as easy to manage—nor to impress. If you want advice, and I hope you will want it—' 'Don't despise your Sisters. You're a little inclined to do that.' 'Remember the Superior of all is the servant of all.'

'You think I'm being nasty, don't you?' she said at the end. 'I wish it were any use. Well, you're going and that's a fact. Don't be afraid to say that you want to come back, and don't forget to enjoy yourself.'

That was an odd thing to say. She might have said almost anything else but that. They were going into the wilderness, to pioneer, to endure, to work; but surely not to enjoy themselves. She could not forget Mother Dorothea saying that.

Yet, now that they were close to it, she remembered again how much she had enjoyed that night she had spent in the

Palace at Mopu when she had come up to inspect it with Sister Laura a month ago. She had not forgotten it since. It was extraordinary how she had remembered it; the feeling of the house and the strange thoughts she had when the General's agent, Mr Dean, showed them over it. It had reminded her of Ireland. Why, when it was entirely different? Was it the unaccustomed greenness, or the stillness of the house after the wind outside? Now, in the forest, she had a longing to feel that wind again.

She began to tell the Sisters again about Mopu. She told them about the Palace, that was only a ramshackle house facing the Himalayas; it had come as a direct answer to their prayers, she said, an answer to their need. They all knew that their Order had no cool place to go to from the Plains; there was no room for them, as every hill station had its convent. '—and this isn't only fortunate for us. The people must need us here. There isn't a school or a hospital, not even a doctor nearer than Goontu.'

While she was speaking, it seemed to her that she was standing on the terrace at Mopu in the wind. She caught at that and dragged it in. 'Sister Laura isn't with us to-day, but she could tell you that, as we stood on the terrace and saw what you will presently see, we felt it was an inspiration to be there.'

Sister Briony and Sister Honey listened with even their breath following hers, but Sister Philippa smiled as if to herself, and Sister Ruth said: 'I wonder why the Brothers left so soon.'

'How lucky we are,' said Sister Honey, 'to be going to such a beautiful place.'

'But I should like to know,' said Sister Ruth, 'why the Brothers went away so soon.'

Sister Clodagh frowned. She had asked Mr Dean that question herself and he had looked at her as if he were going to tell
her, and then shrugged his shoulders and said: 'The school
wasn't a success.'

'No? They have a very great reputation for their teaching.'

He had not answered that, but he turned to her and said:
'It's an impossible place to put a nunnery.'

She said blandly, purposely not drawing him out: 'Difficult, but surely not impossible. Nothing is impossible.' She
tried not to remember what he had said to that.

She told herself that it was because he did not want them
there. That was true. She had felt it while he was showing them
over the house and garden; apart from his rudeness, he was
hostile as soon as they came inside the grounds, he and the old
caretaker, Angu Ayah. Usually Sister Clodagh did not notice
servants very much, but that old woman had made an impression like an impact on her.

She picked up one of the wine-cups from the tray. It was
cold and thick and grey-green between her fingers. It had a
rancid smell that they had noticed as they drank the tea, but
she liked its shape and, in spite of its smell and coldness, she
liked to hold it in her hand.

She looked at the men sitting and gossiping. One of them
had taken off his crown of leaves and stuck a twig of them
behind his ear; the green brought out the colour of his cheek
and it looked as if it would be warm to touch. How often had
she touched Con's cheek and found it smooth and warm; like
the feel of his fingers. His fingers used to play with her hair
behind her ear. 'Your hair's like honey and satin, Clo. Don't
you ever cut it off.' She shut her eyes. The knuckles of the hand
that held the cup were stretched and white.

All last night at Goontu she had lain awake thinking that

they should not have come. She should not have let them come. She had been sent to report on the house and advise on her Order's accepting or refusing the General's offer, and last night she had tossed and turned on the Rest House bed, thinking she had not reported quite truthfully. That uneasy conviction was with her still. Was it a conviction or only a dream? She did not want to answer that question and now Sister Ruth had asked: 'Why did the Brothers leave so soon?'

The young groom stood up stretching and, taking out his leaves, he shook them carefully and gave them to Sister Philippa. They had rough white flowers on them like daphne; Sister Philippa was so surprised that she blushed.

Sister Clodagh put the cup down on the tray and rose, brushing her habit. 'Now how did he know that you are the garden Sister?' she said.

The path led out from the forest and young plantations on to the bare hill where the light dazzled their eyes. They saw the great slope of hill and the valley and hills rising across the gulf to the clouds; then they saw what they had missed at first, because they had not looked as high. Across the north the Himalayas were showing with the peak Kanchenjunga straight before them. They recognized Kanchenjunga but no one remarked on it; but as they stared, they and the hill they stood on seemed to dwindle.

The wind blew, the ponies shifted; a groom blew his nose on his fingers, and still these strange white women sat staring at the snows.

'Kanchenjunga reminds me,' said Sister Philippa, 'of the Chinese house god that always sits in front of the door.' As she said it she looked over her shoulder. The others followed her gaze, and moving together, reined their ponies back on the path.

Under a deodar tree, solitary among the saplings, a man sat on the ground on a red deerskin spotted with white. The colour of the skin and his hands and face and clothes blended with the colour and twistings of the roots of the tree, so that it was easy to see why they had not noticed him before. By his robe and the wooden beads round his neck, they knew he was a Holy Man, a Sunnyasi; there, at the foot of the tree, was the platform of whitewashed earth and string of marigolds that marked his shrine. Among the roots was his bowl of polished wood and his staff, and against the tree leant a hut. He sat cross-legged and took as little notice of them as if they were flies; his head did not move, nor his eyes. In the teeth of the wind he seemed to have on nothing but his cloth robe, his arms and chest were bare and his head was shaved.

Sister Philippa's voice seemed to ring on the air, and the clatter of the ponies' hooves and the creaking of their saddles. They felt curiously abashed and silently followed one another down the path.

2

It was the General's father, the late General Ranajit Rai, who had first made his estate at Mopu. He was the sixth son of the second son of the Governing House; but he had quarrelled with his second cousin, the Prime Minister of the State, and with his wife's elder brother, the Commander-in-Chief, so that the wiser members of his family had nothing to do with him. He found himself lonely, with nothing to do, and he crossed the Range into India to spend the season in Darjeeling. He found that so pleasant that he said he would never go back to the State.

The General Ranajit was given to whims which he called Good Ideas, and suddenly he asked the Government of India if he might lease from them the tract of land which lay beside the frontier, on the slope of hill facing the Range; a sweep of hill from the forest to the River, and the valley in the River basin, and the forest rising on the further bank to the Range. Government wished to compliment the State and also to occupy the General, who was becoming a problem in official circles; they leased him the land, with the clause 'for experimental development' tactfully inserted.

The General liked to make experiments, and he built himself a house, a country palace, on the wild hill a mile above the River facing the greater peaks of the Range. 'It will have the finest view in India,' he cried.

'But who will live in it? And who will pay for it?' asked his aide-de-camp, who was also his Financial Secretary.

It certainly was very expensive. 'But we needn't *live* in it,' said the General, and built himself a modest cottage on the hill above it, round the bluff and out of the wind. It was a cottage of ten or twelve rooms, with ornamental balconies and a fountain in the garden. That had to be carried from Darjeeling; it took the porters eight days to bring it on the route that usually took two, but it was worth it, for the people came for miles to look at it. It was better than going to the Fair at Goontu.

The General called the little house 'Canna Villa' after the manner of houses in Darjeeling, and he dropped into the habit of staying there for three or four days, even a week at a time. He had been known to stay a fortnight and, to make it more pleasant, he had the Good Idea of installing his wife and ladies in the Palace just down the hill. It was pleasant to have the ladies at Mopu, it was convenient and sensible, for there he had leisure to attend to them; soon he left them there altogether and rode out from Darjeeling now and again to see them. It was a good Good Idea, and he felt that his Financial Secretary, who was also his aide-de-camp, should have been very pleased with him for the economical use he had put the Palace to.

'Think of the money we've saved,' he said, 'keeping them all out at Mopu, instead of here in Darjeeling.'

'It was certainly very expensive to have so many ladies here,' agreed the Secretary. 'And sometimes it was rather difficult,' he added. He was also Political Secretary, and lately he had often asked the General: 'Do you have to take them *all* about with you everywhere?'

'All? What do you mean "all"? There are not so very many of them,' said the General indignantly.

'Government doesn't quite understand—' began the Secretary gently.

'Why *not*?' The General had a violent temper, and the Secretary, who was also the Surgeon Adviser, had to beg him to calm himself; too many ladies and too many experiments had played havoc with the General's health. It was a Good Idea to keep the ladies at Mopu.

The people called the Palace 'the House of Women' in those days. They could see lights shining there to all hours of the night, and hear the music; since the General's wife died there was no order kept in it. Picnic parties came down to the River, with carrying chairs and ponies; the ladies wore fine gauzes and had coloured umbrellas; the shrieking and laughing went on until the sun went down and they went back to the Palace up the hill. The people did not think much of them, but it was nothing to do with them.

Soon the General died and was succeeded by his son, the present General Toda Rai. General Ranajit had not liked his son Toda. To begin with, he looked like a coolie; of pure Rajput descent, or so they had always been led to suppose, Toda had the squat figure and slit eyes of a Mongol, and how that happened no one knew, for his mother at any rate was above suspicion. If it had been his father now . . . He had grown to be a model young man, in whom his father's Good Ideas came out in such model things as Progress, Welfare and Improvements. He had served to some purpose in the State Army, was popular with his relations, and had prudently married the wife that the richest of them had nominated. By the time he inherited his father's rather vague estates, he had a considerable one of his own.

But he was far from being self-satisfied; always at the back of his mind he knew that his father, the dashing impetuous scornful Ranajit Rai, had thought him undersized, ugly and dull; that had kept him human and a little wistful in the midst of his success.

Now he was elderly and very rich, very cautious and filled with an intense desire to benefit others. He was at the honourable end of his career in the State, and he decided to retire to Mopu and develop the land and help the people of the valley and the hills.

He found that they helped him immensely. They helped to make Mopu a profitable and prosperous estate; a tea garden was opened on the land between the Palace and the River, and where it was too low for tea to grow, they made him an orange grove, and where it was too high and windy above the Palace, they planted him a nursery of valuable coniferous trees. They gave him cheap and plentiful labour and continued to live their lives as before.

A village grew up around Canna Villa, and now there were enough people to have a market of their own there, instead of going up to Goontu. 'If there was no market,' they said, 'think of the way the General would have to send for his vegetables and fruit!' Everything was peaceful and well arranged; they assured him he had only to smile and grow rich.

These people were not exactly of the State, nor exactly of India; they were free; they lived on the General's estate, but they were not exactly his. They had no laws, and life happened to them with extreme cheerfulness and often with extreme cruelty. The people of the heights were the equal of the people of the valley, and the people of the valley of those of the heights, just as a yak and a pony might look each other in the face and still be different.

On the bony slopes of the Range, the wind blows down the passes, cold with ice and show; there is often a day's march between the villages where the roofs are fastened down with boulders to keep them from the wind. The goats and the ponies and the people are thick-set and solid, built low to stand against it; they are solitary and silent, and they have names like the mountains of their Range; Lashar, Kabru, Kabur, Maku and Kanchenjunga. In the valley, the natives plant their rice and gather their fruit and crops, and fish a little in the River and get drunk at weddings on their own rice beer. They came up from the valley to work for the General; a few came down from the villages below the Range and, once again, they all assured him that he had only to smile and grow rich.

He could not even govern them. They settled their own quarrels with their own blows, and there was no stealing, because the people of the valley had everything and the people of the heights had nothing, and they never mixed; there was no lying, because it was foolish to lie when everything was known to everyone, and there was no pride and no fear. He could not even protect them, because there was nothing to protect them from, except a few leopard and bear in the foot-hills, and these they managed quite nicely for themselves, with their slings and stones and bows and arrows.

'I must do *something* for them,' he said to his English agent, Mr Dean. Then his eye fell on the Palace.

He often lived in Canna Villa, but he would not have stayed a night in the Palace; he did not like it at all, though he was careful to respect it. He considered it a disgrace and yet, in a perverse way, he admired it; it held all the family shame and, mysteriously, some of the family glory as well.

He had turned out the women at once; after all, they had
been behaving badly in a most unbridled way and abandoned
all attempt at being good, even in their fashion. He could send
them away, but he could not wipe them out. Sometimes it
seemed to him that the house had a bad wild life of its own;
the impression of its evil lingered, in its name, in its atmosphere, and, worst of all, in his sister Srimati.

She had been brought up there by Angu Ayah, in the
atmosphere of the House of Women. She was graceless and
beautiful, a gazelle of a girl with great soft eyes, and her father
prudently married her off while she was still very young;
but she never forgot what she had seen and learnt as a child.
When finally her husband had disowned her and she was not
allowed into the State, the good young General Toda Rai had
still countenanced her and let her live in the Palace with her
children until she died. He thought, now, that that had been a
mistake; the house seemed to bring out the worst in her and
she had half killed herself before he persuaded her to leave
it. He had paid for the trip to Europe in an effort to cure her
when she was dying, and he had not been known to put money
into a profitless scheme before. Her death left him curiously
softened; he would do sudden unpractical and unbusinesslike
things, and he had taken her children, legitimate and illegiti-
mate, and provided for them all.

They were not all the cares that Mopu laid on him; there
was Uncle, who had been the great General Krishna Rai, rich
with honours and fame. Suddenly, in late middle life, he had
given them all up, after visiting, on his way back to the State
from Paris, his brother, Ranajit Rai at Mopu. He had never
continued his journey, and now he sat on the hill above the
Palace under his deodar. General Toda could not forget him,
and was bothered by an uneasy feeling that he should go and

do likewise. In the middle of his dinner, he would remember the bowl that the village people filled once a day; trying on his new long coat from London he saw the tattered ochre robe, and at night he woke in his bed and thought of the hut in the wind, with the skins laid on the bare ground. He sent his Uncle a Jaeger rug, but could never find out if he used it; in all those years he had not spoken, and no one had seen him, except in one position on his deerskin mat. He was undoubtedly a very holy man and the wickedness of the house below him seemed all the more dreadful by contrast.

All this was in the General's mind as he thought of his people, and his eye lighted as it fell on the Palace. He had a Good Idea.

He offered the Palace and an endowment to the Brothers of St Peter for the opening of a school.

'This is pro-gress,' smiled the General, as he welcomed them to Mopu. 'You will change the house and make it useful.' But at the end of five months they gave it all back to him. They were curiously reticent. 'There is no scope,' they said. 'We feel we are not needed here. Our energies will be better employed in another place.'

They had changed nothing at all, and Ayah, who by now seemed to belong there, was left in the Palace alone.

3

She was quite alone. The Palace was hidden by the hill
from the village and Canna Villa, from the coolie lines
and the Agent's bungalow, even from Uncle among the firs
above. It was on a ledge cut like a lip from the face of the
hill and it seemed to be perpetually riding into the north. It
faced the mountain Kanchenjunga with the valley and gulf
between.

It was strange how little you noticed the valley or the River
where the green snow water streaked the jelly whiteness of
the stream. You noticed the gulf where the birds flew level
with the lawn; across it was the forest rising to bare and bony
ridges, and behind them and above them, the Himalayan
snows where the ice wind blew.

Sometimes they were like turrets of icing sugar, pretty and
harmless; on some days they seemed as if they might come
crashing down on the hill. On others they were hidden behind
drifts of cloud and a spray floated from one to another; but
however they looked, there was always the wind to remind
you of what they were. The wind was always the same.

That was why the Palace was only one storey high. The General had chosen the site full in the wind, it had no shelter. Its roof came down close to the ground and it had no open verandahs; every space had a thick glass pane. To step into the house was to step into stillness, into warmth even when it was damp and unlit; but after a moment a coldness crept about your shins. The wind could not be kept out of the house; it came up through the boards of the floor and found passages between the roof and the ceiling cloths; at Mopu Palace you lived with the sound of the wind and a coldness always about your ears and ankles.

No one visited it now but Mr Dean, the General's Agent. There was something he liked about it, and in time he came to cherish it. It was a queer Palace, always creaking and straining in the wind, with a sense of power and life of its own. Its thin white walls crossed with beams and red tin roof gave it a look of tidy innocence, but inside it was divided into low little rooms smelling of musk and fungus, and it had a central room, a salon with gilt chairs and a chandelier and powdered blue walls painted with hard gold stars. Only the half-finished class-rooms on the west side showed that the Brothers had been there; no other trace of them was left, except that the bell they had placed on the gong posts hung there rusty and still.

In front of the house was a terrace where no flowers could grow, except orchids and ferns in the cracks of its wall; but, to the right of it, seven roses had grown as high as trees and spread along the drive, making a sheltered walk. In summer the wind smelt of roses and the languorous orange flowers from the groves far below in the foot-hills above the valley.

The drive swept in a curve up the hill and ended in nothing; it was planted with an avenue of deodars and had gate-posts of granite, and scrolled iron gates that opened on to the

hill and a little pony track that led away through the forest.
Through the garden was another track that passed Uncle's hut
and came down the hill, with steps so steep that they were
like a flight of stairs, going down from the forest to the River
against the sky. That was the highest place of all, where Uncle
sat and the coolies rested their baskets on the stones above the
avenue of deodars, and stood up again with their baskets on
their backs against the sky.

The Palace had a garden on the West where the wind was
broken by bamboos planted thickly; there was a terrace cut from
the hill for flowers and more terraces above it running behind
the house, but there only rhododendrons and shrubs like azaleas would grow. On the level of the bamboos was an orchard of
apple trees, and the drive went down past it to the stables and
servants' houses, which were put away on a ledge out of sight.

It always seemed to Mr Dean that there were thickets of
silence in the orchard, that it would not speak though the
bamboos were never still and the wind was always above it on
the hill. It was the one reserved and circumspect place in the
whole Palace, and he liked it with its rows of still green trees
with their arms stretched out.

The rest of the house amused him; he liked to feel its spirit,
and, most evenings, he used to come up and sit on the front
entrance, with its scrolled railing that was too flimsy for the
wind and the great buttresses that banked it like a fortress. He
could easily have asked to live there, but he never did.

He had always disliked what he could easily have; he had
a passion for the untouched. 'There isn't a man who hasn't his
price,' he said, 'and most women are half price.' He could not
help taking them, dirt cheap though they were for him.

When he was a small, fierce though weak little boy, his
mother gave him pennies to buy those lollipops on sticks,

called in the sweet shops 'pommes d'amour', but by vulgar children 'all-day suckers'.

'Mother,' he said, 'I do wish you wouldn't.'

'Why? I thought you loved them so.'

'I do to look at but, as I eat them, they get worse and worse and they leave a nasty taste on your tongue.'

'Then why do you buy them?'

'That's the difficult part. While I can get them, I have to go on having them. It's so difficult to know when you don't want to.'

He was still wise enough to know how difficult it was; because of that he had come to Mopu. For fifteen years he had worked amiably with General Toda and amiably with the people, who amiably understood his habits and assisted him when they could. For this he liked them and despised them a little.

Then one day the General sent for Ayah.

'Ayah, I have invited some ladies to live at the Palace.'

'Ladies!' cried Ayah, her eyes snapping with delight. 'That will be like old times.'

'It won't be in the least like old times,' said the General coldly. 'They're not that kind of lady at all. These are Church ladies.'

'Oh! a *mission*, you mean,' she said, disappointed. 'That won't be any fun.'

'They're not coming for fun. These are nuns. You know what a nun is? They wear long dresses and veils and a kind of a bandage round their chins.'

'Why do they do that?' asked Ayah.

'How do I know?'

'I've seen a bride in a veil,' said Ayah, trying to irritate him, 'and a hospital nurse. Are these ladies married?'

'Does it matter if they are or not?' cried the General. 'You
have seen a nun, so don't pretend you haven't. These belong,'
he looked at the letter, 'to the Or-der of the Ser-vants of Mary. I
have given them the Palace to make a school and a hospital for
the people.'

'You know they don't want a school,' said Ayah, 'and I'm
sure they don't want a hospital. They've never had one before.'

'How do they know what they want till they try?' said the
General tartly. Mr Dean had said the same thing.

'They have all kinds of diseases,' he had pointed out to Mr
Dean, 'they have ringworm.'

'They don't mind having ringworm.'

'Tsst tsst,' said the General. 'They ought to mind. They are
going to have a school and a hospital whether they like it or
not. The Brothers failed me and I don't understand why that
was, so this time I am going to try ladies. I am not in the least
old-fashioned and have no objection to women. Perhaps they
will make a nice school and a nice hospital where the Brothers
did not. They shall be free to all and the people shall all attend
them every day.'

'They were free last time,' said Ayah, 'and no one came.
This time you'd better pay them to go.'

The General looked thoughtful. He had known Ayah since
he was a boy and, though she was blasphemous and alcoholic,
she was quite sensible.

'Two of the ladies are coming the day after to-morrow to
inspect. They will sleep the night at the Palace and you must
get everything ready. I shan't be here myself, but Mr Dean will
take my place. You will get plenty of hot water and tea.'

'What are they to eat?' asked Ayah sulkily. 'How do I know
what ladies like to eat?'

'I have remembered that,' said the General with a smile,

taking up a tin. 'Sausages. They will eat sausages when they come and before they go. Mr Dean's cook shall cook them as I'm taking Antony with me.'

'It would be more polite to leave him behind,' said Ayah, taking the tin.

'Now remember, if you give any trouble, you'll be sorry.'

'I'm sorry now,' said Ayah, flouncing to the door. 'I'm sorry for you. I didn't think you'd be so silly.'

Mr Dean had a note from the General:

Please receive 2 Sister Ladies, Sister Clodagh and Sister Laura from the Order of the Servants of Mary. Don't receive them now as they are coming to-morrow but I am writing this at once as I am going away. Please make them At Home and show them the Palace, where they will make us a school and a hospital, at least I hope so.

'A convent almost next door!' said Mr Dean, when he went to speak to Ayah.

'A convent in the very house. How would you like that?' said she.

He looked at the terrace and thought of the orchard where the hard little apples were on the trees, and at the deep roof and the salon with its French blue and gilt, as if he were seeing them for the last time.

'How will you like that?' he asked.

'Perhaps they won't stay either,' said Ayah, and she and Mr Dean looked at one another.

4

Sister Clodagh had been warned about Mr Dean before she met him. She was warned by Father Roberts before she left Darjeeling on her first visit of inspection.

'He has a very bad reputation,' said Father Roberts. 'I don't believe all I hear, but I believe he's really a very objectionable fellow.' He was in bed with lumbago and groaned as he pulled his pillow more comfortably down. 'He's said to have gone native; lives like one and they say he drinks and is—ouch— bad with women.'

'Let me help you,' said Sister Clodagh, firmly and sweetly, and pressed up the pillows just as he had got them really comfortable. 'I don't suppose we will see Mr Dean,' she said as she helped him to lie back.

'Unfortunately you may have to. Thank you,' said Father Roberts bitterly. 'He acts for the General, who is often away. It worries me that I can't go with you as I meant to. I couldn't get on a pony to save my life.'

'I don't think you need worry. I have Sister Laura with me and we are not afraid.'

'Yes, but you don't understand,' he said crossly. 'You are going into primitive country, almost completely isolated, among people such as you've never met before. We can't get to you in under two days; it isn't even on the route that the trekkers take.'

'We shall be very careful.'

'It won't matter how careful you are,' he burst out. 'You've never had to deal with conditions like this.'

'Tell us about it, Father,' she said to soothe him. 'You have seen the house?'

'It's a Palace,' he said. 'They call it a Palace, but it's a funny place. I don't know. I didn't know whether to recommend it or not, and that's a fact; and usually I know my own mind. You needed somewhere so badly and it's a generous gift; there's all the money to go with it. I gave a lot of thought to it, but I don't know. It feels,' he said slowly, 'like the edge of the world; far more remote than it actually is, perhaps because it looks at such immensity. And the wind! It's very pure and healthy, of course, but—If you don't like it, Sister, you must say so. Don't be tempted by it if you think it's too lonely and too strange. I shouldn't like to think my recommendation had influenced you—' He broke off and twisted his rug into a crumple again. 'Of course you'll be on British Territory and that's something.'

'But will we? I thought it was ceded to the General. In his letter he said "my land".'

'It isn't his. Government have allowed him to lease it,' said Father Roberts firmly. 'Anything else is nonsense. We allow every Tom, Dick and Harry to come over to us and settle and the State won't even grant permits for us to go in, except in rare cases. I believe their side of the passes are picketed and on ours there's not even a policeman. That's what worries me. You're completely dependent on the General. It's lonely and strange, and there's that man Dean—and there isn't a single policeman.'

'I think we shall be able to protect ourselves against Mr Dean without a policeman,' said Sister Clodagh with a smile.

'That wasn't what I meant at all,' cried Father Roberts. She had made him red with anger. 'Well, if you won't be told, you must find out for yourself. Remember you're not infallible, that's all. The Brothers didn't stay, though I haven't been able to find out why. You may find out in a way you don't like.'

When they had ridden down the path to the Agent's bungalow, Mr Dean was sitting on his verandah drinking beer, and on the verandah with him were his dogs, Tibetan mastiffs, his cockatoos, a mongoose, three cats and a hooluk monkey, but no sign of any woman. Sister Clodagh was annoyed that she found it hard to keep her eyes to herself; immediately she noticed that he wore no socks or stockings, but native chapli shoes, and that his shirt was outside his shorts, and he had on, in the house, a huge battered felt hat with feathers round the band. She was glad that she had said nothing to Sister Laura, who was innocently staring.

He did not get up at once, but looked at them over his tankard as if he were very reluctant to meet them. Then he came to them, putting out his hand, the other still holding his tankard of beer.

She looked at his hat and the beer and said in her clear decisive voice: 'You must be Mr Dean.'

'I must,' he said sadly. She darted a glance at him to see if he were laughing, but he was helping her down from her pony carefully and seriously.

'Can you manage?' he asked Sister Laura, who was clumsily sliding from her saddle.

Sister Clodagh said: 'The Sister's not used to riding.'

'So I see,' said Mr Dean, and helped her into a chair. 'Excuse old Feltie. I hadn't a hand to take him off.' He took off his hat. He was so exactly as she had imagined—no, certainly not imagined—expected, that it was ridiculous. Blue eyes, beautiful but with heavy pouches under them, chestnut dark hair, a charming dissipated face—all the trite phrases fitted him; but it was a shock to find that his skin, and there was much of it to be seen, for his shirt was in tatters, was brown and smooth, wonderfully healthy-looking; and his lips were red, almost scarlet, which gave him the berry-stained look of the Irish children she used to play with long ago.

That was when the thought of Ireland first came to her, jerked into her mind by Mr Dean. Long ago she had been a little girl in Liniskelly, where the children were brown and free and had lips of strawberry red like Mr Dean. There had been a boy on the lake shore, a little older than she, who had shown her how his toe-nails turned white under water. Suddenly, clearly, she saw the brown feet that looked green-white in the water and as if they did not quite join the legs above them. She felt his sandy hand holding hers.

She knew she was tired or she would not be thinking like this. Sister Laura was talking to Mr Dean; their voices came to her in a dream, not as clearly as the voices on the shore.

Sister Laura had waited for the Sister to speak, and seeing her leaning back in her chair with her eyes closed, thought that she was tired. 'What curious feathers,' she said with an effort to Mr Dean, looking at his hat. 'I never saw such a collection. Are they all from birds you've shot yourself?'

'I don't shoot birds,' he said. 'These are feathers I pick up as the birds drop them down.' With his finger he touched one and said: 'That was from the throat of a golden oriole.'

'Not *really*?' cried Sister Laura.

'No, not really. We don't have orioles here. It was from the General's canary, but I thought it would please you more if I said it was from an oriole.'

'Well!' fluttered Sister Laura in confusion, and appealed to Sister Clodagh. 'Did you hear that, Sister? Did you hear what he told me when he knew it wasn't true?' There was a puzzled appeal in her voice; her face was like a peony in her wimple. Sister Clodagh came to her rescue.

'Do you shoot much here?' she asked, but her voice was frosty.

He seemed amused and smiled. 'No. When you've shot everything,' he said with his eyes on her, 'it palls, doesn't it?'

There was nothing in that. Or was there? It was the way he said it; it sounded insolent. For the first time she felt a little uncertain, but now he was asking her gently: 'There's tea—and beer. What will you have?'

'Some water, please.' They would take nothing else from him, only some water before they arranged their business and left him.

'A cup of cold water?' said Mr Dean and went into the house to order it. In her nervousness, Sister Laura gave a loud giggle and then sat looking at her feet, avoiding Sister Clodagh's eye.

'We have come to see you on business,' began Sister Clodagh, with a tumbler of cold greenish water in her hand.

'Well, I didn't think you'd come to see me on anything else.'

Sister Laura's tumbler clinked sharply against her teeth. Sister Clodagh sat up rigidly in her chair; then he said quickly: 'I'm sorry. That wasn't fair when you're tired. Cool yourselves down with the water, and then I've ordered some tea to brace you up. Then we can discuss the business before I take you up to the Palace. It's a short ride from here. You know, I'm afraid you'll be stiff to-morrow. I don't suppose you've done much riding lately, have you? Have you any Epsom's? That's the stuff. Sit in your bath with Epsom's; it helps a lot.'

Sister Laura gave another bitten-off laugh and he looked at her in surprise. He turned to his monkey scratching its ears.

They had taken off the topees they wore over their veils, that gave them the look of the pilgrim women in Gothic tales. Sister Clodagh rested her head against her chair. The verandah was shaded from the sun, but outside the trees and the bushes were bright; the colours of the cockatoos were brilliant against the sky, the dogs scratched and the monkey ran, rattling his chain along his pole.

'Couldn't he be loose?'

'He could, and run and bite you to the bone. He's cross, poor little devil. He's full of fleas.'

'Are the fleas bad here in the rains? We were told they were.'

'In the rains and out of the rains. They're worst in spring. I see,' he said, 'you've been making some intimate inquiries.'

A servant, as smart as Mr Dean was shabby, brought the tray. He made the tea in front of them; there was lemon and lump sugar and cream.

'Look, Sister. Lump sugar and cream!' said Sister Laura, and to Mr Dean she explained: 'We haven't seen it since we left England. It's a treat that you are giving us, Mr Dean.'

She caught Sister Clodagh's eye and subsided.

'Lump sugar a treat,' he said almost to himself. 'Of course, they make children of you, don't they?'

'Sister Laura meant that it made us think of home,' said Sister Clodagh, whose quick ear had caught what he said. She put her cup down. 'Thank you, that was a very excellent cup of tea. Now, if you've finished—You know that the General Toda

Rai has offered us this Palace to make a new foundation of our Order here. It's very generous of the General.'

Why 'generous of the General'? It sounded like a silly song. She corrected it. 'It was generous of him. We very much appreciate it.'

'Yes, you'll like the General, Sister Clodagh.' His eyes flicked over her and he half shut them as if he were doing a caricature of her. 'You'll like the General. He also is a superior being.'

Sister Laura gave a gasp, but Sister Clodagh answered him steadily and said: 'I don't know why you're being so rude to me, Mr Dean. I have to talk business with you whether I like it or not.'

'Talk it then, but don't teach it me,' he said like a sulky boy. Sister Laura thought Sister Clodagh was nonplussed. Why did he speak so rudely to her? Sister Laura could not have said herself why she so often made one angry; of course Mr Dean was behaving in an unspeakable way, but perhaps there was something in her voice—

Now Sister Clodagh was saying: 'Perhaps you will show us the way to the house and put us in touch with the servants.'

'How will you get into touch with them? None of them, except the old caretaker, speak Hindustani or English, and she won't help you much.'

'We're going to learn their dialect. I hope by the time we come here, if we do, that some of us will be able to speak it a little. For the present we have an interpreter.'

'That man?' he asked, pointing to Father Roberts's clerk. 'You oughtn't to be with him. I know him. He's a thoroughly bad man.'

'Father Roberts must know him too and he sent him with us,' she said in rebuke.

'Is he a convert? Well in that case I quite understand that you must give him a lot of rope before you hang him.'

'While you are with us'—her words were sharp and exact—'and I suppose you must come with us as the General's representative, I should like you to show us the boundaries of the Palace grounds, so that we shall neither trespass, nor be trespassed upon.'

He gave an appreciative grin and put on his hat and led the way to the horses. Then he stopped and came back to her. 'Try and forget what I said and listen,' he said, 'It's no place to put a nunnery.'

No place to put a nunnery. It sounded odd and uncouth, and he said it again on the terrace when she asked him why the Brothers had left so soon. 'It's an impossible place for a nunnery.'

This time she answered blandly: 'Difficult but not impossible, Mr Dean. Nothing is impossible with God.'

He pointed to the clouds in the north. 'Straight across from here are the Himalayas, the Snows. You think that if you look level you'll see them, but you find that you have to look up, far above your head. Right over you here, is Kanchenjunga. I have never liked anything better than that mountain, Sister, but I don't think you will. Is yours a contemplative Order? Do you live in meditation or whatever you call it? Do you keep solitude?'

Her laugh rang out. 'Our Order isn't in the least like that. We're very busy people. Remember that here we are to open a hospital and dispensary and a school, for children and girls.'

He did not like being laughed at. He said deliberately: 'A school for girls. That's good.'

'You believe in education, Mr Dean?'

'I find uneducated and simple people too disarming.' Deliberately he added: 'You will be doing me a great favour when you begin to educate the local ladies, Sister.'

Sister Laura stared and reddened, but Sister Clodagh answered: 'I have been told already, Mr Dean, that you did not believe in solitude.'

There was a silence. Behind them on the terrace wall the ferns and small orchids shivered in the wind; from their quivering smallness it streamed back into the air. The nuns had to hold their veils down.

'Look at the eagles,' he said.

In the gulf eagles were flying, circling round one small spot in the air. Higher and higher they flew, but still they could not reach the head of cloud that hid the mountain in the north; they could not reach its foot. Circling, they flew a fraction higher; it seemed that they would reach it, but always they were beaten down to be lost in the colours of the valley and they always came up to circle dizzily again.

Mr Dean sent his hat spinning round on his finger. 'I told you it was no place to put a nunnery.'

Just then Sister Laura spoke. She had been listening, and was above herself with shock and surprise and the long shaking ride. 'Oh, how can you say that?' she cried. 'Look at that blue and pearl colour and the light in the sky. It might be Heaven and feels like it too, the wind's so pure and cool. It's an inspiration just to stand here. Who could live here and not feel close to God?'

'Have you written down our notes on the kitchen yet?' asked Sister Clodagh. Sister Laura went away without a word.

'Sister Laura is inclined to be enthusiastic,' Sister Clodagh excused her like a child to Mr Dean.

'I thought she sounded exceedingly sincere,' he answered, and left her.

She stood on alone on the terrace when he had gone. She felt a little ruffled; she was not used to being put in the wrong, and his rudeness seemed to reverberate on the air. Then she forgot him.

The stuff of her sleeves was too thin; the air poured in as she lifted her hands, cold as snow. It ran along her arms. 'You'll have to get used to living in the wind,' Mr Dean had said. Nothing seemed more strange than this feeling of coldness between her skin and her clothes, her hands were goosefleshed and yellow with it. She seemed to be looking at herself from the outside. 'I didn't know until we came here, how yellow we've become.'

Yes, she seemed to be altogether outside herself here; it must be tiredness and the effort of dealing with Mr Dean. She had had such odd thoughts since she saw the house; as soon as she came into it she felt it was alive.

'The General's father used to keep his ladies here,' Mr Dean had said. 'They call it "the House of Women". It will be suitable, won't it, if you decide to come?' He had been rude before, now he was positively hostile, and so was the old caretaker, Angu Ayah.

The woman's face was Chinese, brown and withered like a ginger root: she wore dark blue clothes, a necklace of turquoises and sharp little silver knives, and her hair in pigtails like two grey wires. They had shown Sister Clodagh over the house grudgingly, as if they were trying to keep her away, and, instead of being indignant, she had wanted to say humbly: 'Don't shut me out. Let me in too.'

She had come to report on taking over the Palace and adapting it, and at once she had a fixed determination to take it at any cost and at the same time a violent dislike of the idea of changing it. It was ridiculous. It had been offered to her Order, she had come on its behalf to see with its eyes, and here she was almost siding with this disreputable Agent and a servant against it. She had shared their wild fear that they would change it; the verandahs, that were glassed corridors with geraniums breaking under the window frames, the salon with its gilt and chandelier, the orchard with the grey-green stillness that she had known in the Irish orchards that she had forgotten all this time.

Cosmos flowers were out there under the apple trees; they had grown so tall in that dampness that they had brushed the shoulders of her habit with pollen. Must they be cut down and paths made neat and bordered? Would the Sisters want to cut the empty terrace into beds of patterns; hearts and crosses and initials, as they loved to do? Would they want to prune the sprawling trees that Mr Dean said were roses? Must the stillness be filled with orders and rules and the sound of the bell and the bustle of pupils and patients and work? Then with a shock she remembered that there had been a school here already. It was a foundation of a vigorous flourishing Brotherhood, and not a sign of it was left, except those half-finished walls on the western lawn and the bell hanging between its posts. The silence had closed over it, only these few faint scratches were left.

Her tiredness had gone; she would have liked to go up to that bell and ring it so that it sounded over the hill and across the gulf and down to the valley and up to the mountains. She turned her back on them and looked the ramshackle house over, promising it that it would have to pull itself together now. Already she was itching for the report book that Sister Laura had taken away.

She turned back at the sound of voices. Below in the tea garden the pluckers were going down to the factory with the leaf, their voices were carried to her on the wind. They were women, not like Ayah, but dressed in skirts and buttoned jackets and tartan head shawls; their baskets were shaped like ice-cream cones, and, in the afternoon light, their faces and hands were the same colour as the earth that showed between the bushes of tea. As she watched them, Mr Dean came and stood beside her.

'I shall like these people,' she said.

'Yes, they'll have a lot to teach you,' said Mr Dean. 'Well, if you're quite determined, I give you to the break of the next rains.'

5

On the fourth morning after the Sisters' arrival in October, General Toda Rai sent a message to say that he was coming to call on them; there was a flutter among the younger Sisters as to whether they should curtsey or not.

'I think we should,' said Sister Honey. 'We would curtsey to the Viceroy because he represents the King and is royal.'

'But the General isn't real royalty,' Sister Ruth objected. 'He's more like an Archduke.'

'But one does curtsey to Archdukes.'

Sister Clodagh settled it curtly. 'You'll make our usual little bob if you happen to meet him, but I want you all to go to your work as you would do in the ordinary way.'

'So we shan't even be introduced,' muttered Sister Ruth. 'And why *not*? It's so silly to treat us like children.'

The General's grooms came running down the drive in front of him; they wore uniforms of purple cloth and gold, with puggarees of violet. He rode on one of the small ponies with an elderly aide-de-camp beside him. He was plainly dressed in a dove-coloured achkan and white cotton pantaloons like jodhpurs; he was small and corpulent with a rosy face, and his hair was like a Chinese, cropped and stiff-growing; he had long sparse hairs in his moustache and his finger-nails were cut into points.

'I thought they were Rajputs,' thought Sister Clodagh as she went to meet him. 'He looks like a Tibetan.'

She noticed his earrings, that were diamonds so large that they looked like glass buttons; his rings, the expensive English saddles on the ponies and the fleeces they wore under them that looked odd on the Bhotiya ponies. There were two grooms to a pony, and a peon in the same purple and gold who carried the General's pan-box and his spectacles. She wondered, as she talked to him, how rich he was. He spoke to her in English in a sing-song, carefully dividing up the syllables. She was thanking him for the great gift to their Order. 'It is noth-ing. Noth-ing,' he said.

Perhaps it really was nothing to him, a flea-bite that did not even tickle. He was strange and rich, part of the strange rich State lying behind the mountains. She wondered who had put these ideas of education and philanthropy into his head, as she wondered how he could get such shrewdness and kindliness into such slits of eyes.

She was still in the stage when the faces of the people looked all alike, and now she found, by studying the General's, his mouth and eyes and the lines of his face, that the others seemed to spring into difference and to become faces instead of masks. She was learning to distinguish between the State natives and the hill clans, the Lepchas and Bhotiyas and Limbus; she could single out Jangbir the peon, Nima, the Bhotiya gardener and Toukay the cook.

'I am a great be-lie-ver in good-ness,' said the General. 'This house used not to be at all good. My father used to al-low

some bad goings-on. There is nothing like that about me. I
want you to make the house good.'

'We shall try, Excellency,' began Sister Clodagh. 'We don't
want to change it more than we can help—'

'But you must,' he cried in dismay. 'I want you to.'

'Well, there are one or two things that want to be done.'

She walked with him over the house and gardens, followed by Sister Briony and the aide-de-camp, Colonel Pratap.
To everything she suggested the General waved his hand and
said: 'I app-rove. I app-rove. It shall be done.'

'But who—who is to do this work for us?' she asked him.

'I shall send Mr Dean.'

'Excellency,' she said after a stiff silence, 'if you would send
us the workmen, we can see that they carry out the work
ourselves.'

The General's eyes were lost in their slits as he narrowed
them to look at her, but his face did not change as he said:
'Colonel, you will see about sending men this morning.'

They came out on the drive after the General had politely
tasted the coffee that Sister Briony had made. 'Of course I
don't know if he can take it as he's a Hindu,' she had said to
Sister Clodagh, 'but I think we should offer him something,
don't you?' Her coffee was full of grits, but his face remained
bland and smiling as he drank it. 'Does he ever show anything?' thought Sister Clodagh; the corners of her mouth had
gone wry as she tasted her first mouthful.

'I be-lieve in pro-gress, Sis-ter Clo-dagh,' said the General
on the drive. 'I call a hos-pital pro-gress, don't you? I have
given orders for all the women and child-ren to att-end.'

'If they are ill,' she suggested.

'Ill or well, all the same they will att-end; and all the children will att-end school at once.'

'But, Excellency, we're not ready for them and we hardly know the dialect. How shall we make them understand?'

'They can come and look. It will do them good,' said the General firmly. 'And,' he added, turning to Colonel Pratap, 'isn't there always Joseph Antony, the son of the cook?'

'Oh yes, Joseph is here,' agreed the Colonel.

'Joseph Antony is the son of my Madrassi cook. He was at school for a short while here.' He coughed and went on. 'He is Christ-ian and will wel-come you very much, though he is Roman and you are not. He won't mind for that and will inter-pret you in the school. He speaks English as well as I do,' said the General sadly, 'for I never had the ad-van-tage of going to a school . . .'

Sister Ruth came by to ring the bell. They had kept it where the Brothers had hung it, where the old coolie gong used to hang, between two posts like gallows by the railings. To reach it she had to stand on the horse-block. The top of the horse-block was level with the railings, she had only to take a step to fall into the gulf, to the foot of the buttresses among the bamboos. 'It's dangerous,' Sister Clodagh had said; but it was thrilling to ring the bell, standing on the edge of cloud and sky, with the tea and the valley and the River far below.

Sister Ruth went up to the bell, stepping sideways to bob to the General; Sister Clodagh saw her taking a good look at him, but she did not introduce her.

The General smiled. 'I like to hear that bell. That is pro-gress, isn't it, Colonel?'

'It is very great happiness to have the Sisters here,' said the Colonel politely.

'Good-bye for the pre-sent,' said the General, holding out his hand. 'I shall be away for a lit-tle but if there is any help you need, please ask Mr Dean.' After a moment he added:

'Don't believe all you hear. Dean is a very good fel-low, Sis-ter Clo-dagh.'

Since they came they had been busy unpacking and arranging the rooms. On the first day the clerk had sent word to say that he was very tired after the journey and could not be expected to work, and would the Lady-Sahib please send him some brandy as he was afraid he had taken a chill in the forest. The same message had come every morning since.

'Now what shall I do about that?' asked Sister Briony. 'I only give brandy in cases of great prostration and exposure. He seemed perfectly well yesterday. It would be a great pity to waste good brandy unless he really needs it.'

'He's a lazy wretch,' cried Sister Clodagh. 'He knows we can't do much without him. Mr Dean—' she was not going to say already that Mr Dean was right. 'Send him some ammoniated quinine,' she said. 'That'll teach him. Let's hope this young man Joseph Antony will come this afternoon.'

He came punctually at half-past three.

'Joseph Antony has come,' said Ayah, bouncing into the office.

'Ayah, you must knock before you come in. Where is he?' Sister Clodagh looked at the door.

'Here he is,' said Ayah, pointing downwards, and there was Joseph Antony, not as high as the handle of the door; a black Sambo of a little boy in a yellow shirt striped with pea green.

'Are you Joseph Antony, the son of the cook?'

'Yes, lady.'

Ayah gave him a tap behind. 'She isn't a lady, she's a sister. Say "Yes, Lemini".'

'Yes, Lemini,' said Joseph, taking all of her in, and the room and the box she was unpacking on the desk. 'I have come to teach you the children and I have my box and my bedding outside, because I shall live here with you.'

'Oh!' said Sister Clodagh.

'Would you like to see my box and my bedding, Lady? Sister? Lemini? Would you, Auntie?' he asked Ayah. 'They're new.'

'If you live here what will your father the cook do?'

'He has gone away with the Highness. He gave me my box and my bedding and told me to take it up nicely and come here to you. I am a poor boy,' said Joseph absently, looking at a book of coloured blotting paper on the desk, 'and you must love me and I'll be very good to you.'

'Is this all true?' she asked Ayah.

Joseph scowled, but Ayah said: 'His father has gone and there *is* a new trunk and a bed roll outside the kitchen.'

'How old are you?' asked Sister Clodagh.

'Six to eleven.'

'What did you say?'

'I can remember that I am six,' he explained, 'but my father married my mother eleven years ago, so that I may probably be about ten.'

'Take him to Sister Briony, Ayah, and ask her to arrange where he can sleep.'

'The Fat Lemini who asks a lot of questions?'

'Yes. Sister Briony, Ayah. You must learn to tell our names.'

But Ayah had names for them all. The Fat Lemini, the Smiling Lemini for Sister Honey, the Silent Lemini and the Snake-Faced Lemini for Sister Ruth.

She kept an eagle eye on the furniture, pouncing on them if they moved anything.

'But it's ours,' Sister Honey protested. 'The General gave it to us and we can do as we like with it.'

'Don't you believe it,' said Ayah. 'If you'd been with royalty as long as I have, you'd know better than to depend on that. How do you know he won't ask for it back?'

'Oh, he couldn't do that. He gave it to us. Once it's given it's given.'

'Don't you believe it. They're all the same. How many times would my Srimati Devi say "Here, Ayah, take this" or "Take that" and then, in a day or two, "Ayah, Ayah, where is *my* so-and-so?"'

The nuns laughed. They were always making Ayah tell them stories about the Princess Srimati, and some of them were not altogether stories for them to hear.

In those first days they were happy. The place might, they agreed with Sister Laura, have been Heaven; they were filled with a kind of ecstasy. They woke in the late October mornings before the sun had reached the hills, and saw its light travel down from snow and cloud over the hills, until it reached the other clouds that lay like curds in the bottom of the valley. The mountain stood out, glittering into the air.

'It's the sun on the snow-fields that makes it glitter,' said Sister Ruth. 'The fields never melt and that mist that blows across is a blizzard. It's hard to believe it, it just looks pretty from here.' The wind drove her in to put on a jacket of black crochet wool, edged like a shawl with bobbles of wool.

Now, on the morning of the General's visit, she came out to ring the bell. She stood on the horse-block ringing the Angelus. She must look, she thought, like a fly that had fallen into a green and blue bowl; the midday light ringed the tea bushes with myrtle green; she had not seen tea growing before; it looked a little silly on that wild hill, she thought, like rows and rows of neat green buttons. Who needed buttons on a naked hill? Then far below she saw a pony on the path, with a figure that looked like a little Chinese in a speck of blue and a large flat hat.

'That must be Mr Dean,' thought Sister Ruth, and she sent the bell out with a clang. She should have been saying the

Angelus, but she found it hard in this freedom of space and air not to watch the clouds and the colours and count the peaks of the snows.

They all found it hard. At recreation they walked on the terrace and sat on the block to watch the views, but that was not enough. Sister Honey would stop with a needle in one hand and the cotton in the other, gaping out of the window, and sometimes Sister Philippa would find that it had taken her an hour to pick the cosmos for the altar vases. She was standing in the flowers, red and clove pink and ivory as high as her breast, and her hands were empty.

'Even in my thoughts I'm discourteous and ungrateful,' she sighed. 'We came here to work for God and here I am already neglecting the smallest things I have to do for Him. Very well. I shall go and hoe, myself, what is to be the onion bed.' She worked until her hands were blistered and her back ached so that she could not walk upright.

The first thing they had done was to make a chapel of the small room on the east side of the corridor opposite the bell. They had only a table for the altar, a strip of carpet, a prie-dieu that they had brought with them, and three benches, but it was shaded and peaceful when the schools were empty. A second door led from it to Sister Clodagh's private room, which was also the office.

Sister Philippa had been made Laundry and Garden Sister and had all the outside work and servants to superintend; she looked after the hens and cows and the old pony that General Toda had left for them and whose name, the horse boy said, was 'Love'. There were not many flowers in the garden, the beds were overgrown and the orchard and thickets were a tangle of weeds; the vegetable garden was lost in the grass. 'That must be attended to first,' said Sister Clodagh. 'Then you must clear the fruit trees and after that we will see about flowers.' It seemed an immense amount of work to Sister Philippa, but, as usual, she set about it without saying a word.

Sister Briony had taken the conservatory from her to use as a dispensary. 'It's standing empty, and it's a pity to waste it,' she said. 'I must have somewhere to work in because people are arriving already and I've nothing unpacked. Sister Ruth is upset, she must have a chill on her stomach. It's awkward when the plumbing won't work, and the General had it put in especially for us. I must get at the chlorodyne. Think of all the money they've spent on it and now it won't work; the plumbing I mean, not the chlorodyne. So you must let me come in here where at least the tap runs. It's a nice big place and will do for the present. It's a pity to waste it.'

Sister Briony outdid the most stringent Convent rules against extravagance and waste; she made buns out of the end of puddings and glue out of fish bones, rugs out of rags and pillows stuffed with grass cuttings. Everything was used up and she hated to see the others waste anything. 'Sister, there's at least another mouthful on that herring.' 'Sister Blanche, dear, there's a *whole* thread on your sleeve.'

Now the people were arriving so quickly that they gave her no time to settle her things and make proper arrangements. There was a queue of people; and there was Ayah, who had been told to help her, snipping off bandages right and left and using great dollops of iodine and lint. Some of them had sores and cuts, some were twisted and swollen with rheumatism, but most of them were perfectly well.

'They've made a mistake,' said Sister Briony. 'Tell them, Ayah. The dispensary is for people who are ill.'

At first they were sullen and silent. 'Don't you want me to dress your hand?' she asked one woman.

'No, she doesn't,' said Ayah. 'She could do it herself in her own house, but she has been given two annas to have it done and so she must.'

Sister Briony did not take that in, and soon the sulkiness changed to interest and the interest to delight. 'What is it they like?' she asked. She soon found out. When the dispensary bell rang and she interrupted her work to go to it, it was very often: 'I want to see you make the water pink. Show me the pink water medicine.'

'You had better do it to encourage them to come,' said Sister Clodagh.

'But it's *such* a waste of good permanganate,' wailed Sister Briony.

On the east verandah facing the hill and the path was the Lace School, put there until the new room had been built. Three girls had come with a note from the General.

These girls are to weave and lace and make pretty nice things.

Two were State girls, Maili whose name was really Tirtha, and Jokiephul; the third was a plump little Bhotiya called Samya. Now every few minutes Sister Honey's voice was heard in gentle protest. 'Oh Joseph dear, come here and tell them not to hold the threads with their big toes.'

More than thirty children came to school. There was no room for them on the benches, they had to sit on tins and buckets; some were big boys and girls, some were very small, and the smallest of them all sat on a bucket, which must have been painful, because he was such a baby that the seat of his trousers was still cut out, as was the custom for hill babies. Though his hams, fat as white-heart cherries, were pressed on the sharp edge of the bucket, he smiled and squeezed his hands between his knees, waiting for school to begin. He said his name was Om.

They were all ragged and dirty and sat expectantly in rows.

'They are ready,' Joseph pointed out.

'But I don't know what to do with them,' cried Sister Ruth, who had been given the responsibility of the school. 'We have nothing unpacked; there're too many of them and they smell.'

Joseph began to babble at the children.

'What are you doing?' she said.

'I'm telling them what you said. There are too many of them and they smell.'

'Don't do that, you stupid little boy. I didn't tell you to do that.' She was almost in tears; she had a pain constantly coming and going and she spoke angrily. He looked at the floor, silent as a boot, and the children watched them stolidly.

'What's all this, Sister?' asked Sister Clodagh in the doorway.

'I don't know what to do with them!' she cried again.

'I thought you always knew everything,' said Sister Clodagh.

'It's not fair to give me so many of them and nothing for them to do,' she cried hotly.

'Gently, Sister. That's not the way to speak to me,' said Sister Clodagh. 'It certainly seems to be a very large class. You must start with a few of the older ones. Joseph, tell them that we'll keep the ten oldest ones and the others may run away.'

He spoke to them and they answered emphatically. 'They say they will stay,' said Joseph.

'Tell them they can't. We can't have so many to begin with. They must go away.'

'They say they were paid to come and so they can't go away.'

'*Paid?* Who pays them?'

'The babu has orders to pay every child who comes to school, so they all want to come.'

'Well!' said Sister Clodagh, and could say no more.

Sister Honey came round the partition from the Lace School. 'Sister, may I?' Her eyes were on the children. 'Excuse me, Sister, but may I suggest—'

Sister Clodagh had this pain too, a gnawing pain low down in her stomach. She felt giddy and weak round the knees. 'Yes, Sister,' she said.

'Wouldn't it be a pity to send them away when they have come?'

'They were paid to come,' said Sister Ruth.

'Still, if they like it this time they may come again of their own free will,' said Sister Honey. 'I think I could amuse them for an hour.'

'What could you do with them? They look very stupid to me,' said Sister Ruth tartly. 'Remember they can't speak a word of Hindustani or English.'

'Joseph can,' said Sister Honey, putting her hand on his shoulder. 'You could help me, couldn't you, Joseph?'

Joseph turned ebony with pride.

'There is a blackboard,' said Sister Honey. 'I'll draw things in coloured chalk and they can tell me the name for it, and I'll teach them the English for it. First I'll ask all their names and ages, if they know them, and make a register.'

'You can't call that a lesson,' said Sister Ruth, wishing she had thought of it first.

'You can call it a very sensible idea,' said Sister Clodagh. 'Thank you, Sister Blanche. I'll leave you to deal with them; and you, Sister, had better keep order in the Lace School—if you can.'

Sister Ruth went quickly away without asking for permission. She had to go away. From a little girl she had always had wild tempers, but lately there was something in them that frightened her herself. When she was angry nowadays, she could not help what she did or what she said, because she did not know. It felt like something dark and wet, flooding her brain, like blood. Often she wondered if it were blood; sometimes she actually felt it seeping into her ears and tasted it. She did not know what it was, but she was frightened of it. She was so frightened that she had told no one about it. When she knew it was coming she went away by herself; it was all right if she went away, if she could—in time.

Presently she was able to say, almost calmly: 'It wasn't fair. It isn't fair. She didn't give me a chance.'

For the rest of the day she felt shaken and ill, and she found herself saying over and over again: 'She isn't fair.'

6

N one of it was fair. There was so much to be done, and
work poured in on them before they had time to get
ready for it; and they needed time; first of all to become accli-
matized to living in the high altitude after months and years of
the plains. After the first few days Sister Ruth was always complaining about her headaches; they all had them and felt list-
less and sick. They had not known they were so tired; and still
the patients and the children came, and there was the house
and all the unpacking to be seen to.

They were so tired. The light at Mopu seemed to make the
yellowness of their faces more yellow against their wimples;
their steps sounded heavy in the clear air. They were not strong
enough for the wind; even their clothes seemed grey and dis-
coloured against the whiteness of snow and cloud. Then their
unhealthiness broke through their skins in pimples and spots,
Sister Ruth had a boil on her finger and, one after the other,
they were infected with the mysterious pains and diarrhoea.

'The plumbing must be *made* to work,' said Sister Clodagh.
'I must send for Mr Dean.'

She did not want to do it; she shrank from seeing him again, which was ridiculous, for what could it matter to her what he said? But they had been a fortnight at St Faith's and there was scarcely a change in it; her plans were being defeated one by one and, remembering the ruined foundations that the Brothers had left, she tightened her lips.

The clerk that Father Roberts had given them could not work these outstation men, he did not try; they were not Darjeeling men made servile and easy for money to handle, and he was afraid of them. 'Mr Dean was right,' said Sister Clodagh. 'The man's no use at all.'

They needed coolies, Mr Dean had all the coolies; they wanted wood, Mr Dean had all the wood and the only saws; he had lime and paint and whitewash and wire netting. He even controlled the ponies that went to the depot, without him they could not stir a hoof.

'It's no worse than calling in a doctor,' she told herself. 'It's really as a doctor that I'm calling him in.' Still, she did not want to see him, but at last she wrote to him and asked him to come.

He had heard the convent bell regulating the hours and smiled to himself; he had not gone up to them but, pulling lazily at his monkey's tail, he had smiled at that busy punctual bell. When Sister Clodagh's letter came, he turned it over in his hands thinking how unmistakable it was, with its thick paper, its writing and its set terms. 'To—Dean Esq. Agent of Mopu Estate' and finished 'Clodagh, C.S.M. Sister-in-Charge.'

He put it down thoughtfully on his table, pinning it down with his beer mug, and picked it up again; it had a ring of beer on it and he wiped it and put it in his pocket. He tucked his shirt inside his shorts, pulled Feltie over his eyes, and, standing on one leg, put the other across his pony from behind as he would have mounted a bicycle, and galloped up the hill to the Convent.

'I'm afraid we have no beer,' said Sister Clodagh, 'but we can offer you some coffee.'

'But can you make it decently?' he asked suspiciously, and she, without thinking, shook her head. Sister Briony bristled. 'I don't trust anyone to make my coffee but myself,' he said. 'No. I'll have what you asked from me. Give me some water.'

But he was not rude, he was gentle. She found that she and Sister Briony were pouring out their troubles to him.

'—before we are nearly ready,' cried Sister Briony. 'Things unpacked all over the place, nothing labelled or locked, and that reminds me; all these good cupboards are standing empty because they have no hinges or the locks are broken; and this clerk, this man of Father Roberts, he's no use at all. "How can I mend the hinges when I have no screws?" he says. "Then get screws," I said and gave him four annas; then he brings me half a dozen screws and no change. Screws, dear goodness, that are two annas a *packet* in the plains.'

'You should get rid of the clerk, I think, don't you?' said Mr Dean, not looking at Sister Clodagh. 'Joseph will make you a better interpreter, and I'll send you Pin Fong, the carpenter from the factory; he'll work the men for you and won't cheat you. You say you want to build a work-room and a school?'

'Yes,' said Sister Clodagh. 'We don't want to do more than is necessary but, after the repairs are done, we want to finish the rooms that have been begun as a large class-room and a work-room for our Lace School. And we want to build a chapel later; we're using the room at the east end of the corridor, next to our temporary schools, and it's not very suitable. And *Mr Dean*, Joseph tells us that the people are being paid to come to the dispensary and the children actually paid to come to school.'

'I expect that was the General's idea,' he said.

'Yes, but—'

'He's a wise man in getting his own way, and he learnt a lesson over St Saviour's. It's only until it becomes a habit. Let it become a habit for them to come and they won't remember the time when they didn't, and then gradually he'll leave off paying them and it will gradually become a habit for them not to be paid. They're not really avaricious, it's the idea of getting a present. They're like children, enormously pleased with money, but they don't really want it; and they have children's memories too.'

'He told me he was going to order them to come.'

'Then he knew he wasn't speaking the truth. You can't order these people. They don't know what an order is.'

'Then they should learn,' said Sister Clodagh firmly.

'Why?'

'It's good for them to do as they're told. It's discipline. We all need discipline.'

'Certainly we do,' said Sister Briony.

'Why?'

'You said it yourself. "They're like children." Without discipline we should all behave like children.'

'Don't you like children?' asked Mr Dean.

Neither of them answered, and he said to Sister Briony: 'And that reminds me. May I tell you one thing about your dispensary?'

'Why, yes.' She looked at Sister Clodagh.

'If you get a bad case, a case that seems to you as if it might be dangerous or even serious, refuse to treat it.'

'Refuse?' Sister Clodagh began indignantly. 'But that would be—'

'It would be wise,' said Mr Dean. 'If you had a case that went badly or if one of your patients died, you'd have all the people up against you. You must remember that they're primitive and like children, unreasonable children, and they've never seen medicine before. They'll think it's a kind of magic. Remember, I've warned you.'

There were quick steps outside and Sister Ruth knocked at the door and came in without waiting for an answer. When she saw Mr Dean she stood staring at him from the middle of the floor and said nothing.

'Well, Sister?'

She started and then said dramatically: 'Oh Sister, Sister. They've brought in a woman, our first bad case. She was covered in blood, I've never seen such a sight. She must have cut a vein or an artery. I think it was an artery because it *spurted* blood. I had *such* a time stopping the bleeding. It's the first time I've ever seen bleeding like that, and I really didn't know how to stop it at all, but I managed to stop it at last.'

'Then it was quite unnecessary of you,' said Sister Clodagh, 'when a minute would have fetched Sister Briony, who would have stopped it at once.'

'I said you were to fetch me, if anything came in.'

After what Mr Dean had just told them, their voices were sharp. Sister Ruth turned pale and said: 'I was only trying to consider Sister Briony.'

'You might have considered the poor woman, who, by your description, was bleeding to death,' said Sister Clodagh, dryly. 'Oh, Sister Briony, you had better go.'

She had already gone. Sister Ruth looked from Sister Clodagh to Mr Dean. 'Shall I wait?' she asked.

'We're coming ourselves in a moment,' said Sister Clodagh, repressively. 'I think we needn't keep you.'

As Sister Ruth turned to the door, Mr Dean opened it for her. 'Good-bye, Sister Ruth,' he said. 'I hope your patient does well.'

She looked up at him, her lashes flickered and she dropped them.

He asked her: 'What was the woman's name?'

'It was difficult to understand. It sounded like Samuel, but it couldn't be that, could it?'

'Oh, Samuel. She's a good old lady, one of my best pluckers. I'm very grateful to you, Sister.'

As she stood in front of him, she was almost painfully aware of him. Her shoulders were not as wide as half his chest; she was fragile and white beside him; his flesh was live and bronze like a Red Indian, and there was so much of it; his shirt was short-sleeved and open at the neck, and torn across the arm-hole, and he wore shorts and no socks. Then his colours and his brilliance swam in front of her, she was pleased to find that her eyes were full of tears. She forced them out and made a choking noise and fled.

Sister Clodagh said nothing. He shut the door and they began to talk about the repairs.

He could not attend. He was thinking of her. He had forgotten Sister Ruth, she had pulled that face of anguish at him and he knew it very well by now and made a note that he must avoid speaking to her again; he was thinking of Sister Clodagh.

He looked round the office that was as disembodied as it could have been; it had a desk with writing materials and a shelf of books, an English-Hindi dictionary, religious and school books; a chair for Sister Clodagh and a chair for him and a carpet stool; a green iron safe and a coconut matting on the floor. There was a crucifix but it was like all other crucifixes, and an embroidery frame with a heap of gaudy wools.

Was that really her taste? He looked from those childish colours to her face in its narrowing wimple, the forehead and cheek-bones beautiful and intelligent, the mouth fastidious. She looked cold, almost severe, and yet he thought: 'I believe you're sensitive. Sensitive and warm.'

She spoke to him across the desk, stretching to hand him the papers, and her cross fell on the blotting paper. He stared at it; cheap black wood with a white painted line, but a cross to be worn on the breast, a symbol that meant—how much to her? 'That's what I don't understand. How she believes in that and she must or she wouldn't be here,' and he wondered very much what had sent her into the Order.

She raised her eyes to him as she talked. 'Did you know you have beautiful eyes?' He nearly said it; the charming phrase came almost automatically, but he did not say it. He sat facing her with a curious blankness in his heart; it was a relief when she began to talk again in her dominant school-mistress tones.

'Will you come over the building with me?' she was saying. 'If you'll take this note-book and write down the items, it will help you not to forget.'

Obediently he took the pupil's note-book with its cover stamped with 'Semper Fidelis' in gold, and followed her into the corridor. He felt uneasy. The Palace had become strange; only when they came upon Ayah bawling at the water carriers in the backyard, did he recover himself and know that for all this frosted Convent air, nothing was changed and nothing could be changed.

'Almost you frightened me,' he murmured. 'But it's only because the paint is new. What's underneath will soon come through.'

'How is it going?' he shouted to Ayah in dialect.

'What do you expect?' she shouted back. 'It's just like it was with the others, they're all ill and they're all tired. They need medicine, poor things.'

'You should take better care of them then. What have you been thinking of? I believe they've frightened you out of your wits.'

Ayah laughed. 'Hai! Hai! Hai!' and slapped him on the elbow as he passed. Sister Clodagh was shocked. A native to slap a European in that friendly familiar way! But she had noticed that they treated him as one of themselves. Now he found he could talk to her more easily and his hand strayed to the tightness around his waist and forgetting, he pulled his shirt tails out.

'There is one other thing,' she said. 'I—some of the Sisters—are ill. Sister Briony doesn't know how to treat it and thinks it must be some local infection, as we all have it. Ayah says it's from the water.'

'Darjeeling tummy,' said Mr Dean. 'Yes, we must see to that,' as he had said to the question of the clerk and the wire netting and the kitchen floor.

'And the plumbing is out of order.'

'I thought something would go wrong with that,' he said with interest. 'I hope you haven't been letting any of these people mess about with it or we shall never have it right. It's too bad when you're ill.'

Her face relaxed its tenseness and she smiled. 'Thank you for being so sympathetic over everything,' she said.

'Not at all,' he said politely and added: 'I'm glad to find you're human enough to have—everything.'

Ayah helped Sister Briony deal out his prescription. 'You're ill because you're not used to drinking good water,' she said.

'Indeed we are,' said Sister Briony indignantly. 'We're all exceedingly careful about our water.'

'Calcutta water is bad,' went on Ayah. 'Benares water is worse and it's worse still in Bombay. You had better water in England and Paris, but I still don't call it good.'

'What do you know about England and Paris?'

'Well, I've been there,' said Ayah complacently. 'I'll show you my passport and the certificate the General Bahadur gave me, saying he would pay me two hundred rupees to go across the black water with Srimati Devi and that she was to bring me back to my husband in good condition.'

'And did she?' asked Sister Philippa.

'Tcha no! I got so thin he didn't want me back; he said he'd no use for bones. That was because I found nothing fit to eat; except in France and Italy, the bread. Ah, I can't forget that bread! The horses were good too, but the cows were too big and so of course the milk was coarse and that upset my stomach.'

'Why did the Princess Srimati go to Europe, Ayah?'

'Because she was ill, Lemini, and they were looking for someone to cure her. No wonder she was ill,' cried Ayah. 'I could tell you—hmm. They looked in Paris and London,' she went on hastily, 'and in a place called Baden, and then they sent us to Alassio to rest and then they listened to me and brought her home to make her really better.'

'And what did she do then?'

'Oh, she died. At Darjeeling. That was a great nuisance for us because we had to carry her all the way into the interior. The General Bahadur would have her buried in the State. He thought a great deal of her though—hmm. Not even elephants nor horses can go over some of the passes, but we did. Yes, she died. She was young, it wasn't her time to die.' Ayah sighed and then said cheerfully: 'Let her go. She was always wilful and silly and not much good.'

'Tell us more of what you did in Europe, Ayah.'

'You're as bad as the young masters always pestering me for stories.'

'What young masters?'

'Kundra and Dilip, the eldest sons of Srimati. They are the General's true nephews, the others are not and they are not quite sure about Dilip. Still, let us say there are two. Soon there'll be only one; the elder brother is ill. Did you hear the drums in the night? They were for him. They beat all night while he is ill, if you hear them stop, he's dead.'

All of them listened that night, but the drums beat, hour after hour, until morning.

7

Soon it was quite natural to see Mr Dean in the Convent; soon he began to whistle and walk about in the house with his old hat on his head instead of in his hand, and it seemed no more strange than seeing the other workmen. There was one of them astride the sill in Sister Clodagh's office as she worked; it had warped and he was planing it so that the window would shut; and there had been another moving a ladder from room to room for days, mending the ceiling, they were apt to forget about him perched up over their heads. Mr Dean was always there, showing them how to fit a bolt or measure a door or conferring with Pin Fong. He would flatten himself in a doorway to let a Sister pass, still holding the rule against it, shutting one eye to see if it were straight, never glancing at her; or kneel on the floor, testing the floor boards as their skirts swished by, without turning his head.

He came everywhere; into the office to get Sister Clodagh's signature for a receipt, into the dispensary to mend a tap that Pin Fong did not understand; to the Lace School to explain to the carpenter about the rat that had died under the corner boards, into the school-room to ask if the blackboard were standing more steadily now. The sound of his whistle came from all quarters of the house and, quite often, the sound of his curses; and he would pull his shirt outside his shorts as he worked and leave it hanging there under his disreputable checked coat.

Now they all talked to him naturally, except Sister Ruth, whom he avoided, and Sister Honey who fluttered; she was no more capable of speaking naturally to a man than she was capable of beating Joseph. He knew it and teased her gently, making her blush and flutter more than ever.

It was miraculous how things improved. Pin Fong, the carpenter, was a tall sad Chinese; in his blue coat he looked like a drooping cornflower with a seeded yellow centre; he never seemed to speak, but his men knew what they had to do and worked quickly and well.

The back rooms were mended and divided into cubicles for the Sisters' sleeping quarters, and the door leading to that part of the house was padded with baize to shut out the rest of it; a wall was knocked down between two small rooms to make a large Refectory and the salon was left as a reception room. They put the figure of the Sacred Heart there, where Mr Dean had made a wooden niche for it and painted it in gold. The schools were rising from the ruins on the west lawn and already the statues of St Elizabeth, St Catherine, St Teresa and St Helen were arranged along the corridor, while St Faith herself was opposite the porch.

'There she is,' said Mr Dean, who had lifted her into place for them. 'She's your patron or name saint or whatever you call her, isn't she? Now the old Palace is a proper Convent.'

But it was not. Even with the alterations it was different from any Convent they had known.

Theirs was an Anglo-Catholic Order that had its head-quarters at Canstead in Sussex. Many of them had been pupils at the school and had gone back there as postulants, Sister Clodagh and Sister Briony among them. They all knew the story of how Sister Clodagh had come there, all the way from Ireland as a very little girl, because her mother had been a pupil there before her.

The Order had spread to the East and sent a stream of Sisters to Egypt and Persia and India and China. In India Sister Clodagh had found the same brick buildings, the same green walls and echoing stone stairs; the same figures of saints in coloured plaster, the same close warm Convent smell, mixed with incense and wax polish. The reception room floor had even been laid in wood to match the parquet at home and the chapel had been copied exactly from the chapel at Canstead. The corridors were crowded with girls in neat blouses, the white figures of the Sisters were everywhere, and there was always a subdued busy bustle or else deliberate meditative silence.

Here the house was never still, it strained and spoke in the wind that broke all privacy. There was no such thing as privacy at Mopu, every sound was carried through the house and the rooms were built of windows opening on the endless corridors where the servants and workmen came walking by; and yet sometimes there was that sense of emptiness that was almost frightening, as if the house had swallowed everyone; you could walk in it for minutes and meet nobody. It was as if it had swallowed them up, they and the restraints they had brought to it; they were gone under the old familiarity, their saints tossed down like beads, the bell on its thread of sound snapped off.

The house would not conform; look at the way they tried to say St Faith's and always said Mopu. The flimsy walls did not shut out the world but made a sounding box for it; through every crack the smell of the world crept in, the smell of rain and sun and earth and the deodar trees and a wind strangely scented with tea. Here the bell did not command, it sounded doubtful against the gulf; the wind took the notes away and yet it brought the sound of the bells at Goontu very strongly; pagan temple bells. And everywhere in front of them was that far horizon and the eagles in the gulf below the snows. 'I think you can see too far,' said Sister Philippa. 'I look across there, and then I can't see the potato I'm planting and it doesn't seem to matter whether I plant it or not.'

Then there were the people, the servants and the patients and the children; they were disconcertingly outspoken and familiar; they had no manners at all, because their manners were such a part of them that they ceased to be manners. Mr Dean was like that, he was so like these people that he was almost of them; he had 'gone native' in a way that Father Roberts had not meant. 'And not a bad way either,' thought Sister Clodagh and caught herself up quickly.

At any rate, she told herself, the difference seemed to be stimulating. All the Sisters were living and working well, extraordinarily well; even Sister Ruth was giving no trouble, though sometimes she was pale and silent and had a way of staring resentfully with those green eyes that had such a peculiar glitter. There was fierce competition in the schools; since the first day Sister Honey longed to teach the children, and she would have left her threads and patterns and delicate weaving in a moment if Sister Ruth had given her the chance.

Sister Briony never had a second to spare, and her thoughts were all of the new dispensary that Mr Dean was building for her with such sense and economy; and Sister Philippa was beginning to take a real interest in the garden and had asked if she might borrow the book that Mr Dean said he would lend her on Himalayan plants.

But Sister Clodagh found it difficult to work herself. That first day in Mr Dean's bungalow and in the orchard she had been reminded of Ireland—and of Con. Not reminded, there was nothing to remind her, but they were back again, she had to face that. She had started her old dreams and they were worse for all the years between, when she had not felt a tremor or a touch. She was afraid that she was going to be drawn into it again, but so far she had kept it down, except for the dreams. She tried not to worry, but to let herself drift on the days and be busy with all the work there was to be done.

She told Pin Fong that she wanted work to stop on Sundays; he smiled politely and came on Sunday with his men.

'Why have you come, Mr Pin? It's Sunday.'

'I work all same, Sunday, Monday, Tuesday.'

'But I don't want you to.'

'I want to. Gleat much work to be done.'

On Sundays now the Convent was not quiet, there was incessant tapping and hammering and sawing, and the noise of trowels spreading concrete and the comings and goings of ponies. There were the voices of the men and the voice of Mr Dean; his voice penetrated even to the chapel which was furthest away. Sister Clodagh had to ask him to come at more convenient times.

'I come when there's something that needs me,' he said. 'I'm a busy man, Sister Clodagh, and I can't hang about waiting for this or that reason. Sunday is the day when I'm able to give most time to the work as the factory's closed. Let's get on and finish it and then you needn't be bothered with us any more.'

'You know it isn't that. Sunday with us is a day of quiet,' she said. 'And we find it disturbing to hear you when we're in chapel.'

'In chapel you oughtn't to hear me,' he said gravely. 'If you were truly in prayer nothing could disturb you.'

She stared at him in amazement and then left him and went back into the empty chapel.

How dared he answer her like that? She knelt staring at the mountain framed in the window. How dared he? She was too angry to pray and sat down with her hands in her lap trying to control herself. As she sat there her anger seemed to leave her tired and irritated. She looked at the narrow room; it had seemed peaceful, almost pretty, with its window hung with creepers, its shining benches and the altar bright with cosmos flowers; now she found herself thinking that if the mountain had a voice, it would be like Mr Dean's, magnified a thousand times, disturbing the world instead of one small whitewashed room, and she found herself wishing that it could. She liked it, she gloried in it; she had lived too long with the delicate and small and petty.

Then she knelt down and pressed her fingers into her eyes, and her hands into the back of the bench in front of her and her knees into the floor. How could the years she had given to God be small and petty? She tried to think how, to Him, the mountain was as infinitesimal as the sparrows; instead she thought how the eagles, filled with His life, were beaten down before it.

It seemed to press through the window and fill her eyes with startling clearness like a railway poster, white painted with blue on a blue sky. She got up to look for Sister Briony.

'We must fit curtains to the chapel window,' she said. 'The light is far too bright.'

8

Sister Clodagh thought that the time had come when she could speak to Mr Dean about the Holy Man on the Convent grounds; they had established themselves now, she felt, and it was not only the Holy Man; the path with the stone steps was a short cut to the factory and the River and, all day long, people could be seen on the sky-line. Anyone climbing the steps stood straight into the sky, and the wind in their clothes and the sky with its scarves of cloud and the trumpet shapes of the trees, made the figures like gay and flimsy dancers cut from paper.

They were very distracting. Sister Honey and Sister Ruth could watch them from the school verandahs; the coolies rested their cone baskets on the stones, the women sat down in parties to smoke, the ponies climbed the steps like cats and sometimes there would be Tibetan monks in red and blue robes, their shaved heads flashing and shining in the sun with sweat.

'We ought to put a grotto there,' said sentimental Sister Honey, 'a grotto so that they might drink. We have a lovely statue of dear St Vincent de Paul coming to us from the senior pupils at Canstead; he would make a beautiful grotto, wouldn't he?'

She was talking to Mr Dean, who said: 'Why should they want a grotto when they have a stream?'

'Oh, well—' Sister Honey was confused and then said: 'If the saint were over the grotto, wouldn't they think of him while they drank? Think of the good thoughts they would have if they thought each time of St Vincent de Paul who sent them the water.'

'Come to that,' said Mr Dean, 'it was God who sent the stream.'

He often tripped her up like that, to see her blush and stammer and contradict herself, but he did it so very gently that she liked it and continually invited it.

'And this is St Juan of Aliros,' she would say, taking him reverently from his packings. 'He was martyred at fifteen years of age with swords and arrows, and all the gutters of Aliros ran with blood.'

'They couldn't have,' said Mr Dean.

'Couldn't have? Why not?'

'Aliros has no gutters.'

It was not very reverent of him, but still she liked him; it was impossible to believe that anyone so kind in small things could really mean to be unkind in big. 'I *think* he's only teasing,' she said to Sister Ruth. 'I suppose his face is wicked, though it is so charming; but then that's how one would *expect* it to be, wouldn't one?'

'What do you mean?' asked Sister Ruth.

'Well, he has a very bad reputation,' Sister Honey sank her voice. 'I suppose I shouldn't tell you, but I think you ought to know. Sister Laura talked about it and that's why Reverend

Mother wouldn't let her come back here. Father Roberts warned Sister Clodagh against him and, that first time they came here to see the house, he behaved very badly; Mr Dean, I mean, not Father Roberts. He said something to her about the women here. Sister Laura said she could hardly believe her ears.'

'What was it?'

'She couldn't quite catch it, but he told her that he had educated the local ladies or something like that. You can tell he's not really a good man, the way he *exposes* himself,' said Sister Honey with a shudder. 'I do think that Sister Clodagh should make him wear more respectable clothes when he comes here. I'm afraid he's not at all a good man.'

Sister Ruth's eyes were fixed on the figures on the sky-line, but she did not see them. 'I don't believe a word of it,' she said. 'I don't believe it's true, but if it is it won't make any difference to me.'

The people took to sitting on the path to watch the nuns; they laughed and talked about them and handed round cigarettes and made a party of it. They embarrassed them acutely.

'It's not pleasant to be talked about and laughed at in a language you can't understand,' said Sister Ruth resentfully, and Sister Clodagh said: 'I can't wait for the General. I must speak to Mr Dean.'

'That man, the Sunnyasi or Holy Man,' she asked him one afternoon, 'surely he's living on our ground.'

'He was here first,' said Mr Dean.

'Yes, but I don't think the General should allow him to live on the land that he's given to us.'

'*We are the people selected by God,*' he began under his breath. '*Having from the beginning, distinctions and rules—*'

'What did you say?'

'Nothing.'

'I should like you to ask the General to turn him off.'

'He couldn't do that. It wouldn't be polite.'

'That's ridiculous. A dirty, ragged old man like that. I don't suppose the General knows he's there.'

'On the contrary,' said Mr Dean with a gleam in his eye, 'he knows only too well. That old man worries him quite a lot.'

'Then he should turn him out.'

'In these parts we're rather proud of our Holy Man,' he said. 'Besides it would be a little difficult for the General to turn out his own uncle, wouldn't it?'

'His *uncle*?' said Sister Clodagh.

'Yes, he was General Ranajit's elder brother.'

'I can't believe it!'

'He was the Grand General Kundra Rai with all sorts of titles and orders. He lent General Ranajit the actual money to lease Mopu. He'd been decorated by four foreign governments and he was asked to London for the Jubilee; Queen Victoria's I mean, not King George's. I've never heard him speak but they say he talked several European languages.'

Sister Clodagh was speechless. After a while she said: 'Does he never speak at all?'

'I've never heard him. The people take him his food but they say they don't know when he eats or sleeps, he's always in his place under the tree, facing the Himalayas. The people come for miles to see him.'

'I wanted to ask you about that too,' she said. 'Is there a right of way through our grounds?'

'Not that I know of, but it would be difficult to stop them using it.'

'But if they have no *legal* right?'

'It's become a custom. What harm do they do you? If you're afraid they'll trespass, you needn't be. They won't come one step nearer unless you ask them in.'

'They sit and stare,' she said.

'Only because they think they're on their own ground. You'll make them feel very foolish if you suddenly tell them it's yours.'

'But it is ours,' she said. 'I don't want to hurt their feelings, and of course I can't offend the General about the Holy Man, but at the same time—I don't know quite what to do.'

'What would Christ have done?' he asked softly, tipping his hat over his eyes, and went to the window, where he stood whistling.

He knew she was angry. Without looking round he could feel that, but he did not know that she was considerably dismayed.

Who had taught him to speak like that? To catch her out with her own arguments, to speak with an authenticity that she recognized at once, that was unanswerable?

Without another word she let the people go and come; but every time she saw the line of figures against the sky her own words seemed to come back to her and the more she thought of them, the less she liked them.

9

One day, at the end of the afternoon, Sister Clodagh came out to sit on the terrace; she had been hard at work since it was light; even harder than usual, as Sister Ruth was in the infirmary and she had most of her work to do.

Already the Goontu bells were ringing, but there was still an hour before she need ring for the Angelus and Vespers, and she sat down on the horse-block to rest her mind and legs.

The wind blew the clouds quickly and lightly across the sky and filled her sleeves and veil. Sister Philippa and her coolies were working on the high terrace; she could see them talking, but the wind took the sound of their words. The birds flew from the orchard and landed on the railing before they launched themselves into the gulf; there was no one else in sight. The emptiness on the path was unusual; where had all the people gone to, she wondered, why was there this stillness and waiting?

Then she heard a throbbing that came from the hill, from the forest. At first it was only a throbbing, then it came nearer, separating into drum beats, a tom-tomming that was low and exciting. It came nearer and louder and above it she heard a flute.

A procession of men came from the opening in the forest, walking between the sapling firs to the steps, moving along the sky-line. One carried the drum and the flute player was beside him, she could distinguish him with his hands to his mouth; a boy danced in front, waving a muffler that he used as a scarf, and after them came the men in twos and threes. There were a great many of them and some of them carried the poles nailed with strips of cloth that she knew were prayer flags.

They turned left to the long road to the River, passing below Sister Clodagh at the foot of the terrace; at each buttress the procession curved out and in again like a looped snake. She looked down on the heads passing below her and the flags stiffening in the wind and the feet moving with the drum. Those were the only sounds, the drum and the feet and the wind in the prayer flags.

She saw that the men were all young, in their teens or twenties. Some of them had their heads uncovered or wore round black hats, and these wore long coats and pantaloons like jodhpurs. Others were quite small and squat, they had Tibetan robes and their hair was cropped or plaited down their backs. 'That's odd,' thought Sister Clodagh, 'that Hindus and Buddhists should be walking together,' for this seemed some sort of religious procession; with its flags and the drums and the silence; none of them were speaking a word.

She thought they were beautiful, walking between the tea on the narrow grass path; their cheeks were olive and ochre brown, their eyes brilliant. They made her think of the groom in the forest with the leaves behind his ear, and then she noticed the young man walking alone behind the others. As he walked he kicked the stones away from him and slashed at the bushes; he looked as pretty and naughty as a child, though he was nearly a full man; tall and beautifully built, not like a hill man but like a young Rajput.

He slashed with his cane at the bushes, and she was suddenly back, walking down the Wishing Lane at home with Con; the green damp lane that led from the House gates past Skinners Farm to the lake, and Con was slashing at the hedge to show his temper.

'What's wrong, Con?'

'Oh, everything.'

'What specially?'

'Oh, nothing. You wouldn't understand.'

The shadow of the hill fell on the lane and the ferns trembled under his stick.

'Is it—is it money, Con?'

'What else ever is it?' and he burst out: 'Desmond's well out of it, I must say. He's doing wonders with Uncle Nat; he's in Michigan now opening a new branch. And because I'm the eldest son, I can't go. I'm a hundred times quicker than Des and I've got to hang round waiting for this.'

She saw the Kelly lake and the village at its northern end where the houses were reflected in the water, in their odd patched colours and sunk roofs; the land was marsh that ended in the reeds of the foreshore or hill with heather and gorse and rock. The few fields were going to waste because Con's father could not afford the men to work them; the stables were three-quarters empty and the House itself not much better, with the rooms shut up and only the two rough girls and Pat, who was butler and groom and handyman as well.

'I'll have a little money, Con, when—when I marry.'

She could hardly say it, the red crept up her neck and her footsteps seemed to be hammering in her ears as she walked with him down the lane, but he only answered gloomily: "Tisn't a little money it wants, it's a fortune and then it would be a waste." She dug her nails into her hands.

She must have done that again, because she gave a little cry of pain. She was sitting on the horse-block, and now the head of the procession had reached the corner and turned and wound back on the lower plane of the path that went backwards and forwards across the hill, going down until it reached the River.

She heard beads clicking and turned, her eyes still dazed, to see Ayah standing beside her. She smelt garlic and an underlying tang of wine.

'Ayah! You've been drinking again.'

'Of course I have,' said Ayah. 'I thought perhaps with the garlic you wouldn't notice it. We've all been drinking, we've had a lovely funeral feast. It's very sad, but nobody could call it unexpected and crying won't bring him back. It's much better to decide who shall have his things and how to divide the tips.'

'Is someone dead?' asked Sister Clodagh startled.

'It's the General's elder nephew. His heir, the young General Kundra Rai.'

'Oh, Ayah! Yes, of course, the drums were quiet last night.'

'And two nights before that. You don't notice much, do you? He's been dead three days.'

'But the General sent us fruit and vegetables this morning and said nothing.'

'Why should he? It's nothing to do with you,' said Ayah kindly. 'Why should you bother yourselves with a thing like that?'

'But his heir?'

'That's why they're making all this to-do. They took the body down to the River before it was light. They'll burn him there on the further side. That's the new heir, walking behind.'

'The young man alone at the back?' asked Sister Clodagh stupidly.

'That is Dilip Rai, he is now the little General. He was nothing until this morning,' said Ayah, 'he wasn't even legitimate, not to be certain, that is. This morning they decided that he was legitimate and he is now the heir. I know what I know all the same,' said Ayah darkly.

'No one has ever bothered with him,' she went on. 'He lived in the General Bahadur's house, but I don't think he likes the boy at all. He gave him a Bengali tutor to teach him English reading and writing. I think it was a pity to give him a Bengali tutor, their ways are not our ways, poor things. The little General doesn't look like his uncle, does he? He's as pretty as my Srimati Devi. Of course I shan't tell who his father was,' said Ayah with a hopeful look at Sister Clodagh, 'not if you were to ask me all day and all night.'

'What did you say is the young General's name?' was all that Sister Clodagh asked.

'Dilip. Dilip Rai. He's clever as well as pretty. He was going to school in England.'

'To school? But he's quite grown up.'

'He was going to school,' said Ayah firmly. 'He was going to a school called Cambridge, but now he won't do anything of the kind. He'll be put into the army and married.'

Sister Clodagh watched the procession going down through the tea, the men becoming smaller and smaller until they were no bigger than ants; she was not sure if she could hear the drums or not, whether it was her own pulse throbbing in her ears.

She thought of them fording the River; perhaps the body was already on the further bank and they were waiting for the young heir to arrive before they lit the pyre. They would stand by the forest, under the gloom of the trees, by the cold pebbles of the River. He would stand there too, moody and sulking.

Con used to play ducks and drakes across the lake, scaring the geese and making them draw up their necks and hiss. Perhaps the young General would play ducks and drakes across the water with the little stones.

Sister Philippa touched her gently on the shoulder. Ayah had gone. 'Shall I ring?' asked Sister Philippa. 'It's after six.'

That night Sister Clodagh could not sleep. She could not help thinking of the funeral on the River bank, of the boy Kundra's body and the men busy round the pyre and their torches under the gloomy trees. She had seen many people die, but until now she had never known a young foreign death, foreign in colour and in creed. It seemed very terrible to her in the night; she lay awake, wondering and sorrowing. Her thoughts grew confused; sometimes it was the young General who stood on the bank where the torches shone into the water; sometimes it was Con, standing in their porch at home outside the white door with the light on his face. The trees gleamed where the wind tossed the flames, the laurel bushes moved and rustled beside the step.

It was morning when she slept and then she dreamed; she was not rid of them then; they were in her dreams and in an odd way they were one; they were beside her, but they kept their backs to her. They had mirrors in the palms of their hands and they were talking to themselves, and she was trying to attract their attention over their shoulders. She could not make them listen because she could only echo what they said. She woke with such a feeling of distress, that she got up and dressed and went into the chapel.

10

Mr Dean came up to the Convent in the rain, wanting to see Sister Clodagh. Sister Ruth answered the bell and asked him to wait in the reception room, looking half away from him as she always did.

'I'll wait here,' he said. 'I've something with me for Sister Clodagh.'

With a startled glance she saw, beyond him, a young hill-girl standing in the porch, her hands on the handle of her umbrella, a tin trunk beside her on the ground.

'I'll tell her. Is that—' said Sister Ruth and went away to find Sister Clodagh.

She was in the school-room with Sister Honey who had run in to take charge while Sister Ruth answered the bell.

'Don't you think Om's mother should sew his trousers up?' asked Sister Honey, looking at him tenderly. 'Do you think it's quite nice?'

A month ago Sister Clodagh would have agreed with energy and precision that Om's trousers should certainly be sewn up, but now she murmured vaguely: 'He's only a baby,' and fixed her eyes on the enticing shape in the split of his seat. 'It's a good idea really,' she said, 'and *very* clean.'

With difficulty she detached her gaze and went to Mr Dean.

'I've brought you this girl,' he explained. 'Her name is Hasanphul, but we call her Kanchi. She's seventeen and it's time she was married, but she's an orphan and as you see she's too pretty. Say Salaam to the Lemini, Kanchi.'

The girl salaamed. She was like a basket of fruit, thought Sister Clodagh, piled high and luscious and ready to eat. Though she looked shyly down, there was something steady and unabashed about her; the fruit was there to be eaten, she did not mean to let it rot.

'Why did you bring her to us?' Sister Clodagh asked and her eyes took in the pointed little pears of the girl's breasts under her thin jacket and the flaunting banana yellow of that jacket.

At her tone his eyes lit up. 'It's a common species,' he bantered her. 'Besides, isn't it your business to save souls? I thought you might like to try your hand on this one.'

She said sharply: 'You are *not* to speak to me like that, Mr Dean.' It was too sharp for an order, it was almost a plea, and he said at once and sensibly: 'I'm sorry. Every evening when I come home I find her sitting on my verandah. She dresses herself up and puts flowers in her hair and is becoming an absolute nuisance. If you could keep her here and teach her a little sense, I'll try and make her uncle arrange her marriage. She has just this one uncle who'll be more than glad to get her off his hands; he has daughters of his own, and if she's cloistered for a few months she'll be more desirable. She's been behaving so badly that no one wants her.'

'That's all very well,' said Sister Clodagh, 'but I don't think we want her either.' She looked at Kanchi very doubtfully. The ring in the small nose moved quickly up and down, catching the eye as the girl stood there. How could she take this unwilling, ripe, breathing thing into her house? 'Couldn't she go into some sort of service?' she asked.

'She's a little trouble-the-house,' said Mr Dean softly. 'I thought no one would have patience with her—excepting you.'

Sister Clodagh did not answer. 'I never knew that natives could be lovely until now,' she thought. 'There's this Kanchi, and little Om with his white-heart bottom, and the young General Dilip Rai,' and she thought that this girl was fit to stand beside him in her colours and softness and youth. In these days Sister Clodagh was young and soft herself and she stretched out to Kanchi and took her hand. It was warm and reluctant and unexpectedly hard.

'Very well, we'll try,' said Sister Clodagh. 'I'll take her to Sister Briony who will find her somewhere to sleep.'

He watched them go. Kanchi was carrying her umbrella and trunk and at her dutiful back he smiled; then he looked up and saw that Sister Ruth was watching him through the glass. He went to the edge of the porch and stood there, looking at the dripping gutters and feeling in his pocket for matches. Behind his back she came up step by step along the corridor and flattened herself against the glass, looking down on him. Now he could not see her, but he was aware of her out of the corner of his eyes, and he had an almost irresistible instinct to whip round on her. Instead he lit his pipe, and under cover of his hands, he stole a glance at her; he saw her face pressed against the glass, curiously elongated and flattened, her eyes shining. Then at the frip of Sister Clodagh's skirt she vanished.

'I've left her with Sister Briony,' said Sister Clodagh. 'I think for the present she'd better go into the Lace School with the other girls. I hope she'll settle down.'

'I hope so.' He beckoned to Phuba to bring the pony. 'Well, I mustn't keep you, and I have to go up to the Villa and see the General.'

She hesitated. 'He was very devoted to the boy who died, wasn't he? Is he grieving?'

'Yes.' He took the pony's reins. 'It's hard to tell with these people, they keep face so well, but he's grieving. Kundra was a fine lad.'

'But the other boy—' she said almost timidly. 'He looks as if he could be fine too.'

'Oh, you've seen him, have you?' He did not ask where or how. 'He's been badly brought up and spoilt; the General doesn't know how to make the best of him. I don't know who would,' he added thoughtfully. 'He was here with the Brothers; though it was for such a short while, they managed to make him very enthusiastic. I'm sorry for the boy, he's naïve and very disarming. They don't know how to deal with him and the General won't listen to advice.'

'The Sunnyasi, he's one of the family and surely they'd listen to him,' she spoke out of her interest in the boy. 'Wouldn't he help?'

Mr Dean smiled. 'You don't understand,' he said. 'He doesn't concern himself with things like that. The fact that Kundra dies and Dilip has to go on living is nothing to him.'

'You can't call that holiness,' she cried.

'It's a different kind of holiness,' he said.

'It's inhuman.'

'I think that's what he means it to be,' he answered, pulling down his stirrups. 'Well, thank you for taking in my little lovebird.'

He was looking at her with the same gleam in his eye, but she had not heard him. She was thinking of the girl again and

Sister Briony's face when she had seen her. Kanchi had not said a word, her lids were dropped over her eyes, but she saw everything; she had done what Mr Dean had told her like a little dog, but Sister Clodagh remembered that reluctant hand and the quick breaths agitating the nose ring. She looked swiftly at Mr Dean and met his eye.

'You're sure there's no question you're dying to ask me?' he mocked.

She hesitated. Then she answered firmly: 'None.'

He laughed and put his leg over his pony. 'Then good morning, Saint Clodagh,' he said, and, hitching up his feet, clattered away in the rain.

11

By the end of November the house was finished, except for the class-rooms and dispensary and the chapel. The Refectory and the cubicles and guest rooms were ready, the corridor floors mended and oiled, not a pane was missing in their windows; the roof had been painted a glistening red and the grass on the terrace squared and cut. Inside and out, the house was decent and shining, only the salon was left with its old French colours, and the life around the back doors was as strong and noisy as ever.

Mr Dean was seldom in the house now, but he came up every evening to see the work on the west lawn and usually he came out on the terrace to report to Sister Clodagh.

'I can't tolerate him any longer,' she said on the morning he had brought Kanchi to them. 'I don't see why I should. Why should he suddenly be rude and mock at me like that?' Secretly she knew the answer to that, she had known it as soon as she had uttered that wretched 'None'.

'But I *couldn't* have asked him that,' she cried. 'I'd taken the girl in, against my own judgement for charity's sake. What

more could he expect. Naturally I couldn't help wondering—'
She made up her mind that she would not speak to him again.

But she had to listen to his reports on the work; she had
to direct it and though that 'Saint Clodagh' still rankled, she
seemed to be talking to him most evenings of the week. They
talked of plans and dimensions and the difficulty of getting
seasoned wood, of a leak in the passage and the sink for the
chapel cloakroom; but Sister Ruth saw their faces turned
to one another, full of interest, earnestly talking, and she
watched them hungrily. Sometimes he would take a catalogue
out of his pocket and show it to Sister Clodagh, pointing to
an illustrated window catch or a fertilizer for the garden, and
she saw their heads close together as they bent over the book.
She never failed to watch them, but she never dared to go near
enough to hear what they said. It was at the time that she had
to tidy the class-rooms and get the work ready for to-morrow;
usually she had Kanchi and Joseph then for English, and she
would leave them with a column of letters to write and step
out on to the grass, walking softly round the corner of the
house. She could hear nothing in the wind, only see them pac-
ing backwards and forwards, Sister Clodagh holding her veil
down, Mr Dean's hat over his eyes, while Phuba and the pony
waited on the drive.

Kanchi and Joseph knew very well why she left them. Into
Kanchi's eyes would come a little flicker, she looked sideways
at Sister Ruth, wetting her pencil with her tongue; but Joseph
would keep his eyes down and work busily at his letters.

It was a new habit of Sister Clodagh's to come out after
tea. That was the time, in these short evenings, that the sun
went down, leaving the valley and the foot-hills first, drawing
away from the hills higher and higher until only the sky was in
light. The light spread in ripples; they lapped the terrace while

the tea and the bamboos were lost in the dusk and the buttresses had heavy shadows against the walls. The sun flashed on the corridor windows and dazzled her eyes as she looked at the people going down the steps; the workmen going to their homes, the garden coolies who had left their spades in the earth until tomorrow. She turned to Mr Dean with a smile, but best she liked to be alone with the garden, in its brilliant light that would presently change to dusk.

This was the time that she used to walk on the shore at Liniskelly or, if the men were coming home early, on the lawn, or go through the fields with the dogs. In the greyness the waves lapped the shore and the boats were getting ready to go out; in the fields the dogs ran on, the chestnut sweep of the setter Roderick's tail busy among the rabbit warrens, Gamble and Morna, the spaniels, breaking the bracken; and on the lawn, the light fell from the lamp in the drawing-room and she heard the car wheels on the gravel and smelt a cigar as her father came home.

'Father, is Con coming over?'

'Well, the old man's coming in to play a game with me. How should we know but the young one might be along?'

Often Mr Dean found her with that softness on her face, and the girls going home from the Lace School had to step up to her before she heard their salaams. 'Salaam, Lemini, Salaam.' How long had they been standing there, Maili and Jokiephul giggling into their shawls, fat Samya fidgeting with her umbrella? 'Salaam, Lemini. We'll find you in the morning.'

She was fond of these people. She could not remember when it was that she began to think of them as people; not as natives, persons apart, but as people like themselves, and she was beginning to see with their eyes. Ayah's brown hands carrying a bowl of water no longer seemed alien, but, rather, her own hands stretched out to take it seemed insipid. There was a richness in the brown skins that she liked; in the peasants' red and brown, in the children's coloured rosiness, in their cheerful Mongol faces.

Every Wednesday, she and Sister Briony went to the market, with Joseph as a go-between. The market was in the village square, which was not level but slanted up the hill under the wall of the General's house. Sister Clodagh found that if she were not careful, she would look at it and begin to wonder about the young General and then fall into a day-dream.

They walked between the booths with the people, and there was so much to look at that they were a long time over the things they had come to buy. There were the Bhotiya women at the stalls with their bowls of curds and butter tea; Sister Briony stared at their jewellery, at their girdles and necklaces that were like breast-plates, and their earrings and a coronet they wore of blue and red beads in their hair, which was oiled and plaited round their heads.

'It's like a tiara,' she breathed. 'Fancy finding tiaras here! And you wouldn't think, with all that money, they'd need to keep shop, would you?'

Sister Clodagh liked the kingfisher colours of their clothes and their aprons which were striped and plaqued with embroidery at the corners, and the corn and green of their sleeves.

'What is it they daub their faces with?' asked Sister Briony. 'It's brown, but do you think it's *rouge*?'

'It's pig's blood,' Sister Clodagh told her and Sister Briony shuddered.

The State men had cropped heads and round black hats; their women were dressed in print skirts and jackets, the Italian folds of their shawls falling about flat gilded faces. Then there were the Lepchas, Ayah's people, who were lazy and lusty and bawdy, who wore dark crossed robes and their back hair in two pigtails; their men wore pigtails too, though they had no hair on their faces. The men all wore earrings and had a passion for Homburg hats, Lepchas, Bhotiyas and Tibetan traders. 'Why are they all so much dirtier than the women?' Sister Briony wondered, 'they positively stink'; and she held her large hand-kerchief to her nose as she stopped to stare at a Lama, dirtier than them all, shouting at the crowd for alms, while his disciple walked behind him, bellowing even more loudly.

There were odd things to buy and to find in that far cor-ner of the world. Among the eggs and grain and fruit and oil, were yaks' tails and umbrellas and Lucky Strike cigarettes and Roger and Gallet soap; there was a second-hand bottle shop and a cloth shop with prints from Manchester and Japan, printed with patterns of feathers and shells and moons and stars and daisies. There was always a side-show going on, a story-teller or someone dancing to a drum and a metal fife.

When the village children first saw the nuns out of school they pretended to be frightened and run away, but soon they followed in a pack at their heels, talking about them with Joseph.

'What do they say?' Sister Briony asked, smiling indul-gently at them.

'They say white teeth look funny in white faces, and they want to know if it's true that you have no ears.'

'No ears! Of course we have ears.'

'Then why do you keep them bandaged up?'

'How do they think we hear if we have no ears?' asked Sis-ter Clodagh.

'They think she hears with her mouth,' he said, pointing at Sister Briony. 'It's always a little open; but they don't know about you, you keep yours so tight shut.'

'Ridiculous children,' they said, but they went down to the Convent, both feeling a little displeased.

Sister Honey knew all the children; long before Sister Ruth who taught them could tell them apart, she knew all their names and ages and which were brothers and sisters and which were good or naughty. Every day she saw Om to the gate because she thought he was too young to be trusted down the steps alone. 'He can hardly do more than toddle,' said she indignantly, 'and his mother never knows where he is.'

Hand in hand they would go to the gate at half-past eleven and at four, and they talked to each other all the time, though they hardly knew a word of one another's language. Outside the gateposts the children had drawn a sort of hopscotch on the ground and Sister Honey had been known to pick up her skirts when no one was looking and hop there with the best of them.

'Oh dear. There's the bell. I must go,' she would cry. 'Why, it's twelve o'clock already.'

'Stay, Lemini, stay,' the children cried, catching hold of her veil and her habit and her hands.

'Really I must go. That's the Angelus.' Reluctantly she turned away from them, her veil fell into prim flat folds and her lips moved quickly, as she hastened to say her first 'Hail Mary' and the Office of the hour. They went quickly away behind her back.

They had a great respect for holiness, these children, as whole-hearted a respect as they had for Bhûts or ghosts; not one of them would go near the Sunnyasi and they would not have dared to stay with Sister Honey while she prayed.

It was amazing how quickly the hours came round; it seemed that the bell had hardly rung when it rang again.

'Really, no sooner have I started than I have to stop,' said

Sister Philippa, looking feverishly at her half-cleared flower beds, 'and there's so much that has to be done.' Sister Briony complained that she took time from the laundry to work in the garden, certainly she took it from her own recreation, but she had to interrupt her work it seemed to her continually, she hardly found time to work at all. She took to going into chapel at the last minute, not even waiting to wash her hands. 'What am I thinking of?' she said, 'interrupting my *work* to go to *chapel!* What has come over me to make me think like that. It used to be, it ought to be, the other way round.'

But she was beginning to love her work in the garden. The winter green of the trees and hills was mixed with the frosty colours of the ground; it was hard for the coolies to drive their spades into the earth, the stream seemed to run more slowly and the wood cracked on the bonfire, where she offered up the last stems of the cosmos before returning them in ashes to the beds. Her cheeks burned from the sun and frost as she lay in bed at night, and the walls of her cubicle were bright with visions, not of saints but of flowers.

Nowadays Sister Ruth was often ten minutes late ringing the bell and sometimes none of them noticed except Sister Briony, who was as punctual as any bell under any circumstances. Sister Clodagh herself was sometimes curiously absent-minded as she read the prayers; occasionally she said a prayer through twice, and once, at the end of Compline, she kept them kneeling there for nearly ten minutes. Then she stood up with such a gentle apologetic smile that she did not look like Sister Clodagh at all, and they glanced at her, half awed, as they bobbed to her for their good-nights.

They left her standing by the altar with the candle snuffer

in her hand, but for a long time the candles flickered and smoked in the wind of the open door before she put them out.

12

Father Roberts was to ride out once every two months from Darjeeling and spend the night at St Faith's; it was the best he could do for them, he had a wide parish of his own. 'I wish he could have been with us for All Saints,' said Sister Briony. 'It's one of the happiest days of the year and this year it will seem very empty, I'm afraid. Still, the sacrifice is all the greater, and Our Lord will make it up to us in other ways, I'm sure. Let's be glad Father Roberts can come at all. I'm sure we all need his visit.'

He came in the third week of November and the day of his visit was like a day from another world, their own world that they had done so long without. It was a long joyous day of services and prayers. On the evening of his arrival, tired though he was, he heard Confessions and next morning celebrated Mass. All work was put on one side; the girls and children in the schools sat in orderly and excited rows. Kanchi was sent for to the office, even the workmen came in for their share when the building was inspected. The nuns were suddenly alert, their faces exhilarated and their eyes bright; even their footsteps sounded crisp and the air was disturbed by the constant ringing of the bell. Father Roberts blessed the temporary little chapel in a special service, and took Vespers and Evensong. Sister Clodagh knelt with the other Sisters in the first row. He seemed very tired. She noticed that he prayed for 'Our Gracious King Edward' and that his hands were shaking. 'He's too old for such arduous work,' she thought.

He felt her eyes on him once or twice. '*I don't know what there is about her,*' he wrote afterwards to Mother Dorothea, '*that I find so puzzling.*' '*It's a kind of innate superiority,*' Mother Dorothea wrote back. '*She has always felt herself just a little better than anyone else. What makes it so hard to deal with, is the fact that she undoubtedly is. She has great gifts and one can't deny it. But one day I think she'll learn to know herself. I have always found that it is wiser to let God teach His own lessons in His own time, haven't you?*'

In the early morning of the third day he rode away up the hill. They stood in the porch to see him off.

'I must congratulate you, Sister,' he said. 'You've been more successful than I believed was possible. All the work seems excellent. Excellent. I'll be here in January.'

When he had gone, the Convent sank back into its everyday life; the stimulus died down, quiet closed over it and hardly a trace of his visit was left. Sister Philippa, working late in the dusk on the high terrace, missed saying her Office altogether.

13

Sister Clodagh had made up her mind that rainy morning that she would not talk to Mr Dean again, and how easily she had drifted into it. She had tried to keep up her barrier, but it was so easy to slip into talking when she was with him, that she forgot it; he was so refreshing to talk to after the sameness of the Sisters, such a change that, even when he talked about Kanchi, it was hard to remember that she was offended. She could not be bothered with it; she did not try to bother in these happy relaxed days, she simply let herself drift with the present or sink into the past.

It was like practising the piano; at first your fingers feel cold and stiff, and the notes seem a little sharp on the air and the phrases stupid and meaningless. Then you are warm, it flows, it becomes music and it seems to take you where it flows. It was getting to be a habit with her, to let her mind flow away, to spend minutes and hours back in the past with Con.

When Mr Dean came into her office and put two canvas bags on her desk she looked up at him with an absent smile; she seemed so far away that he nearly said to her: 'Where have you been? Where are you?' Instead he clinked the bags sharply together as he put them down.

'What are those for?' she asked at once.

'The thin one is from me for Kanchi's keep,' he said. 'I suppose ten rupees a month would do it, and ten for all you're teaching her. Anyhow, I've put in twelve notes to last her six months.'

'But you needn't do that, you know,' she said. 'We're endowed.'

'I foisted her on to you, so it's my responsibility. I'd thankfully pay twenty rupees a month to avoid being worried by her, but you needn't let that go any further. The other is money I've extracted from her uncle for her dowry. It's not as imposing as it looks, as it's mostly in four-anna bits and pice, but I want you to keep it like that for her. I'll get some more from him later. You see, if I pay her dowry the husband would certainly think he'd been cheated, it's got to be small and authentic in bits and pieces like this. Is she being a nuisance?'

'She's settling down amazingly well. She's very good.'

There were only two things in the world that Kanchi cared about, and one of them was herself. It was for that reason she stayed at the Convent; she knew she had been behaving very foolishly and that Dean Sahib had been right to bring her here, but she had to be careful or she might have betrayed herself again.

It was not for nothing that Kanchi had those ripe sweet cheeks and that honey-coloured skin. Dean Sahib had saved her so far, now she had to save herself; to save herself up for something that glimmered on the far horizon, that she could not put into words. She was doing well with the nuns; that was easy because she was quick and glib. She helped Ayah with her work in the mornings before she went to the Lace School, and nothing could have annoyed Ayah more than that; and after the schools were closed she did light work for Sister Briony. She went over the morning's dusting with a feather brush that Sister Briony had given her. In the cold light that came through the glass panes, the colours of her sleeves and veil moved like wings; and if one of the men came by, a peon or a house-boy, or one of the workmen, he seemed to be constrained to stand watching her; and as if the feathers of the brush had tickled him, a slow delighted smile came into his face and he would forget the hammer he had been sent to fetch, or let his tray tilt further and further, until the milk dribbled out of the jug and Ayah pounced from a doorway.

Kanchi flicked on with her brush, the lids of her eyes and her small smile making the shape of three half-moons in her face.

In the Lace School the girls sat on the verandah with their cushions while the new school was being built. Samya, the Bhotiya girl, was glossy with health and grooming; Maili was plump too, her nose ring gave her the appearance of a charming little bull, but there was something about Kanchi's waist, the demure supple knot of her skirt length that stole the eye away; and there were far too many excuses, Pin Fong told Mr Dean, to go past the verandah from the men.

'You behave. I'm watching you,' said Mr Dean, and Kanchi kept her eyes on her bobbins. She wanted to stay, for a time at any rate. Dean Sahib was right, she had made a little silly of herself and that was better forgotten. She wanted to stay here, where the food was good and she was filling out into even more delightful curves; where her presence was pleasantly annoying to Ayah, and she was gaining prestige by her monkey cleverness in making this lace and learning the Catechism.

She was taking pains to impress the nuns and the grieved and puzzled way she looked at Mr Dean was very well done. He smiled at her and said: 'That's a good girl,' and added: 'If you give them any trouble, mind, I'll send you back to your uncle.' When she had been there a day she said she had never been so happy in her life; when she had been there a week, she wanted to become a Christian.

'Isn't that wonderful!' cried Sister Honey. 'In one short week!'

'Almost too wonderful,' said Sister Clodagh. 'We'll have to wait and see.'

'Sister, I don't want to discourage her.'

'A little opposition won't discourage her if she's really sincere,' said Sister Clodagh. 'You can teach her some Scripture if you like, providing her uncle doesn't object, and she can see Father Roberts when he comes.'

Her uncle had no objections. 'Teach her anything you like,' he said generously. 'I don't suppose it will do her any harm.'

Though Sister Clodagh spoke in such a *lukewarm* way, as Sister Honey said, with the help of a dictionary and grammar that the Brothers had left behind she began laboriously to translate the Catechism, some prayers and a few easy hymns to be used in the school. It was slow, difficult work; it was hard not to dream as she did it, and she seemed to get very little done at a time.

'What are you working on?' asked Mr Dean, as he tied the money bags, catching sight of the grammar. Without asking he looked at the book spread on her desk and read '*Love thy neighbour as thyself*' and the translation beside it. 'You've got that wrong,' he said. 'That's not the imperative. Let me show you.' Below it in her writing he saw her notes. '*Have I hurt anyone in any way? Have I tried to do to others as I would like*

*them to do to me? Have I considered others as more important
than myself? Have I spoken kindly to others, never saying anything that would hurt another's feelings? Have I thought kindly
of everyone?'*

'Very salutary for you and for me,' he said, 'but are you
going to translate it all? It'll take you a month of Sundays.'

'It's for Kanchi and others like her,' she said. 'Kanchi says
she would like to be a Christian.'

'Do you believe her?'

'Of course it remains to be seen if she's sincere,' she
answered coldly.

'And meanwhile, you're doing all this work for that
improbable pea that is Kanchi's soul. Good God, Sister, don't
you know trash when you see it?'

'No one's soul is trash,' she said steadily. 'Everyone is valuable to God.'

'I should like to know just what He'd give for that thieving,
self-seeking, shallow little opportunist.'

'He gave Himself.'

'Have you no sense of proportion?' he cried, and then: 'Do
you really believe that? Sister, the people here worship the
mountain. They think it concerns itself with them. They're
silly, aren't they?'

She was silent, her lips set, and he repeated: 'Everyone is
valuable to God. What's the use of teaching them that?'

On impulse she asked him: 'What would you teach them,
Mr Dean?'

'I wouldn't teach anyone,' he said thoughtfully, 'but if I
were you, I should teach them poverty.'

'*Poverty?*'

'Yes,' he said slowly. 'Poverty. All of them. We're all hoping
for something better, if not here, in another world. Teach us

me. Look at our Holy Man; he has a good English blanket and skins to lie on, and there's never been anyone holier than he.'

They had noticed that the Sunnyasi had a great fire and Sister Clodagh had seen a snow leopard skin hung outside his hut, but he still sat motionless in front of it, his face turned to the snows.

Joseph collected broken apple wood for their fires and the ponies brought in logs from the forest. The wood was stacked in the passage and the house smelled of it, and the Sisters found chips of bark and moss in their skirts at night. The ponies, coming through the forest, had fringes of ice on their eyelashes and the hairs in their ears frozen stiff; when they breathed, they smoked through their nostrils like dragons, and Sister Philippa used to give the old pony 'Love' a seer of hot milk when he came in.

The air grew so fine and cold that the hills and the trees and the house shimmered in it and the nuns, in their white veils, seemed to wear haloes as they worked. Sister Clodagh thought their faces had changed, that it was not only the light that made them shine, and she sent down a very favourable report to Reverend Mother.

On Fridays they fasted until three o'clock, and kept Saturday, when the schools were closed, as their day of silence; in the cold, at that altitude, to fast was nearly unbearable. Every Friday by middle day she was on the point of ordering coffee and bread at the very least, but every Friday they had managed to hold out and she had not ordered it yet. She had meant to ask about it in her weekly letter to Mother Dorothea, but she had only asked for a dispensation for Sister Ruth as she did not seem well.

On the second Friday in December she had a feeling of light-headedness, as if, when she walked, she were standing still and the air flowed past her and the ground spread away in rings under her feet. She seemed ringed with air in which there was no colour, only a sense of colour; of the white walls and the green trees and grass, the dots of nuns wearing their black winter habits and a blue whiteness that was the air itself. She felt her own heart beating, a suffocation in her head and she thought suddenly that if she were one of the eagles flying in the gulf she would feel like this, seeing on tilted wings the colours of earth and snows and sky. However she soared and struggled, the gulf pressed down on her, and she gained not an inch on the mountain.

The sense of fright came back to her that she had felt in the Rest House at Goontu; restlessly she left her desk and walked round the Convent in this strange ringing and flowing, trying to still the fear in her mind. 'It's because I'm hungry,' she thought. 'We shall have to give up the fast here. I'll find Sister Briony and tell her to get coffee.'

She went to the dispensary, but there was only Sister Honey putting belladonna on a hill-woman's breast; at the smell of the belladonna she almost vomited and went hastily away.

The lace workers were sitting together on one mat to keep warm; they blew on their fingers before touching the bobbins and Kanchi slipped her hands in her sleeves as soon as the Sister turned her back. Sister Ruth had Joseph for an English writing lesson; in spite of her breakfast she looked cold and blue. Joseph was writing the letters of the alphabet, his pencil kept on squeaking on his slate, and at each squeak Sister Ruth drew her brows together and winced; then Joseph gave her a humble and sorrowful glance and delicately, with his tongue out, would try the pencil again.

Sister Briony was busy in the kitchen and yard. 'I had to come out,' she said, 'to store away these apples. I couldn't leave them lying about. Sister Blanche has taken over for me.' Her skirts were tucked up out of the wet and Sister Clodagh could see her great feet, hobbling with chafecracks and chilblains. She was putting the apples on the shelves, arranging them in rows so that they did not touch one another.

'Are they worth all that?' asked Sister Clodagh.

'I'm not really storing them, I'm just putting them here until I have time to make them into jam.'

'Aren't they too bitter for jam?'

'Oh, no! We mustn't waste them. If they're too bitter for jam, they'll make jelly if I put plenty of sugar.'

'But wouldn't that be a waste of sugar?'

'I shouldn't use the best sugar. There's the country sugar they sell in the market and I can buy that. It's quite pure, and at any rate it will be thoroughly well boiled.'

'So long as you're sure you won't give us all typhoid—'

'Oh, no! Besides, we've all been inoculated.'

'And it would be a pity to waste that, wouldn't it?' said Sister Clodagh. Sister Briony annoyed her this morning, how could she be always and consistently the same? Not hunger, nor surprise, nor atmosphere could move her, she followed her own nose cheerfully, for ever in her cheerful, familiar little rut. Without asking for the coffee, she left her and walked down the corridor.

The boards of the floor seemed to widen and narrow as she walked and the panes of glass to pass by her in a blur, until she came to the front door which was open. There the wheeling colours resolved themselves into a young man sitting on a pony in the porch.

It was the General's nephew, the young General Dilip Rai. He and his pony had been in the porch for a long time; he had not seen a bell-pull before and there was no knocker, it was so quiet that he did not like to shout. His pony sniffed the flower pots on the steps and pushed one with his nose. Hot with horror, the young General reined him back.

He looked at the crucifix. He recognized it and he expected to find it there, for the Brothers had had one and these were real Jesus Christ ladies, but he wondered what the holy water stoup was for; it looked too small for drinking and he thought perhaps it was for flowers. His Great Uncle had marigold and melted butter and pots of curds and milk on his shrine; he thought this one would have been all the prettier for some marigolds.

There was a box marked LETTERS and underneath 'Servants of Mary'. That was a strange idea to put the servants' letters in a box; in his house none of the servants could read or write so that it would have been no good to send them letters, but perhaps here, where he had heard they were all so clever, the servants had already been taught to read and write and the Sisters gave them their orders by letter. He supposed that the principal Sister was Mary.

Ayah and Joseph had told him that the nuns were called Mother and Sister, just as the Brothers had been Father and Brother; it made him blush to think of calling them that, but he had practised it aloud and he wished one of them would come.

When he saw Sister Clodagh coming down the corridor, he dismounted; his pony rubbed its face on his legs and dribbled on his shoe; as she came to the door, he was rubbing one shoe over the other trying to make it clean.

He was just as she remembered him, in the dark fitting achkan and the gold earrings, but now he had come so close he seemed suddenly much more of a man. He carried a hat and gloves and stick, and he smelled of cigarettes and there could have her up and teach her a little here. Though I'm not I.C.S., my Uncle is a very important man.'

'I think,' said Sister Clodagh, 'that you had better tie up your pony and come with me.'

In the office he put his hat and gloves on the edge of her desk and then picked them up, blushing, and put them on the carpet stool. When he sat down, he took another piece of paper from his gold case.

'Before I came to you,' he told her, 'I wrote out my timetable. Please read it and give me your advice. I want to study far harder than with the Brothers. You will see that I have decided to study every subject, every day, and not spare myself. In that way I shall get on.'

She took the paper. He had written it carefully on both sides and drawn the hours in red ink:

5 a.m.–7 a.m.	Algebra and Geometry and Arithmetic with the Mathematical Sister.
8 a.m.–10 a.m.	Studying Religions, especially Christianity, with the Scriptural Sister.
10 a.m.	Art.
1 p.m.–3 p.m.	French and German with the French and German Sisters (if any).
3 p.m.–4 p.m.	Physics with the Physical Sister.

She laid it hastily down on her desk, without reading any more. He was looking at her searchingly. 'Do you think my ideas are any good? Will you let me come? Of course I give you carte blanche and all that to alter it in any way, if you think so. You see I mean to study earnestly, I must prove to you my energy and interest.'

quiet that he did not like to shout. His pony sniffed the flower pots on the steps and pushed one with his nose. Hot with horror, the young General reined him back.

He looked at the crucifix. He recognized it and he expected to find it there, for the Brothers had had one and these were real Jesus Christ ladies, but he wondered what the holy water stoup was for; it looked too small for drinking and he thought perhaps it was for flowers. His Great Uncle had marigold and melted butter and pots of curds and milk on his shrine; he thought this one would have been all the prettier for some marigolds.

There was a box marked LETTERS and underneath 'Servants of Mary'. That was a strange idea to put the servants' letters in a box; in his house none of the servants could read or write so that it would have been no good to send them letters, but perhaps here, where he had heard they were all so clever, the servants had already been taught to read and write and the Sisters gave them their orders by letter. He supposed that the principal Sister was Mary.

Ayah and Joseph had told him that the nuns were called Mother and Sister, just as the Brothers had been Father and Brother; it made him blush to think of calling them that, but he had practised it aloud and he wished one of them would come.

When he saw Sister Clodagh coming down the corridor, he dismounted; his pony rubbed its face on his legs and dribbled on his shoe; as she came to the door, he was rubbing one shoe over the other trying to make it clean.

He was just as she remembered him, in the dark fitting achkan and the gold earrings, but now he had come so close he seemed suddenly much more of a man. He carried a hat and gloves and stick, and he smelled of cigarettes and there was a line of hair, almost like a moustache, on his upper lip; he might be seventeen, she thought.

She looked at him without speaking and tried to think just why it was he made her think of Con. She could hardly bear to look at him. Con had fair hair and a skin almost too white for a man but the quality of him was there in the young General waiting to speak to her. Con was in America; he was over forty, but she could not believe that. He was far more here, in this young Rajput, fumbling with his hat and gloves.

'Good morning,' he said, 'I want to see the Superior Sister.'

He spoke English naïvely, as if he were not quite certain of the effect it would produce, and at the sound of his voice, his little horse put its face against his arm.

'I'm the Sister Superior,' said Sister Clodagh. 'What—what can I do for you?'

'I want to be a student here with you. I want to study a lot of learning. I have heard about you, that you are all very clever. I want to study mathematics and history and poetry and languages. Have you a Sister to teach these things? I have a note from my Uncle to you, to ask you to encourage me.'

'I'm very sorry,' said Sister Clodagh, not taking the note. 'We only teach children and young girls.'

'Why?'

'A convent doesn't take men pupils.'

'That's not very polite to men.'

'We don't mean it like that. It's the custom. The Brotherhoods are for teaching men, the Convents for the girls.'

'But there aren't any Brotherhoods here now, so that I think you should teach me. Jesus Christ was a man,' he added, looking at the crucifix.

'He took the shape of a man,' she said, trying in her light-headedness to choose adequate words.'

'But you needn't count me as a man,' said Dilip Rai. 'I'm only interested in studious things. I needn't count as a man.'

She looked at his height and his slimness and his face with its delicate moustache and at his hands, hairless and small, but unmistakably a man's.

'How can I be a student if you don't help me?' he asked. 'Please. My Uncle was going to send me to Paris and London and Edinburgh, for all of which I have introductions and a very great admiration. I was to go to the University of Cambridge; now that my brother is dead my Uncle says that I mustn't go. I thought if I studied and learnt quickly, he might change his mind and think me so clever that it would be a pity not to send me after all. How can I do that if you won't help me? My dear tutor, Narayan Babu, has gone away and the Brothers have gone away too; I have no one left but you. And there is something else. I have to marry and have a baby son; it is our custom that my Uncle should choose my wife, but Narayan Babu has taught me that is old-fashioned and I am modern, I want to choose my wife myself. I should like to marry a girl that you have taught and then, if you teach me too, we should enjoy our culture together in our own home. I should like to marry a Bengali; I have only known one Bengali, but I think they are very intelligent, don't you? In fact, I cut this out of the paper. Of course it's only an idea, you may not approve, but would you please read it and give me your advice.'

From a gold cigarette case he took out a cutting:

'Wanted, for a fair complexioned girl, now studying B.A. knows music and knitting, a gentleman of position, preferably I.C.S. or other adequate post. Apply Box—'

He watched her expression as she read it. 'Don't you think that might be a favourable idea?' he asked. 'You see, it says she is studying B.A. and even if she's not a girl you've taught, we could have her up and teach her a little here. Though I'm not I.C.S., my Uncle is a very important man.'

'I think,' said Sister Clodagh, 'that you had better tie up your pony and come with me.'

In the office he put his hat and gloves on the edge of her desk and then picked them up, blushing, and put them on the carpet stool. When he sat down, he took another piece of paper from his gold case.

'Before I came to you,' he told her, 'I wrote out my timetable. Please read it and give me your advice. I want to study far harder than with the Brothers. You will see that I have decided to study every subject, every day, and not spare myself. In that way I shall get on.'

She took the paper. He had written it carefully on both sides and drawn the hours in red ink:

5 a.m.–7 a.m.	Algebra and Geometry and Arithmetic with the Mathematical Sister.
8 a.m.–10 a.m.	Studying Religions, especially Christianity, with the Scriptural Sister.
10 a.m.	Art.
1 p.m.–3 p.m.	French and German with the French and German Sisters (if any).
3 p.m.–4 p.m.	Physics with the Physical Sister.

She laid it hastily down on her desk, without reading any more. He was looking at her searchingly. 'Do you think my ideas are any good? Will you let me come? Of course I give you carte blanche and all that to alter it in any way, if you think so. You see I mean to study earnestly, I must prove to you my energy and interest.'

'I must consult Sister Briony,' said Sister Clodagh. 'In a day or two, when we have talked it all over, I'll send you a note to let you know our decision.'

'But I want you to tell me now,' he cried in dismay. 'My Uncle goes away to-day and I want to tell him before he leaves. Why should there be any difficulty? I can start now. I have brought my pony's feed with me, and I have eaten before I came so that I could stay a nice long time.'

She looked at him helplessly and rang her bell.

He was asked to wait in the salon that he knew well; but not with the floor polished and smelling of wax, and the chairs standing primly round the wall and the lamp burning quietly in front of the figure of the Sacred Heart. He liked the lamp, he thought it was a pretty red colour, the red of rhododendrons in the spring. As he stood there, Kanchi came in, flicking with her brush and, seeing him staring at the shrine, with lowered lids she came to dust it, which she was strictly forbidden to do. The gold of the niche and its gold rays and the gold in her nose ring shone in the warm light, and he stood there thinking how delightful and pretty they were until the office door opened.

'This is a wild place,' Sister Briony had said, 'it's an uncommon place and, yes, we must expect to have to do uncommon things.'

That was a surprise after what Sister Clodagh had thought half an hour ago; Sister Briony should have wanted to do what had always been done before.

'As the boy says, he has no other means of learning and we don't want to offend his Uncle, Sister. I don't see how we can refuse. He might turn us out. Why not try it, and meanwhile you could write to Reverend Mother and Father Roberts.'

'Ye-es,' said Sister Clodagh. 'As you say, we mustn't offend the General, and yet—' She was curiously reluctant to allow him in. It was somehow bound up with the fear of the morning.

'In any case I should ask Mr Dean. He's so nice and sensible, and yet they tell you such terrible things about him that he would be sure to know the very worst about the boy. He seems a nice young man. He stood up as I passed through the reception room and I thought that encouraging in a native Royalty. He doesn't seem in the least spoilt. Let's ask Mr Dean.'

He was not enthusiastic when Sister Clodagh consulted him. 'Won't you be letting a cuckoo into your nest?' he said.

This was so exactly her own feeling that she stared.

'Apart from that, you may have trouble with Kanchi.'

'I don't think that,' she said. 'She won't see him, and she knows very well that she's a little servant and he's the General's heir.'

'I expect she knows the story of the king and the beggar maid all the same,' he said. 'I wasn't thinking only of Kanchi. You've never done anything like this before, and it's letting a new element into your lives. Don't you think you've got enough to digest already?'

She looked at him stiffly and for one of the few times in her life she felt herself flushing; she could feel it tingling her face and neck under her wimple. 'I only asked you to tell me something about the boy.'

He said: 'You don't need me to tell you you must keep him off religion. That boy can never be converted to Christianity.'

'We're not in the habit of trying to convert our pupils,' she answered icily.

'You ought not to be able to help it,' he said.

15

'I should like to do something for the children,' said Sister Honey.

Sister Clodagh looked up. She had not heard Sister Honey come in, and now the Sister was standing beside her, twisting her hands together and speaking very earnestly. 'I *feel* I could do something for them.'

'You do a great deal already.'

'I play with them and help in the classes sometimes; but—' Sister Honey turned pink, 'I feel I'm only there on *sufferance*.'

'You have all your own work to do. Isn't that enough? I expect we could find some more girls if you feel that you could manage them.'

'But it's the *children* I should like to help. Not of course that I'd ever neglect the girls, and I think you'll allow that they're getting on well. I'd thought of some kind of a clinic for the children; some kind of welfare work, Sister. My time isn't *fully* occupied. I mean I could find time to do it without neglecting anything and it goes to my heart to see them so ragged and dirty. If I could teach the mothers to care for their babies and keep them cleaner—'

'How would you get them to come to your clinic?' asked Sister Clodagh. 'The General's away, and we haven't the money to pay them, as he did to start the schools and patients.'

'Well, I'd thought of giving them little presents,' said Sister Honey blushing, 'just to begin with,' she pleaded. 'Penny toys and those little flannel coats that are sent out by the box-full. You remember, Sister, we brought some with us and we could easily ask for more. And I had thought—' the words came tumbling out, 'that now the new Lace School is so nearly finished, the girls could move in there and I could use the part of the verandah they're in now. Mr Dean could put up some shelves and I could take a table from the house, and the people needn't come inside at all, but could wait in the class-room, if I could have an afternoon a week when it isn't being used. Sister Briony would help me. I could talk to the mothers about keeping the babies clean, and give them ointment for their eyes, because their eyes are shocking, aren't they? And their ringworm is too. And I could weigh them and give them clean clothes and—'

'One minute. One minute,' said Sister Clodagh. 'This must be thought out carefully. You mustn't go so fast.'

'But it *is* a good idea, isn't it, Sister?'

'It's a damn fool idea,' said Mr Dean. Sister Clodagh had asked for the tables and shelves for the clinic which Sister Honey was to be allowed to start as an experiment under Sister Briony's eye. He measured the wall for a set of shelves. 'You'll be sorry for this, see if you're not.'

'What makes you say that?' asked Sister Clodagh coldly. 'It seems to me that Sister Blanche may fill a very much needed want by this work.'

'Remember what I told you when you opened your dispensary? Sister Briony's a sensible woman, but Sister Honey is not, saving her presence.' Sister Honey gave a little squeak of dismay. 'You know yourself you've got no sense,' he said, smiling at her. 'These babies are born like flies and die like flies; the mothers think that's right and natural, but if you start monkeying about with them and *then* they die, just you wait and see what happens.'

'If they're ill she won't touch them,' said Sister Clodagh. 'They'll go to Sister Briony in the usual way. Sister Blanche will only treat things like sore eyes and sores, and try to teach them a little hygiene and give them clean clothes and soap.'

'You're not going to let her *wash* them?' cried Mr Dean in horror.

'Of course I shall encourage them to wash,' said Sister Honey.

'Damn it all, don't let her start tricks like that,' he said earnestly. 'Let her put muck on their eyes and plaster their sores if she must. If you want to do good you might give them pure oil and warm clothes, but you must stop her at that. Scratch any mother and you find a savage, but scratch a savage mother and I'll not answer for what you'll find.'

Sister Honey was inclined to be tearful and pout, but Sister Clodagh said thoughtfully: 'You must remember to go carefully, Sister.'

Sister Honey told Sister Briony.

'He's perfectly right,' said Sister Briony, 'and just you remember it, Sister. Don't let me find you carrying out any fancy ideas of your own. Mr Dean knows what he's talking about. We want you to do good, not harm.'

'As if I would harm them,' said Sister Honey, smoothing one of the flannelette coatees as tenderly as if it were a baby itself. 'As if I'd harm them when I love them so.'

16

It was on Christmas Eve, when they had been out in the forest cutting boughs, that Mr Dean sent Phuba up with a parcel. The Sisters' feet were soaking when they came in and, even after rubbings and dry stockings, they could not get warm. They gathered round Phuba, stamping their feet and wrapping their cold hands in their sleeves. He was a tall old Bhotiya with a pigtail hanging to his hams and, like Mr Dean, he wore a felt hat of no shape at all, but in his he had a peacock's feather.

'It's a parcel for us!' cried Sister Honey.

'Not for us,' corrected Sister Clodagh. 'Mr Dean knows better than to send us presents. It's for the Order.'

'That's splitting a hair,' said Sister Ruth boldly, but, as if she had not heard her, Sister Clodagh opened the parcel. Inside were five pairs of Tibetan boots, knee high and made of felt and worked with wool and lined with fleece.

'Ahh!' whispered Sister Briony, going down on her knees as if they were something holy. 'Dear goodness! Just feel the warmth and the fleece and the softness. Blessings on the dear,

dear man. Now I shall be able to get about on my poor feet without wanting to cry at every step.'

But Sister Clodagh was looking at them doubtfully as if she had half a mind to send them back. 'I wonder if we ought to take them. These are gifts to us, not to the Community.'

'I don't agree,' said Sister Briony. 'I don't agree at all, if you'll excuse me saying so, dear Sister. Mr Dean knows how our work has been spoiled and crippled, yes really crippled by this cold. I don't know how many things I've been forced to leave undone because of hobbling so badly on my poor feet. I shall put on a pair at once and thank God for them and Mr Dean.'

She sat down there and then on a stool and, grimacing, took off her own leather boots and drew on the largest pair of Mr Dean's. 'He must have measured us up very nicely,' she chuckled. 'I always have difficulty in getting fitted, but these are plenty big enough for me.'

'And didn't he make me call you one by one across the yard when the mud was soft?' said Ayah in huge delight. 'And he measured the footsteps and wrote it all down on the paper he keeps in his hat.'

Sister Briony's feet looked an elephant's in the high felt boots, but her face wore a look of bliss. When Sister Clodagh saw that they did not show too much under her habit and that the colours were not really too bright, she told the others that they might wear them too. Sister Ruth did not try hers on, but sat apart with them, touching them with her finger and looking at them; there was something tense and childish in that look that gave Sister Clodagh a sudden shiver.

'Come along,' Sister Briony said to her. 'We have all this litter to clear and supper to eat before we can start hanging the boughs. Pick up your boots and get on.'

'Don't you *touch* them,' said Sister Ruth turning on her. 'Don't you *dare* lay a finger on them.'

Sister Briony was folding up the parcel paper and undoing the smallest knots in the string, and did not hear her, but Sister Clodagh watched her sharply.

'I wish we could do something for Mr Dean after all he's done for us,' said Sister Honey. 'Couldn't we invite him to the carol singing, Sister?'

'No,' cried Sister Ruth fiercely. 'That wouldn't do at all.'

'Sister Blanche was speaking to me and not to you,' said Sister Clodagh, still watching her. 'Mr Dean can certainly come to the carol singing if he likes. The service is open to everyone who cares to come.' She saw her face darken, but she picked up the papers and carried them away without answering.

Joseph had been given boots too; his had come in the Christmas Box from Canstead. When he saw them he licked his lips uneasily.

'Look,' cried Sister Honey. 'They've come all the way from England. Joseph, aren't you a lucky little boy?' and Joseph's heart sank as she showed him the laces and the toe-caps and the beautiful welted soles. He felt he was bound to keep them always with him, and, after that, Joseph could be seen trotting on his errands with his beautiful English boots hung round his neck.

All the servants had presents.

'These are extraordinary people,' said Ayah. 'I don't understand them.' She folded the cardigan that had come for her in the box. 'They buy coolie blankets for themselves and sleep on thin cotton, and this, that they *give* to me, is thick wool and good bone buttons; and yet they don't owe me anything, they always pay my wages on the first of every month.'

Sister Honey had spent hours in making a Crib for the children; she had put it inside the porch as there was no room in the chapel, and it was made of spruce and bamboo boughs strangely mingled together. The figures for it had been sent from Canstead too, and she made them change colour by holding strips of coloured talc across a light. She made a rosy Bethlehem dawn outside the Inn, or a strong noon in yellow, or moonlight, shadowing with blue the tinsel star. The people thought it was wonderful and Sister Honey was gratified by their numbers, but she did not know that Ayah had invited them with promises of a free show and free tea. There were the women in their respectable gowns, the men who were so dirty in comparison and, most of all, the children.

'Why have the devils with wings come to mock at the poor baby?' asked the children, pointing to the angels.

'The baby is the Number One Lord Jesus Christ,' Ayah told them.

'But He hasn't any clothes on! Aren't they going to give Him anything? Not a little red robe? Not a bit of melted butter?'

'This is His Mother,' said Ayah, showing them the little porcelain Virgin in blue and white and pink. 'He is her child.'

'*That* isn't true,' said the women, measuring the baby with their eyes. 'He's too big to be possible. Probably He's a dragon, a bhût in the shape of a child, and presently He'll eat up the woman.'

They were all afraid of bhûts, Hindus and Buddhists alike, and the little Christian Joseph would not go down to Mr Dean's house alone at night because of the bhût who lived on the road.

All day the people came softly in and out; the porch was full of voices respectfully low, and of feet coming and going. A tide of love and liking seemed to lap the Convent; it was in Ayah's dark skirts as she went to welcome them in, and it was in the china figures under the boughs of spruce; it came from the children's happy faces as they crowded round, and was in the nuns' voices as they spoke to one another and in the candles they had lit before the Crib. All day Sister Clodagh had felt that sense of success and love and again she wrote glowingly to Mother Dorothea.

At midnight Sister Clodagh read the Christmas prayers and psalms. The new harmonium had come; the ponies had carried it down, two harnessed together under its weight. When it was uncrated, the packing straw was frozen stiff, but it was not any the worse, and when Sister Honey practised on it, the music rolled down the hill. The wind carried it over the trees and across the gulf; in the village they woke to listen; it came in through the windows of the General's house and reached Mr Dean as he sat at his dining-room table drinking the whisky that the General had sent him for Christmas. Sister Honey had not played for a long time and, even after practising, sometimes there would come, instead of a note, a long breath of wind or a sudden vibration that startled the room and jarred the window panes.

The chapel was festive; they had laid branches along the sills and crossed them at the foot of the statues, and on the altar were the few precious sprays of holly that had come from the hedges at Canstead. After prayers came the carols, that were always sung by the Sisters on the first hour of Christmas morning. Sister Briony, Sister Philippa and Sister Ruth had risen in the front line, Kanchi and Joseph from among the empty seats behind them, Sister Clodagh stood by the altar facing them, when the door opened on the night and Mr Dean came in and with him the young General, Dilip Rai.

The harmonium gave a long wail and a jar, the singing wavered, the book Sister Clodagh was holding dipped closer to the candle flames; then her voice rose:

'I sing of a maiden
That is matchless,
King of all Kings
For her Son she chose.'

Mr Dean kicked over a chair as he moved in near the door; Dilip, shocked and blushing, picked it up and set it on its legs. Sister Briony, still singing, stepped from her place and offered them the sheet of words, and Mr Dean began to sing. Sister Clodagh thought his voice was unnecessarily loud, but it gave impetus to the Sisters, who sang loudly too, their crosses rising and falling on their breasts as if they were panting. Now there was a warmth and rush in the singing, their faces reddened, the harmonium notes seemed to swell in the room and the boughs trembled. The meek familiar carols were almost shouted into the night.

Mr Dean was enjoying himself, but Dilip's eyes were full of wonder. He looked at the altar with its lace and holly, the candles shining on the brass cross and the statues above the boughs. Sister Clodagh watched his face as she sang.

On that last Christmas, Con had given her a silver brooch. He was not good at giving things in proper season, but he had always bought her a great many presents. She remembered once, when they were in the High Street at Pantown, he had stopped and said: 'I want to give you a hat.'

Pantown! They always drove to Pantown in the lorry because there was usually a netted pig or a steer to take in. 'It's market day. We're taking in the bull calf. Like a lift?'

The lorry had no side windows, the wind blew in a hurricane, and the rain trickled to where she sat between the old man and Con, tweed shoulder to tweed shoulder. Often her cheek touched Con's shoulder, the short gold hairs that were clipped on his neck were close to her lips. They swayed and bumped, hip to hip.

'*Do* keep your skirt off the gears,' said Con. 'Listen to the brutes! You wouldn't know it, but one day I'm going to have a Bentley,' and he shot a glance at his father across her.

In the High Street he said, 'I want to buy you a hat.'

'You can't. Don't be silly, Con.'

'I want to. Come on.'

The harmonium finished the last line, pelting ahead of the singers. In the silence she looked up. 'Number six, on your sheets. "Once in Royal David's city".'

The only hat shop was Strayne's; it had cream blinds edged with lace and a tapestry chair in the window, and a bowl of anemones on the floor. Why on the floor?

> '*He was gentle, meek and lowly,*
> *Tears and smiles like us he knew.*'

Tears and smiles! That was the year that hats were shaped like pudding basins and pails. Con was difficult over them.

'That one's like a bucket. Take it away. No, thank you, that's too much of a flower-pot altogether.'

'What kind of a hat *do* you want, sir?'

'Well, I had in mind a very little one; grey with something bright and soft on it, like feathers and diamonds mixed.'

But the brooch had come on Christmas Day. He gave it to her outside, after church. 'Here's something for you.' He walked away to talk to the other men.

'Con, come back. Come back for a moment. I want to speak to you.'

The music had stopped again. They had come to the end of the carols and they were waiting for her. She knelt; they all knelt, she could see Sister Honey out of the corner of her eye, the soles of her feet in Mr Dean's boots were turned upwards. Mr Dean sat down noisily and Dilip Rai very quietly, Kanchi looked through her fingers at them.

Sister Clodagh was the last to leave the chapel; she put out the candles dreamily. As they went out one by one and the room grew dim, the night and the stars seemed to come closer to the windows, pressing cloud and gold against the glass. Now only the red lamp was burning in front of the altar; it was the colour of cherries; Dilip would have called it the colour of rhododendrons, he always said 'red as rhododendrons', 'white as rhododendrons'. He had been taking lessons for ten days now.

She knelt down before leaving the chapel. 'Con, come back. Come back for a moment. I want to speak to you.'

There was a scuffle outside and a small scream, and steps ran past into the house. She went to the door but there was no one there, only the young General and Mr Dean a little way off, standing with their ponies under the porch.

Dilip Rai came up to her at once and said: 'Sister, may I congratulate you on the birth of Christ?'

'Thank you,' she said, not knowing what else to say. She saw Mr Dean smile in the light of the porch lantern.

'I was so glad to come,' Dilip said. 'I heard the music, and went down to ask Dean what it was, and he brought me to see. I hope you did not mind. I am very much interested in Jesus Christ.' Sister Clodagh stiffened and he said quickly: 'Have I said anything wrong?'

'No-o,' she answered, 'but we don't usually speak of Him so casually.'

'Then you should,' said Mr Dean loudly. 'He should be casual, and as much a part of life as—hic—your d-daily bread.'

She ignored that. 'We want to thank you for the boots,' she said. 'Sister Briony will tell you, far more eloquently than I can, how very much we needed them; and now we have a present for you. Real holly sent to us by our Mother General at Canstead. It was picked from our hedge there; we have only a few sprays, but we kept them for the chapel and for you, because you have been so good to us.'

The young General, who had been thinking, asked: 'You have a feast to commemorate His death, haven't you?'

'Yes, at Easter. His death and resurrection,' said Sister Clodagh, holding out the holly to Mr Dean who made no movement to take it.

'In the history of my country,' said Dilip gravely, 'there is a superstition that, if a man asks for his shoes and umbrella when he is dying, he will come back from the dead.'

Mr Dean gave a loud guffaw, and Sister Clodagh saw that he was very drunk, holding on to his saddle and watching her and Dilip with affectionate amusement. She was shocked to her very bones, and for a moment could only stand there, staring at him. Dilip, with his head bent, was drawing a circle on the gravel with his toe; he was quivering with shame because Mr Dean had laughed at him.

His laugh had broken the silence. Though the house was quiet it seemed to be full of people; behind Dilip Rai it lay with a teeming life of its own. She had a sudden sense of dismay that came from the house and not from Mr Dean, a sense that she was an interloper in it and the Convent life no more than a cobweb that would be brushed away. The house had its own people, strange bare-footed people who had never had a Christmas, nor a star, nor a Christ. Dilip fitted them, standing in the porch with his horse as if he had just come through the forest. '*The grandfather kept his women here.*'

She seemed to hear the door opened in the night, and hear them coming, running, gauze hurriedly twisted round their bosoms, flowers seized and pinned in the hair, feet with anklets chiming, hastening to the door. She heard them come and she heard their voices, whispering as they gathered their finery, coming to the door to welcome Dilip Rai. *'This house used to be not good. I give you until the rains break.'* The Brothers had left their ruins in the grass.

The holly pricked her hand. Dilip was looking at Mr Dean now, with an interested face.

She said: 'How dare you come here—like this?' He only smiled, holding on to his pony. 'How dare you be with that boy—or come here to our service to-night?'

Still he smiled and she saw that he wore a sprig of holly in his buttonhole, and at once she remembered the scuffle she had heard outside the chapel and the faint scream. Could it have been—couldn't it have been Kanchi? She put out a hand to push him away, trembling with disgust.

'You're—' she said furiously. 'You're—you're unforgivable.' Then she said vindictively, between her teeth: 'You're objectionable when you're sober, and abominable when you're drunk.'

'I quite agree,' he said, and taking his pony went down the hill. They saw Phuba rise out of the shadows and take his other arm. Presently they heard him loudly singing.

'I sing of a maiden
That is matchless,
King of all Kings
For her Son she chose—'

The words shivered the shadows, mocking their Christmas; even the rustling of the leaves seemed a titter and the house whispered, insinuating whispers, under that bawdy singing.

'Don't listen. Don't listen,' she cried.

But Dilip was listening attentively. 'I do like his voice,' he said. 'It's so nice and loud. I think it's lovely, don't you?'

17

When Sister Ruth answered Sister Clodagh's bell she found her standing in front of the window, throwing crumbs to the birds. These January days were as quiet and sombre as if there were a Lent in the hills and they were fasting of their colours. Even the grass had turned to a grey-green, but the bamboo stems shone as yellow as a blackbird's bill.

The blackbird had come to Sister Ruth's mind when she saw Sister Clodagh feeding the birds; now the earth was so stiff and hard, their cries sounded all the short day. They were strange birds, she thought, minahs and Himalayan thrushes and hoopoes, bolder than starlings at home. Sister Clodagh threw the crumbs farther and farther until the hoopoes were on the lawn in the shape of the crest they wore on their own heads, and their voices filled the air as they pounced and jostled and choked and fed.

'Aren't they hungry!' said Sister Clodagh. She had heard the door open, but she spoke out of the window and her breath steamed on the air.

'I've tried them with a coconut,' she said, 'but they don't like it. They love this mutton fat.'

She was only talking for time; over and over in her mind she was thinking of what she must try to say. She did not know in the least how she was going to begin, how she could put it, and she stayed by the window throwing the crumbs and talking; just talking. Sister Ruth stood by her without speaking. 'What do you want me for? What have you got to say?'

At last, Sister Clodagh shut the window and said: 'I want to speak to you. Come and sit down.'

Now they were facing each other across the desk and Sister Ruth sat on the edge of her chair, upright, plainly on the defensive. Sister Clodagh looked at her, trying to find some clue that would show her how to begin. If only she could light on something to say that would make the Sister's body relax and the hands in her lap unclench themselves, and take that stony expression off her face. She was so strung, so rigid, so still and filled with fear that Sister Clodagh said, almost without having to think: 'I've been worried about you for some time. I feel that things are not right with you.'

A wary look slid into Sister Ruth's eyes. 'In what way?' she asked.

'You look so ill.' Sister Clodagh seemed almost to be pleading. 'You've got terribly thin. I know you're trying to keep up for all our sakes, but I think you really must go in with Sister Briony and see the doctor.'

'I shan't see the doctor,' cried Sister Ruth violently. She had sprung to her feet and stood over the desk. 'I'm perfectly well, I'm stronger than I've ever been and you know it. You know it but you're trying to make out—' she choked and then stood still. 'I'm sorry, Sister,' she said, dropping back into her chair. 'I didn't mean—to be rude, but really I'm perfectly well. I—I haven't been sleeping, that's all.'

'If you haven't been sleeping,' said Sister Clodagh watching her, 'there must be some reason for it. Can't you tell me? Is something worrying you?'

'Yes. Yes, that's it.' Sister Ruth wet her lips. 'I—I *am* worried.'

'Don't you think you could tell me about it?' For a moment it seemed to hang on the air; Sister Clodagh waited breathless, not daring to speak; then she leant forward across the desk and said: 'I'd like you to tell me if you can.'

At once the eyes flickered away from hers. 'I can't speak of it—to anyone,' said Sister Ruth.

It was like trying to catch hold of something slippery, that slipped out of your hand. Sister Clodagh tried to keep her voice kind and even. 'Won't you try?' she said. 'I'd like to help you. You know you can trust me.'

'You didn't want me to come here,' said Sister Ruth. For the first time she looked directly at Sister Clodagh. 'You'd use anything I told you to get me away. How can I trust you?'

'That's absurd, Sister.' In spite of herself Sister Clodagh's voice rose. 'I only want to feel that you are well and content.'

'How can I be content? All of you, wherever I've been, have been against me. None of you have ever wanted me.'

'Don't you think that's your fault as well as ours? If it's everywhere you've been? It must be in yourself, Sister. Won't you let us examine it and find out—'

'At St Helen's they didn't want to lose me.' Sister Ruth said it loudly. 'It was just that I felt I couldn't stay. You can write and ask them if you don't believe me. And Reverend Mother said to me herself before I left, that she was sending me with you because I was so quick to learn the language and because she liked my methods in the school.'

'Of course she did,' said Sister Clodagh, groping carefully after her. Then she asked warily: 'But knowing all this, what makes you say that none of us want you?'

'You don't want me,' cried Sister Ruth. 'Don't pretend you do. From the very first minute—' she pulled herself up sharply.

'Don't you think,' asked Sister Clodagh carefully, 'that you're letting things run away with you? I feel that you're letting yourself give in to this idea. You know, you must know, it isn't true. I feel the same for you as I do for all my Sisters, that you are more to me than myself—'

Sister Ruth said nothing; she looked at the carpet, but a faint smile crept round her lips. There was a pause and then Sister Clodagh said: 'I think this is really all to do with somebody else. I think you have let yourself fall into thinking too much of Mr Dean.'

Sister Ruth started and then set her lips. She looked at Sister Clodagh in obstinate silence.

'Please answer me carefully. Why did you give that holly buttonhole to Mr Dean on Christmas night?

'Why did you?'

Sister Ruth shivered suddenly. She tried not to, but as she sat on the chair she shook violently. Sister Clodagh pressed her. 'You must answer me. Why did you give it to him?'

'I didn't.'

A look of intense relief made Sister Clodagh's face almost luminous; then, as she looked at the Sister it faded. 'I think you did,' she said.

'I didn't. You can't make me say that I did. I haven't given him anything.'

'What can I say to you?' asked Sister Clodagh. 'Sister, what is the use of talking to me like this? You gave it to him outside the chapel on Christmas night. Sister, don't you realize what you're doing? What you're running the risk of losing in yourself? Sister, you must, I must, make you see before it's too late.'

Again that indescribably baffling look came into her face. 'All the same, I've noticed that you're very pleased to see him yourself!' she flung at Sister Clodagh.

Sister Clodagh's face blazed. She half rose in her chair and then she sank back into it again, holding her desk.

'You're trying to tell me I'm not fit to be a nun,' cried Sister Ruth. 'Well, let me tell you that no more are you. You should never have entered either, and you know it for all your honours and success. Wonderful Sister Clodagh. Clever Sister Clodagh. Admirable Sister Clodagh,' she mocked, 'and all the time you're worse than I am and that's why you're trying to bully me.'

She stopped for breath and then, staring at Sister Clodagh, a horrified amazement came into her face. 'What—what have I been saying?' she said in a small wondering voice. 'What have I said? What have I been saying?'

'If that was in your mind, it's better said,' said Sister Clodagh. 'I think you're out of your senses.'

Sister Ruth cowered away in her chair. 'I lost my temper,' she said. 'Sister, I lost my temper. Forgive me. Please, please forgive me.' She began to weep, silently, without a handkerchief, letting the tears pour down her face, not wiping them away. There was something theatrical in those tears, pouring down her thin white face, and her thin body that might have been whipped, curled in the chair; yet Sister Clodagh had a feeling that at any minute it might rise and sting her again, and she had a sudden shudder of repulsion.

'Listen to me,' she said at last, when she could trust herself to speak calmly. 'I don't know, I can't decide now, what to make of you. The very fact that you could speak like that, even in temper, shows that there is something very wrong somewhere. It isn't what you said of me, but the state of your mind that worries me. I shall have to think, and I want you to think too; if there's any way that you feel you could be helped, will you come and tell me? Try to take more time every day for prayer; try and forget yourself and not to brood.' There was still no expression on Sister Ruth's face, only the tears falling helplessly down; Sister Clodagh felt she was not even listening. 'Would you like to write to Reverend Mother?' she asked.

She waited but there was no answer. 'Think it over and come and let me know. At least you must feel, with her, that she has no personal feelings against you. Try and believe the same of me; that you are as much to me as any of the others; in fact I have been thinking far more of you than any of them.' As she said it the words seemed to have a double meaning. 'As for Mr Dean, there can be no need and you have no business to speak to him at all; you must see that it's all-important that you should get over this feeling for him. When you came to us, Sister, you were very young and inexperienced, or you'd see what's plain to us all. In spite of his charm and his kindliness, Mr Dean isn't a good man; you must take him for what he is and not try to glorify him into someone he is not. When he speaks to you he has a way of making you think he's interested in you, but that's only a manner, he doesn't really mean it. When he came to chapel on Christmas night he was drunk.'

At that Sister Ruth's whole face flamed; she put her hand up to her wimple as if she were choking and shut her eyes while the tears ran under her lids. 'May—may I go?' she whispered.

'Go into the chapel,' said Sister Clodagh. 'You can use my private door and no one will see you. Go in there and I'll come to you presently.'

When she went in, after she had sat going over and over what she had said, there was no one there.

A few days after, she sent for Sister Ruth again. The Sister waited with the air of a martyr in front of her desk.

'Sister, I've been thinking a great deal about you. I want you to believe that.'

'I believe it, Sister.'

'I want you to write freely to Reverend Mother. I shan't look at the letter, of course, and her answers will be your own business. For the moment I shan't write to her myself, because I think the best way for you will be to go on quietly with your life and work here.'

'There could be no worse punishment,' said Sister Ruth.

Sister Clodagh looked at her sharply. 'You're making things very difficult for both of us,' she said.

There was no answer. Then Sister Ruth said: 'Am I to write two, or three pages to Reverend Mother? Have I to do it now, or may I finish my class-work first?'

Sister Clodagh picked up her pen. 'You may go,' she said and began to write.

It seemed an age that the pen scratched and she tried to keep her hand steady on the desk. Then Sister Ruth turned and swept out of the room.

18

The General Dilip Rai and Joseph Antony worked at tables side by side in the small extension beside the new Lace School. Joseph was a sop to propriety and he could not understand why his school hours had been lengthened, nor what this strange jargon was that went on over his head. He was learning to write English, the General was learning to write French.

'*Avez-vous le crayon de mon oncle? Non, mais j'ai la plume de ma tante et le papier de mon cousin,*' wrote Dilip Rai.

'*A–at–cat–chat,*' wrote Joseph.

They worked in an atmosphere of soft whispers and titters from the Lace School on the other side of the partition where Kanchi, Maili, Jokiephul and Samya sat at work. They were not allowed even to peep at the General, but it was because of him that they giggled and spoke in whispers, and because of him that the lace-making, and the arrangement of the head veil and the new blouse print had become suddenly thrilling.

Every few minutes Joseph was called away to help in the school or in the Lace School itself, though there they had learnt the meaning of 'nice-good-bad-careless-unpick-and-do-it-again' and could even say 'do not hold the thread in your big toes'; Joseph had taught them that himself and it had saved him a great deal of trouble. 'Dew not haould e'tred e'taus.' Joseph always wanted to please Sister Honey and he dared not displease Sister Ruth; there was something about her that he did not understand.

She was as sharp as Sister Honey was sweet, but it was not that; it was the way her eyes seemed to narrow and glint as if she were going to strike you, and her teeth made her look as if she could give a sharp bite, and the frightening still way in which she talked. Sister Honey really loved him; sometimes she had to punish him and that made her miserable.

'Joseph, I—Oh, Joseph dear. I'm afraid I have to punish you.'

'It's all right, Lemini. I don't mind. Really I don't. Don't you think about it. You just go on and punish me.'

'He's the *dearest* little fellow,' said Sister Honey.

'I think he's sly,' said Sister Ruth.

She thought them all sly and tiresome and grating. 'He's sly and the children are rude and I don't trust Kanchi at all.'

'You're right there,' said Ayah. 'Now some people, they think she's pretty and don't trouble to see any more. Well that's not likely to happen to us,' she said chuckling. 'I'm an old woman now and no one could call you pretty with those teeth.'

That stung. Once people had called Ruth beautiful, but now she thought she had never been so ugly; how could she help it with this strain and misery? Her eyes were stretched with watching, but she had to watch. Every moment of the day, *They* needed watching if she was to keep herself safe. She dared not relax for an instant and she had to know what

Sister Clodagh was up to. She had to find excuses to go past her door, to walk up behind her, to follow her, and she was getting so tired. Even at night she had to get up and listen and softly push the door to see if it were locked, to see if Sister Clodagh were asleep or only pretending; she dared not sleep herself in case Sister Clodagh or *They* came upon her while she was asleep.

Sister Briony brought her a glass of milk. 'Sister Clodagh says you're to have this every day at ten,' she said with a sniff.

Sister Clodagh had asked her: 'Have you noticed anything peculiar about Sister Ruth lately?'

'She thinks a great deal too much about herself,' Sister Briony had answered promptly. 'She's broody and neurotic.'

'Do you think it's only that? You don't think there's anything—odd about her? Sometimes lately I've fancied—'

'I shouldn't encourage her, Sister, if I may say so. She's full of her own importance and she likes to make the most of her ailments. Look at the way she fussed about that hill trouble and the headaches when we first came; all the Sisters had them, and we never heard a word from them, did we?'

'Still, she does look terribly thin. I think she needs building up in this cold. Give her a tonic, and extra milk in the morning and evening. And you might keep your eye on her. I'm not quite at ease about her.'

When Sister Briony had gone, Sister Ruth poured the milk out of the window. Sister Clodagh had sent it especially for her, a harmless-looking glass of hot milk, but quickly and furtively she poured it away.

There was one thing now that was continually in her mind. In eight months she was due to go to England. After five years abroad, the Sisters of their Order returned to the Mother House for six months.

She was to go in eight months, but Sister Clodagh might send her before if there were any more of these interviews in which she gave herself away. That was the terror of Sister Clodagh, she was the person that undid all her resolutions, that made her forget; the very one before whom she dreaded to give herself away, the very person who made her do it. 'Steady. Steady. You're quite all right if you go steady,' she told herself, and then Sister Clodagh would smile and say: 'Well, Sister,' and it would rise up in her again, and before she had thought she had rapped out an answer. And all the time *They* were watching. She looked over her shoulder; a dozen times a day she caught herself doing that. One day it would be noticed. 'What do you keep on looking at?' Already she had seen Joseph look after her, puzzled as to what she could see.

All the time she had to be so careful. She could not, would not be sent away from Mopu; even to herself she dared not add 'and Mr Dean'. At first that was hardly a thought, only a deep stirring in her mind, a warm and happy feeling she had never known before. Then Sister Clodagh had put it into words; that had been as terrifying as if she had shouted it in front of them all; she had trampled all over it but she had not trampled it down. Now that it was spoken it was alive, real; she almost thought it was real and now she did not know what she had imagined and what was real. It was so alive that she was frightened of it and yet it filled her with a tumultuous joy. She did not know what she could do to keep it, she could not even say it, but she hugged it to herself all day and night.

All that she knew was that when the time came she would not go. When the time came she would have a plan, but meanwhile it was 'Steady. Steady', and trying not to look behind her and watching Sister Clodagh and trying not to think of *Them*.

'Lemini,' Joseph twitched her sleeve, 'I have written out this "a-at-cat" until there's no black place left on my slate to write it on any more, and the General Bahadur has finished his French.'

'Yes, Sister,' said the General, smiling and showing his teeth. 'I have written out the whole of the exercise and I have learnt it by rote while I was waiting for you to finish your daydream.'

'Sister, it's nearly half-past twelve and you haven't rung the bell,' cried Sister Briony at the door. 'Whatever are you thinking of?'

None of them noticed the game of cat and mouse that was being played on the other side of the partition; Kanchi peeped round it to look at the young General and listened through it to hear his voice and put her face under it to see his feet. She had put on a blouse of purple cotton printed with stars and the colour of her veil was a brown, half pink, half cinnamon.

19

Sister Philippa brought the seed lists to the office. In the evenings she had spent hours making them out. Her work in the garden was almost at a standstill now; the January and February days were all alike, they went like a procession of the nuns themselves, unrelieved by any colour; there seemed to be no life or movement in the earth but the wind tearing at the trees and bamboos. Still Sister Philippa was in the garden while it was daylight, planning and marking, turning up pieces of earth and littering the ground behind her with scraps of paper that the wind blew away, so that she had to draw her plans all over again. She called Nima up from his warm quarters at all hours and she would stop in the middle of talking to him, looking to where the snows lay hidden under the clouds; wrinkling up her eyes at the place where Kanchenjunga was wrapped away, while Nima waited with his eyes watering in the wind. She had a collection of pots ready for seed in the shed that Mr Dean had put up for her and she spent a great many hours there; best of all she had the catalogues of spring and summer flowers and her lists of them to make.

'That cow is sick and you haven't even seen it,' said Sister Briony. 'The boy says she has been off her feed for days. There's nothing you can do in the garden now, so you might attend to your other work.'

'Lemini, you've a great hole in your skirt, did you know?' asked Kanchi pertly.

It was so difficult to decide what to have. Roses for instance. Mr Dean said she would have enough roses from the trees on the terrace and that no other kind could be better for colour and scent. 'They start with copper-coloured buds and go into flame and orange and rose and apricot, and when they die they turn cream. There are thousands on a tree, Sister, higher than the house. I can smell them down at the factory. I've only seen one other place where roses grow like that, in the Nishat Bagh in Kashmir.'

'Have you seen those gardens then?' cried Sister Philippa. 'Do tell me about them. Have you seen the Shalimar?' But the roses in the catalogue had such tantalizing names and the descriptions were so beautiful that she had to write down a few. 'I must see what "Lady Hillingdon" is like and this "Golden Dawn" that they say has forty-five petals and this lovely sounding "Shot Silk".'

She had visions of the hill behind the house white and gold with daffodils and jonquils, but Mr Dean said that bulbs in this damp climate were extravagant, they rotted and had to be renewed every year, and that the spring was so brief and had so much already packed into it that they were more trouble than they were worth. 'If you plant hill crocus, it'll cost you nothing, because the boys can bring the roots wild from the woods, and Pin Fong can get you some Chinese lilies, if they are bringing them over this year in spite of the war. They're so like jonquils that you can't tell them apart.'

'I should very much like some lilies, and I'll arrange about the crocus roots,' she said, but she wrote down daffodils and jonquils all the same.

She planned to plant sweet peas with a border of petunias; it said in her book that the scents together were exquisite, and she decided to have red Japanese peonies with gypsophila for contrast; the peonies were rather expensive, but their description was magnificent. Then there were lupins, delphiniums and larkspurs and stocks; all the colours of snapdragons, nigella which was love-in-the-mist; pansies and the portaluca she had grown to love in the plains; mignonette and verbena, candytuft and phlox.

Sister Briony told Sister Clodagh, in front of all the Sisters, that the laundry was late again. Sister Philippa smiled apologetically and looked out of the window where the azaleas crouched on the bank, swept by the wind, and her expression changed to acute concern. Sister Clodagh followed her anxious eyes.

'And must she allow our washing to be hung out anywhere as it is?' asked Sister Honey primly. 'It's altogether too suggestive.'

'Don't be ridiculous,' said Sister Clodagh sharply; she was a little worried. 'There's no one to see it.'

'Except the mountain,' said Sister Philippa quite gravely. 'I never thought of that. I won't let it happen again.'

The Sisters laughed, but Sister Philippa said: 'I was more right than I knew when I called him a household God. He's everywhere; before and about and in our house.'

Sister Honey opened her lips in dismay waiting for Sister Clodagh's quick answer to that, but she went into her office without speaking.

'That sounds irreverent to me,' said Sister Briony as soon as she had gone, 'and, talking of irreverence, do you know you've been late for chapel every day this week? I don't know why Sister Clodagh hasn't noticed it. I think she's far too patient and kind to you all and you take advantage of it.'

'Seed lists already?' said Sister Clodagh, when Sister Philippa came in. 'Surely it's too early?'

She seemed reluctant to be disturbed, but the Sister answered firmly: 'Not for the bulbs and the fibres I need; and I have to get the compost for the rose-beds.'

'What rose-beds?' asked Sister Clodagh.

'I'm going to make some. They have to be dug down three feet, you see, we shall need extra labour for that, and then all this stuff put in. Then I have to mulch the rhododendrons before they come into flower and I want to see if I can improve the wild ones by putting in some of those red and white Splendours; I've told Nima to get me two coolies for that as I can't spare the regular ones. It's my idea to turn the present vegetable terraces over to flowers, and make the vegetable garden down below the stables where it can't be seen. That's what the extra list is for; and here are the herbs for the herb garden I've planned to put round the new chapel; we might as well start it now as the building will go up quickly. Only simple herbs, lavender and sage and mint and rosemary—'

'But, *Sister*.' Sister Clodagh looked at her in bewilderment. 'All this would take months—'

'Not if I have enough labour. I can get any amount of coolies from Mr Dean.'

'But think of the cost!' Sister Clodagh tapped the lists in amazement. 'The seeds alone are beyond any allowance we can possibly expect, and you've put down bulbs and herbs and roses and creepers.'

'The creepers are *not* included,' said Sister Philippa. 'They'll have to be extra. I'm putting up frames for the honeysuckle outside the bathroom and cookhouse doors where they'll get the soapy water; and I want to try morning-glory, though I'm afraid we're too high for it.'

'Of course we're too high. Half the things in this list couldn't grow here.'

'I think they could.'

'It's very, very unlikely.'

'I should like to try,' said Sister Philippa obstinately.

'We can't afford to try. You'll have to be content with the things that Nima's had here before. I'm sure that this year Reverend Mother won't want us to spend very much on the garden. I'm sorry, Sister, but it's impossible.'

'It's absolutely necessary if the garden is to look as it ought to,' said Sister Philippa loudly. 'It's the very least I can manage with.'

Sister Clodagh was puzzled. She looked at the Sister sitting opposite her, at her pleasant wise face with its benevolent forehead and eyes. Reverend Mother had said: 'If you want advice, ask Sister Philippa, she's wise.' She had always been the most sensible and even of them all; she spoke so seldom that she was listened to, and what she did say was worth hearing. Sister Clodagh remembered that several times lately she had had to speak to her two or three times before she answered; and Sister Briony was always complaining now that she neglected the cows and chickens and the laundry work. There was something vague and untidy about her dress, too, there were patches of mud on her skirt round her knees, and the tear in it was not mended. Her cheek had a smudge of dirt on it and her nails were black.

'I don't know what's come over you, Sister,' she began. 'You bring me these schemes which would cost hundreds of rupees in labour and plants and you know perfectly well that there is

him. He's so vain,' she mocked, 'like a peacock, a fine black peacock. I'm going to call him Black Narcissus.'

'But he isn't black,' said Sister Honey, who had laughed and felt mean for laughing. 'He's only a dusky olive colour.'

'They all look alike to me,' said Sister Ruth loftily, and she answered Dilip ungraciously and said: 'I don't like scent at all.'

'But don't you think it's rather common to smell of ourselves?' he pleaded. 'To tell you the truth,' he said shyly, 'I'm trying very much to improve myself. Have you noticed any difference in me the last few days?'

'I've noticed that you're not getting on very fast with your French,' answered Sister Ruth. 'Now, General, will you write out from memory the present indicative of the verb "aller", to go.'

It seemed suddenly and utterly fantastic to her, that she should be requiring French verbs from this dark young prince, in his shimmering coat; working in the smell of his narcissus scent made her head reel, and she went to the window, looking out across the terrace. She could just see the factory roof far down below and the streamer of smoke from its chimney; as she looked down, her eyes hardened and she squared her shoulders; then she leant against the sill, her chin on her hand, one finger tracing the line of the wood; she smiled, a curious little absent smile, and now her eyes were wide and softly green.

The young General seemed very beautiful to all the nuns. When he came galloping down the drive, flashing under the deodar trees, he might have been a forerunner of the spring and summer days that were so long in coming. They had seen so little colour in the winter that he seemed almost startling, and he came so fast, his pony's mane rising in the wind like a crest, its tail streaming over the sky and clouds between the trees.

Sister Clodagh had let more than she knew into the Convent with the young General Dilip Rai.

He was outside everything they had considered real; he was the impossible made possible. He was fantastic. His white pony was a stallion of the famous Tangastiya breed; it galloped up and down the hills, and when he galloped it on the narrow paths of the high ground, his head looked to be above the clouds, and the trees below the path brushed his knees. His coats and jewels were fabulous, and he was as naïve and charming as the youngest son in a fairy story. His people were fantastic too, heady and strong with their crude bright clothes and goblin faces, and they also rode these white and dappled stallions.

'Have you noticed,' Sister Philippa asked once, 'how important these people are? How they've impressed themselves on us, compared with the natives in other places we've been in?'

They and the General were not too fantastic for the country; nothing was too strange for the mysterious and impenetrable State and the ice mountains and the dark forests and the valley with its easy luscious fields.

Sister Honey stopped in her work to listen eagerly to the children saying their lesson in the next room, as if they belonged to her; Sister Philippa straightened her back from her frozen beds and stared across the garden, seeing it in summer, and Sister Ruth watched and waited for Mr Dean. Sister Clodagh's face was so softened and changed that Mother Dorothea would not have known her.

'Sometimes she looks half asleep,' said Sister Briony. 'Really, I'd think she had liver if she didn't look so well. She's as flushed and clear-skinned as a young girl!'

If Sister Briony noticed anything unusual about the Sisters, she thought spring must be coming and they needed dosing; all she thought about the General was that he should not be allowed to wear his best clothes in the morning. She was far too busy to look out of the window or to stop and think about people, except as legs and arms and heads that needed bandaging and eyes and stomachs and chests that came to be treated.

Sister Clodagh was very angry when she heard that Sister Ruth had nicknamed the young General 'Black Narcissus'. She was angry and astonished at its neatness; what had made Sister Ruth echo her own dream with a name? In her dream, Dilip and Con had held mirrors in the palms of their hands, and she had tried to attract them but could only echo what they said. And now Sister Ruth had put her dream into words.

Often now, it was Con and not the young General who sat at her desk, while she was in her chair stitching at the wool picture of St Francis and the animals; there was not the gulf and the snowline beyond the windows, but the lawn and the veronica hedges, the foreshore and the lake and the low green mountains.

'Con, won't you ever finish? Pat's had the boat waiting for the last hour.'

'Lord, girl, can't a man write a letter in peace?' They smiled at one another across the room; there was such happiness in that, that she had to turn away and look at the lake and the boat with patient Patsy in the stern.

In summer they were often out with him on the lake after brown trout, or fishing the Upper River when it was not let, or else at the small stream that ran out on the lake. Every year the cousins came over for the shooting, and there were the long days on the mountain with the guns and Roderick and Morna and Gamble matching themselves against Con's springers.

'Call in your mad dog, Clo. Is it the Waterloo Cup you've entered it for? Take it home and cut off its tail just behind its ears. It's corrupting my beautiful Joey.'

'Joey! *That* rabbit catcher!'

Cousin Michael's wife, Mary, eyed the men and said: 'Well, Clo, I suppose very soon you and Con—?'

'You and Con.' Everyone was thinking that. Everyone was waiting. The Byrnes at Clough House, and the O'Driscolls at Fosse, and the Misses Barradine at Castle Maine, and Lady Truebridge, who was her godmother. 'These emeralds are for you, child, when you marry Con.' There were the Malley girls, Moira had been making eyes at Con since she was in socks; and the Riordans and the Shephards and the Monks, and young Jerry Caldecott who was the next Lord Toome, as mother was always pointing out. They were all waiting and wondering.

It was in the winter she saw most of them; that last winter every face had been an open question. Hounds met three mornings a week and Con had let her ride Thunderer as well as having her own Peewit. 'Be careful of that horse, he's the family fortune.' Con kept by her side and showed her the way when she let him. 'Be careful, Clo. Mind him at the break. Keep behind me if you can.' The dances and the hunt balls were in the winter, and the Misses Barradine's games party, and the tenants' dance which was the only kind of entertainment Con's people ever gave; that last one had made her stiff with self-consciousness, scenting congratulations in the air. 'Miss Clodagh and Mr Con, isn't it?'

But in the blessed summer months they were shut away by themselves; Con's father was not the only one who withdrew into obscurity and let the house and the fishing and the shooting. 'Our house is a byword now,' grumbled Con, that last summer. 'Even the agents can't recommend it. No one will take it now.' She was glad of it; it kept him there, and every evening his whistle came over the hedge.

Father looked over his paper. 'That's Con.' Mother put down the fleecy knitting. 'Now not too late, dear.' As she closed the door she heard mother say: 'Oh dear, I'd like them to settle something before next winter.'

They walked down the hill and leaned on the bridge to watch the stream run into the lake. She always remembered how, in the fields, the rabbits showed white scuts and undercoats as they played and the geese shone like pearls in the mud, and a gull over the lake showed white wings as it turned to the shore. She always remembered those small shining pieces of white.

'It isn't even a life for a man,' said Con. 'There isn't anything in it for me. What do I get out of it, waiting for the old man to die? Seeing him toil and slave for a house that's falling to pieces over his head. The rot's in and the land's gone to weed and he won't see it. He'll kill himself for it and I'm expected to do the same. Why? Because we've always been here; because of a lot of old dead and buried men. What do I care what kind of blood I've got, when I haven't a penny to bless myself with? What do I care if the land's been ours for a thousand years when it isn't worth a halfpenny now?'

'But Con, you know quite well you're proud of it and love it.'

'Love it! When he dies, and it's the sober truth I'm telling you, Clo, I shall let the whole thing go and clear out to Uncle Nat. I've written and told him so and he agrees with me. Fond as I am of the old man, there are things I won't do. As soon as he goes, I go. I never want to see the place again.'

The water seemed to flow away from her, the geese, and the clouds seemed to run together into a blur. 'Think of all there is to do in the world,' cried Con. 'God! Sometimes I can't wait for it all. Clo, doesn't it make you itch to get away?'

'I don't want to go away,' she said. 'I want to stay here, like this, for the rest of my life.'

'Please, Sister,' the young General was saying, urgently from her desk. 'In this passage

> *"Laudate et benedicite mio signore et regratiate;*
> *Et seruite a lui cum grande humilitate"*

how do I translate "*Et seruite*"?'

She was sitting at her embroidery frame, the blue thread of St Francis's eye in her hand, and the unstitched eye still staring at her from the canvas.

'Sister, I've asked you twice,' said Dilip plaintively. 'What is the right translation for "*Et seruite*"?'

Kanchi looked for him every day, she watched him ride up and give his old coat to the groom so that it should not be seen, and pull down his cuffs and straighten his hair, and touch his earrings to be sure they were in place. Then he took up his books and went in to his lesson, leaving a waft of fragrance on the air, that made Sister Briony say: 'Tsst! Tsst!' and fetch the pine disinfectant.

If he saw Kanchi he smiled at her because she was young and pretty like himself, and because he knew that she desired him. He thought that was perfectly natural, but at present, with all his schemes and ambitions, he had no time for anyone but himself, and he smiled at her and went in to his lesson.

Kanchi dropped her lids at once, but after he had gone, she raised her eyes to his back and they were bright with tenderness and greed.

21

Father Roberts had put off coming until now, and after tea on the day of his visit he walked on the terrace with Sister Clodagh. He kept his hands behind his back, the wind blew the short hairs on his head into bristles and sent his cassock streaming out behind him like a skirt.

'I hope you're pleased,' said Sister Clodagh.

'Ye-es,' said Father Roberts doubtfully. 'It all seems excellent; very excellent. Yes, it certainly seems that. But—' he stopped and looked directly at her. 'Is anything worrying you Sister?'

'Why do you ask that?' she said steadily.

'I don't know, but you seem changed. Yes, you all of you seem changed, except my good friend Sister Briony and she's always the same.'

'In what way are we changed?'

'I don't know,' he said slowly. 'I can't quite say. I've noticed it with each one of you. It's difficult to explain. I feel as if you were all hiding something from me. Nothing's happened, has it?'

'Nothing.' She hesitated. 'I told you that I had been worried over Sister Ruth, but she has been writing to Reverend
Mother, and I think she's better; and Sister Philippa has been
overworking herself, but I think that's all.'

'I hope it is.' He still spoke doubtfully. 'You don't think it
was a mistake to allow the young General to come—I mean
the novelty of it—but no, no it couldn't be that, and I don't
see how you could have done anything else. I feel something's
upsetting you. Do you know in chapel this morning, I suddenly had the feeling that I was alone. That not one of you was
listening to me.'

'*Father!*' said Sister Clodagh.

'I did. Sister, if the place is too much for you, you will
say so.'

'But, Father, I don't understand. I thought we'd made such
progress here. That you'd be so pleased.' She was touched to
the quick.

'It's difficult to explain,' was all he said. 'To-day, I somehow
felt I'd lost you. You're none of you as single-hearted as you
were.'

22

After Christmas night Sister Clodagh felt she could never see Mr Dean again; that this time she would not and could not tolerate him. He had come up as usual to see the buildings, but she had hardly seen him. She did not think he was avoiding her, he gave her the same twinkling smile when they did meet, but she always arranged to be busy when she saw him coming down the drive. Now, in answer to her enthusiastic letters to Mother Dorothea, a packet enclosing the chapel plans had come. Reverend Mother had written: '*From your report we think the time has come when you may safely embark on the building of the chapel. You seem to have been very successful in the organizing of St Faith's.*'

Sister Clodagh had been worrying all night over Father Roberts's odd words, but now she went humming to the window and opened it; she felt alight with happiness and hope. '*You seem to have been very successful in the organizing of St Faith's.*' As she leant out of the window she could hear the men busy on the class-rooms, a saw working, tapping and hammering, and the noise of someone pounding mortar; she could hear the workmen's voices, and the chanting of the coolies as they dragged a roller on the drive, and the children in recitation in the school. Sister Briony came round the corner, her keys swinging and her veil wrapped round her shoulders; she gave some order to Sister Philippa who came up from the stables to meet her, and then their busy figures parted and they went back to their work. A pony trotted past with a load of wood, and a man came down from the General's house with a basket of vegetables on his way to the kitchen. Sister Clodagh gave a satisfied smile and closed the window.

She felt that she must go and tell them all that the chapel was to be begun, that she had had a letter of commendation from Reverend Mother, who so rarely praised, that here was a reward for their work; but before she moved, with her hand still on the window catch, an unpleasant thought struck her. 'You may safely embark on the building of the chapel.' She could not possibly embark without Mr Dean.

All their conferences must begin again; she would be drawn into talking to him, and she had said firmly that this time he had gone too far and she had no more charity to give him. She stood there, her eyes on the carpet; she thought of Sister Ruth and the finished, careful work he had done for them before; she thought of his crude, peculiar opinions and his sudden rudeness, and then of the way in which he had dealt with all their troubles, of his gentleness with Sister Honey and the help he had given to Sister Briony and Sister Philippa. And then she thought of the new chapel, that was to be the centre of their lives, and the crisp new plans on her desk; it was the final establishment of the foundation, and she sat down at her desk and wrote a note, and then went to find Sister Briony.

'Sister, I have a letter from Reverend Mother that has made me very happy. We are to start on the chapel, and I've

'What else can we do?' she answered.

'I *don't* understand why he was so rude.'

'He wasn't rude,' said Sister Clodagh. 'He was serious.'

The next day he did not wait to ring the bell and be announced, but came straight down the passage to the office, where Sister Clodagh and Sister Briony were going over the accounts. He pushed everything on her desk to one side and spread out his plan.

'I've got it,' he said, 'I've got it exactly. This is how it should be. This is the chapel you should let me build for you here.'

They looked at it, all three together for a very long time. 'But it isn't a chapel at all,' said Sister Briony, raising a bewildered face. 'It's more like a temple.'

'Of course it is,' he said. 'This is the East, you're dealing with an Eastern people. Christ Himself was an Eastern Jew. Now listen. It should be built where the path comes out from the forest on to the hill, just above the Sunnyasi's shrine.'

'*Not* near that shrine,' cried Sister Briony.

'Yes. He's taken very nearly the best place, but not quite the best; just above him is the highest place of all, the best place to see the snows. It'll be made so that the path comes right through it, and the people are going and coming through it all daylong.'

'People coming and going through it all day long?' she echoed doubtfully. 'What an extraordinary idea!'

'Yes,' he said, firmly. 'Built there it would be above everything, above the valley and the clouds and the trees, the highest point of all; you'd always have to go up to it. You see, these are not exactly walls and not exactly pillars; they're placed across the corners to break the wind and give shelter without shutting it off. On the outside I thought we should letter them with stories in the local writing, so as to make them interesting; but inside they should be plain white, and you should keep them very clean, because between them the clouds will show, and on fine days the snows. On the floor you should put straw; yes, I think that would be most satisfactory to kneel on and at the same time clean the people's feet, and encourage them to rest there.

'Here's your altar, in the shelter of this pillar. I've made it a rock, like Peter, and the mica will shine in it to remind you how his faith shone in his strength. Your lamp and your flowers will be safe there from the wind. From outside at night, the lamp will make it look like a lighthouse in the dark, and from inside you'll see stars in all four spaces. Look, your bell is under the dome; it will sound deep and rounded from there, not like the silly clapper you have now. You'll find the birds will nest there as a matter of fact, and though that sounds nice it will be a damned nuisance, but perhaps it'll be good for you, because you'll continually have to clean and change your straw. You can console yourselves with thinking that it's a chapel, not only for you, but for all life. All life,' he repeated, reverently, 'which is God.'

There was an amazed silence. Sister Briony was looking uncertainly from him to Sister Clodagh, her mouth a little open; Sister Clodagh's head was bent over the plan; and then behind them came a deep satisfied sigh. Behind them stood Sister Ruth with the letters for the depot in her hand.

She did not look at Sister Clodagh but at Mr Dean. 'That's beautiful,' she said, in her tense voice. 'It's more than beautiful, it's holy. Oh, Mr Dean, that's the chapel you should build for us here.'

He looked uncomfortable at once, and took off his hat and began to rearrange the feathers in its band. Sister Briony rustled indignantly and Sister Clodagh said: 'Thank you, Sister. Please give me the letters and go back to your work.'

Sister Ruth did not move.

'Sister, didn't you hear me?'

Sister Ruth said slowly: 'I suppose you're not going to build it. You're going to miss a chance like this, of making something beautiful and—and fitting, just because it's something new . . . something you haven't thought of yourself. Oh, Sister, you can't let it go.'

'I don't think we asked for your advice. This isn't anything to do with you.'

'Oh, isn't it?' cried Sister Ruth. 'I'm as much a part of the Order as you are. It's as much my chapel as yours, and I tell you it must be built. I'll write to Reverend Mother myself. I'll fight you with every breath in my body.'

'Sister!' Sister Clodagh's voice cut across her coldly and sharply. 'Control yourself. Remember where you are and who you're talking to. I must apologize, Mr Dean, for such an exhibition of hysteria.'

There was a snap of light in Sister Ruth's eyes, she flung herself forward across the desk. 'You—' she cried, 'you—' Her hands groped in the papers and found the alabaster paper weight. Sister Briony screamed and Mr Dean caught her hand as she lifted it; she shrieked and opened her fingers, and it crashed to the floor. Red to his ears, Mr Dean stooped and picked it up, and she began to sob in sharp, terrified whimpers.

'Take her out, Sister,' said Sister Clodagh, who had not moved. 'Thank you, Mr Dean.'

Sister Ruth turned to the door, her hands hiding her face, and Sister Briony, stiff and outraged, went after her. Mr Dean put his hat on slowly and hitched up his shorts. He said deliberately: 'They say your bark is worse than your bite; all the same I think it must be a pretty nasty bite.'

She stared at him in surprise and saw that his whole face was dark and angry.

'Taking charity as love,' he bantered her, 'you speak in a very uncharitable way. Almost like one of us heathen.'

She was too surprised to defend herself and he stood and glared at her.

'As you don't like my plan, give it back to me,' he said.

'Why! are you angry about *that*?' she said, light breaking on her face.

'Don't be foolish,' he answered shortly.

'I do like it, but you must see that it isn't a chapel.'

'It's what a chapel should be,' he shouted. 'I didn't think of it. I read through Matthew, Mark and Luke and John to find out for myself what Christ would have thought of your dadoes and your closed door. I didn't find any mention of you any-where. You and all your sacred mystery. A chapel shouldn't be sacred, I tell you, Sister Clodagh, but as free and useful as the path I put it on.' He stopped and looked at her, and the anger left his face. 'There, it's all right,' he said. 'I don't expect you to understand me any more than I can understand you; but I respect you and that's the difference between us. I'll build you any sort of chapel that seems to you best.'

He saw her eyes suddenly bright with tears, and she bent her head.

He stood by the desk, awkwardly silent, and then he said: 'Come, at least stick to your guns,' and took his plan and tore it up.

23

The General sent six cherry trees for the garden; they came by a runner, their roots done up in a hard lump of clay.

'*I do not know if they will grow where you are*,' wrote the General, 'but I should like you to make an experiment with them and try.'

'I'll take them out to Sister Philippa at once,' said Sister Clodagh. 'How pleased she'll be.'

Sister Philippa was not in the garden: Nima said she had not been out all day. 'That's very funny,' said Sister Clodagh. 'She must be busy in the laundry. Put these in the shed, Nima, and I'll go and find her.'

'More work,' said Nima, morosely, but there was a gleam in his eye as he tapped the clay lumps with his finger-nail. 'The Lemini will like these,' he said.

The laundry was an outhouse towards the stream and, as Sister Clodagh came round the bamboo clumps, she saw smoke pouring from its chimney, and from the stream came the smack, smack, smack, of wet clothes on the stones. As she opened the door she smelt charcoal and steam, steam streamed past her into the cold air, and the smell of irons on hot linen rose from the tables. The dhobi and Sister Philippa were both ironing, he in his white coat at the table, she pressing the elaborate folds of their wimples on a small board.

'You're very busy,' said Sister Clodagh.

'We're behindhand again,' said Sister Philippa tersely.

'Can you spare a few minutes all the same? The General has sent us some cherry trees to try in the orchard. Come and look at them.'

Sister Philippa put down her iron; for a minute it seemed that she was going to say something, then she followed Sister Clodagh.

'They look like dead sticks, don't they?' said Sister Clodagh. 'It's hard to believe that all their roots are twisted up into that knot. Do you think that you'll know what to do with them?'

'Nima will know,' answered Sister Philippa, in a curiously flat voice. 'Where would you like him to put them?'

They looked at her in surprise; she was not looking at the cherry trees but out through the door of the shed, and there was something fixed and hopeless in her face that made Sister Clodagh say: 'Sister, what is it? What's happened to you?'

'I was going to ask if I might speak to you,' said Sister Philippa.

Nima stood the little trees carefully in a corner and dusted his hands on his knees and went out.

'Tell me what's wrong,' said Sister Clodagh.

'There's nothing wrong. Sister, I want to be transferred.'

'*Transferred.*' In sheer surprise Sister Clodagh's voice was shrill. For a minute she could say nothing else.

'Yes,' said Sister Philippa firmly. 'I want you, if you will, to write and ask for my transfer at once.'

Sister Clodagh could only look at her. She was still standing at the door looking out, her hands dropped limply at her sides and in the dark shed her face seemed very pale and set. In that resolute flat voice she said again: 'If you will, at once.'

'But *why*?'

'I was becoming too fond of the place. I was too wrapped up in my work. I thought too much about it.' Sister Clodagh noticed that she spoke in the past. 'I had forgotten,' she said.

'Forgotten what?'

'What I am.'

'You mean—'

'Yes,' said Sister Philippa, 'I am a religious. I had forgotten that. I was putting my work before my religious life. I was losing sight of God in it. I was losing the spirit of the Order. I've been thinking it over, you see,' she said with a wry smile, 'and I must go at once.'

'I don't see that,' said Sister Clodagh, after a moment. 'Now that you know and you've realized the danger, you needn't go. Surely, now is the time to stay.'

'I daren't stay.'

'Isn't it a pity to give in?'

'Not when it's something more important than yourself,' said Sister Philippa. 'Mopu had run away with me, I was obsessed with it and the mountain and my work in the garden. Yes, I think I was really obsessed. There's something in this place, I don't trust myself here. I mean it when I say I daren't stay.'

Other words seemed to surge up in Sister Clodagh's mind. *'If the place is too much for you, you will say so? You're not as single-hearted as you were. You're not the sort of person who'll admit you're wrong. Isn't it a pity to give in? Not when it's some-thing more important than yourself.'*

'I think I understand,' she said; but to herself she mur-mured: 'What am I to do? What am I to do?'

In the corner of the shed was a shelf with a row of pots and boxes and in their carefully sifted soil were wooden tags for the names of seeds. She began to arrange them, raking over the earth with the sharp points, sticking them neatly in the corners.

What was she thinking of? What had she been think-ing of? It was difficult to say exactly. Of all these months she had only a vague blown pattern in her mind; the work had gone on, the work had been done by Sister Briony and Sister Philippa, and Sister Honey, and Sister Ruth, and Mr Dean; she had directed it and done some of it herself, but she hardly knew when or how; most of the time she had been away. 'I was obsessed by my work in the garden,' that was the wise Philippa. 'I must do something for the children,' and the hunger in Sister Honey's eyes. And Sister Ruth; what a carking anxiety Sister Ruth should be to her at this moment, and to-day she hardly thought of her at all. 'I had forgotten.' She had forgotten and had let them all forget. Again she said, as she raked the earth backwards and forwards; 'What am I to do?'

'I think there are only two ways to live in this place,' said Sister Philippa, 'you must either live like Mr Dean or like the Sunnyasi; either ignore it completely or give yourself up to it.'

'Which is which?' asked Sister Clodagh, and she added: 'Neither would do for us.'

'No,' said Sister Philippa, 'that's why I say we oughtn't to be here.'

'Well, we are here,' answered Sister Clodagh, 'and I don't think it will help matters if we run away.'

Sister Philippa did not answer, and presently Sister Clodagh said: 'You know if I ask for you to be transferred, it will be a bad mark against you.'

'That's all the better,' said Sister Philippa. 'That's what I need.'

24

It was at the beginning of Lent that they noticed that Sister Clodagh had changed. After the long winter, spring had come at last, not a tender spring, but troublesome and hard. The wind cut until it hurt, it had swept the clouds out of the valley; the snows were stark in the hard clear sky and the bamboo leaves seemed sharp as thorns. Skins felt brittle and dry, voices were harsh and the smallest things were hard to bear; the restrictions of Lent seemed unendurable. Sister Clodagh would not relax any of them.

In Lent it was rice and beans and lentils, lentils and rice and beans at every meal. The familiar brown pots appearing on the table made themselves important by their very monotony. 'If only we could get fish,' said Sister Briony, 'I'm sure we should all be better tempered.'

'Nonsense,' said Sister Clodagh. 'We should eat what we can get and be thankful. This is a convent you're catering for, not an hotel.'

That was not fair. Sister Briony grew very red in the face. Her work here was exactly the same as at St Helen's or St

Mary's or St Ursula's itself; exactly the same, if not better, and no one, not Reverend Mother herself, had ever complained to her before.

'I don't know what's come over Sister Clodagh,' she said, more to herself than Sister Ruth, who was helping her turn out the store cupboard. 'I'm worried about her. These last few days she's changed completely. Whether it's the change of food, or this horrible wind or Sister Philippa's going that's upset her, I don't know, but she's quite different. And the way she's working! She's like a machine. One of those Roberts.'

'Robots, you mean.'

'That's what I said, Roberts. I've always had a horror of them, nasty, unnatural things. Yes, she reminds me of a Robert.'

'She's a bully,' said Sister Ruth.

Sister Briony whipped round on her at once. 'Don't you let me hear you talk like that,' she said. 'Anyone else would have sent you packing long ago, let me tell you that. I myself advised her to. You ought to be too ashamed to speak, I should think, the way you disgraced yourself and all of us in front of Mr Dean.'

'That's my own disgrace and I can bear it as I want to, I suppose,' said Sister Ruth.

'What one religious does is done to the whole Order,' said Sister Briony, 'you know that. In the Community the weakness of one is the weakness of all. Doesn't it say that in the Rule? And the honour of one is the honour of all. Sister, you can't have forgotten that.'

'I called her a bully,' said Sister Ruth, 'and I mean it, because we have enough to bear out here without making it worse; aren't the work and conditions trying enough for anyone without all this extra meditation, and getting up an hour earlier and cutting down our food?'

'It's only for Lent, you know that.'

'Well, I think we'll be dead at the end of it,' said Sister Ruth.

'None of the others are grumbling,' said Sister Briony. 'I never thought I should live to hear one of our Sisters talking like this. Though we don't understand, we may be perfectly certain she has a very good reason for everything she does. It isn't for nothing that she was made the youngest Superior in the Order.'

'There isn't a name that could suit her better,' cried Sister Ruth. 'Sister Superior. Oh, very superior indeed.'

'Really, you should send her away,' said Sister Briony when she reported her to Sister Clodagh. 'It shocked me to hear her speak of you like that. I wish we had sent her down with Sister Philippa.'

'I haven't been severe enough with her,' said Sister Clodagh. 'In fact, I think we've all been getting lazy and undisciplined.' Sister Briony swallowed and said nothing. 'That reminds me, we were late again this morning. You're responsible for waking everyone. I was in the chapel waiting for you for half an hour.'

'I'm sorry, Sister. I'm so tired that I sleep too soundly and that's a fact. Mr Dean says the spring here is very trying and I think we're all feeling it. And that reminds me, angry as I can't help feeling with Sister Ruth, I don't think she's well. Perhaps that isn't altogether her fault. She's not sleeping. I hear her at night and at times I've seen her in a kind of shivering fit. I'd really like her to see a doctor. I wish we had sent her down with Sister Philippa.'

'Well, we didn't and we can't help that now. After Easter I'll see what I can arrange; she might go back with Father Roberts. Did you give her a tonic?'

'Yes. She's so rude if I ask her about herself, but don't you think that she might be excused from early chapel until she's better?'

Sister Clodagh hesitated. 'No,' she said. 'On the whole I think it's wiser not to single her out in any way. She needs discipline.'

'She certainly does,' sighed Sister Briony. 'Dear me, how odd it feels without Sister Philippa. But no one's indispensable, are they? And we should all feel glad that we're able to welcome Sister Adela. Poor soul, she must be worn out with all she's suffered.'

The first impression of Sister Adela was one of height; not a graceful height like a tree, but of a prop or a lamp-post or a figure on stilts from Hallowe'en with a carved-out turnip for a head. Sister Clodagh frowned at herself for thinking so, as she rose to meet her. 'Poor thing, she must have suffered!' she thought, and felt ashamed.

Sister Adela had been at St Agnes's in Canton. The Convent had not closed down during the bombing and she and another Sister had been wounded. When she turned her head, a scar showed, running down from her chin under her wimple towards her ear; it was raspberry coloured and still angry, and she carried her arm stiffly from a wound in her shoulder. She had been evacuated to India and the doctor had recommended that she should be sent to the hills for a long period; the escort that had taken Sister Philippa to Darjeeling had brought her back.

'You see, she's found her way safely to us,' said Sister Honey, ushering her into the office.

'I hope it didn't jolt you too badly coming down the hill,' said Sister Clodagh. 'Our ponies are sure-footed but they're rough. You must be very tired.'

'I'm accustomed to bad journeys,' answered Sister Adela. 'In China we often had to go very far between our schools and if we'd wasted time thinking whether we were tired or not, we should never have got anything done.'

'Really,' said Sister Clodagh. 'In that case you'll be able to join us for supper. I was going to suggest that you went straight to bed.'

'Oh, I think she should go straight to bed,' Sister Honey interrupted, 'she's really very tired and she's eaten almost nothing all day.'

'But didn't Sister Briony send provisions?'

'She sent meat pies,' said Sister Adela. 'This is Lent and today is Friday.'

Sister Clodagh coloured and said nothing. These last few days she had been examining every least thought and feeling, examining them all in an effort to get back to the atmosphere that she felt that they had lost. In chapel she had tried to stand outside herself and listen. Was it her imagination that the prayers sounded almost strange, as if she had not heard them for months? That it was an unfamiliar feeling to go down on her knees and pray, instead of the most natural thing of her life? She had tried to throw her earnestness and appeal into her voice, but she noticed how the Sisters' eyes strayed and how very often they seemed to be following her with their lips, but with their minds far away.

She had spoken to Sister Briony about sending the Sisters to St Ursula's after Easter in turn for their annual Retreat that had been postponed from Christmas. 'Yes, Sister,' said Sister Briony, 'but wouldn't it be better to let them go in the rains or in the winter when we haven't so much to do? I'd thought of having a spring cleaning, all these fires have made the house so dirty.'

'How is Kanchi getting on with her Catechism?' she asked Sister Honey. 'Does she understand anything of it? Do you think she will be at all ready to see Father Roberts after Easter?'

'I think so,' said Sister Honey. 'I haven't heard her through it for a little while, I've been so busy. Sister, have you seen how Om's little brother is improving? He hasn't a single sore left. Do come and look at him!' She held up the sleepy baby for Sister Clodagh to see.

'Look, his eyes are so small that they disappear into fat when he smiles. Look, he's smiling now. He knows me. What darlings these babies are! How different from the skinny little dried-up things in the plains, aren't they, Sister? Look, he's trying to catch my finger. Oh, I couldn't love him more if he were mine.'

'Don't you let me hear you talk like this again,' said Sister Clodagh in a sudden rush of feeling that was almost panic. 'You're getting entirely too sentimental over these children. You must control yourself, Sister, or I shall have to stop them coming here.'

There was Sister Ruth going out to the terrace, her jacket huddled round her thin shoulders; she would stand by the railings looking down to the factory, searching the path that wound up between the tea, looking to where the hill hid the way to the Agent's bungalow. When she saw Sister Clodagh, she drew herself up and walked quickly away to the class-rooms.

Sister Clodagh was beginning to look haggard. She had driven herself and the others hard these last few days; she had tightened and narrowed her very thoughts, and worked and kept vigil at night, but still she found time to think. She had stopped her walks on the terrace and the hour she spent at her embroidery frame; if she woke in the night she got up at once and went to the chapel, and still she found time to think. In the middle of her work, in the middle of giving her orders, at her desk or at meals, even in chapel, her thoughts would catch her unawares. She would find she had been sitting for half an hour with her pen in her hand, or that Sister Briony was waiting for her to speak, or the young General was looking at her, patiently waiting for her to finish her sentence.

In the second week of the month when the moon was full, the mountain glittered into the air by night as well as by day. She had a window in her cubicle; she had deliberately given that cubicle to herself, and now she lay and stared at the mountain, until she dressed again and went into the chapel.

How often she had seen the first light creep on the green ceiling of the House of Novices at Canstead, defining the tops of the cubicles where the others lay happily sleeping. How often she had heard the first blackbird in the garden and known another night had gone, and she had not shut her eyes. She ached with sleep and still she could not shut her eyes. That was not in her first year; then she had been too sore and proud and angry; but it was impossible to stay in the Order like that, bit by bit they had drawn it all from her; but her pride was always left; she had never lost that, and they did not know that night after night she lay awake, listening to the chimes of St Joan's clock from the great hall below.

She still did not know how this had come on her again. It had seemed to radiate from the feeling of the wine-cup in her hand that day in the forest; she had looked up from it and seen the young groom with the leaves behind his ear; she had looked at him and thought of Con and then of her doubts and worries in the night.

In the old days at Canstead, peace had gradually come to her; she had been drawn into the life of the Order and had found in it more than she had ever thought that life could mean; it had come to be her life and so it would continue to her death. That must be; nothing else could ever be, and desperately she had been fighting these last few days to find that peace again.

Now she looked at Sister Adela and said nothing; but face to face with a Sister fresh from the older branch of the Order, the first house in India, she realized how far they had gone from it this winter. Even these small things, meat pies in Lent, Sister Honey interrupting her, were signs of it, and Sister Adela missed none of them. She was suddenly glad that Sister Adela had come, that already she had criticized in that unbending voice, that she was looking coldly at Sister Honey. They were eyes with a fanatical light in them, they were eyes that would see more than there was to be seen.

'I'm glad that you've come, Sister Adela,' said Sister Clodagh. 'I think we need you here.'

25

Sister Adela met Mr Dean for the first time in the passage leading to the nuns' private rooms. She stopped, dramatically barring the way, and said: 'What are you doing here? You can't come in here.'

With the hand that held two spanners and a piece of rag, he took off old Feltie. 'You're the new Sister,' he said. 'How do you do? You'll get used to me in time. I'm not prying. I've come to mend a loose joint in your pipe.'

'My pipe? What pipe?'

'The lavatory pipe,' said Mr Dean blandly. 'Now, may I go in and see to it?'

'You must send a workman. I've told you, you can't go in there.'

'The mistri can't deal with it,' he said patiently. 'He has tried. I count plumbing of sorts among my other gifts, and I swear to you, Sister,' he said with his eyes twinkling, 'it's only the pipe that I'm interested in.'

Sister Adela clapped the door to behind her. 'I must see

Sister Clodagh about this,' she said. 'Until then, I forbid you to go in there.'

'Very well,' he said, putting on his hat, 'but in fairness I must tell you that the plug won't pull till I do, and I'm going away in half an hour and I shan't be back for three days.'

"This is something that I've never heard of," cried Sister Adela indignantly before Sister Clodagh's desk. 'I never expected to be asked to tolerate this.'

'Why should you object to him more than to any other workman?'

'He's not a workman, that's why. You should have heard the way he spoke to me!'

'How did you speak to him?' asked Sister Clodagh. 'He's usually respectful unless he's provoked, and then he only does it to tease.'

'Why should I tolerate it?'

'We have to,' answered Sister Clodagh wearily. 'We can't manage without him. I don't think you realize the conditions here, Sister, our complete isolation and the difficulties of finding adequate help. These hill-people are peasants, agriculturists; they haven't learned to be skilled workmen and they're not good carpenters or smiths or plumbers. We're dependent on Mr Dean and he has been very good to us. Perhaps it will help you to understand, when I say that I call him in very much as I should call in a doctor. You didn't refuse to see a doctor when you were ill, did you? In the same way it's necessary that Mir Dean should go into our private part of the house and repair that pipe. He does so when the rooms are empty; you only met him this morning because you haven't taken up your work yet.'

'You mean he comes here often?'

'There's still a great deal to be done. He's building the chapel for us and the class-rooms are not finished yet, and he's

helping me with some translations because he speaks this dialect as well as he speaks English. He comes when it's necessary.
He seems odd and rude, but he's really very kind.'

Sister Honey found it hard to swallow Sister Adela's com-
ments. When she came into the Lace School, her eyebrows
went up above those gaunt all-seeing eyes.

The Lace School was nearly finished; the workmen were
busy on the interior which smelled of whitewash and wood
shavings. The girls moved their mats round the room out of
their way and Sister Honey's chair and table followed them.

There were two separate conversations; the shy whispering
of the girls broken with giggles, and the burring noise made
by the men when they tried to speak softly to one another in
their deep voices. Often while they were planing a piece of
wood in the vice or tarring the plinth of a door, they stopped
to watch the fingers at work on the bobbins and the curious
result of knitted threads that the Lemini prized enough to pay
for it. Then one of the girls would notice that she was watched,
and would droop her head under her shawl and make secret
glances at the others; the folds about her face made a deeper
shadow, the warmth of her cheek came up under the brown
and the ring in her nose glinted as she trembled with inward
laughter; Kanchi would toss her head and say a few words to
the others that the men would catch and a slow smile would
spread from face to face round the room, and then the man
would be transfixed with his mouth a little open until Sister
Honey looked up, when he would drop his head and, too hastily, begin to work again.

Sister Adela said nothing, she stood by the table fingering
the patterns.

'You find all this a little unusual, Sister?' said Sister Honey
at last, with a deprecatory wave of her hand.

'*Very* unusual.'

'It's only until we're settled. It was *expedient*,' said Sister Honey impressively. 'I wanted space for my clinic and the girls would have caught cold on the verandah.'

'Would it have done them any harm to have caught cold?' answered Sister Adela.

Sister Honey flushed and answered as Sister Clodagh had done. 'We're living under primitive conditions—'

'You forget I was at the opening of St Teresa's in the hills. There we had to start from the bare ground; we organized the labour and the workmen, and as they built room after room, we took them over and finished them ourselves. There were no Europeans there either, except a French doctor, and,' finished Sister Adela, 'I never remember seeing him.'

She went down the new corridor that joined the schools to the main building and turned to the right by the statue of St Elizabeth; she stood there for a little while to get her breath, for she was still weak and the altitude made her breathe too quickly. St Elizabeth had a robe with a glaze like blue linen, and the porcelain roses in her lap gleamed beside her hands that were like a doll's.

'Don't you think she's awfully pretty?' asked a voice beside her.

Behind a partition screen which had been pushed back, a young man sat at a desk writing busily in an exercise book; in front of him stood a pink text book that read *French Without Tears,* and he was copying from it, with his tongue at the corner of his mouth. He was dressed in pink too, but as pale as a shell, and he had amethyst earrings as large as sixpences stuck in his ears. Her eyes travelled from his shoes, over his pantaloons and achkan to his head, measuring his size, and hardened into hostility.

'What are you doing here?' she asked him as she had asked Mr Dean.

'At present I'm doing the verb "s'asseoir", to seat oneself.' He put down his pen and smiled at her. 'But to-morrow I'm going to read a child's easy book called *Les Malheurs de Sophie*. Do you know it? Have you read it? Can you read French? Are you a Sister or a Mother? I do so want to meet a Mother.'

'Who are you?' demanded Sister Adela.

'I am General Dilip Rai. How do you do?' he stood up and bowed.

'General?' Her voice was suspicious though her ears had rung with the names of generals and warlords for the last months. 'What have you done to be made a General?'

'I didn't make myself one. It was my brother.'

'Well, what did he do?'

'He died,' said Dilip simply.

'You mean you inherited the title. I've never heard of any-one *inheriting* a military title. What did he do to be made a General in the first place?'

'He was born,' said Dilip. 'He wasn't made a General, he was born one. I would have been born one too, but my Uncle wasn't certain if I were legitimate; now it has been proved that I am and I am now allowed to be General as my brother was. He is dead and I am to inherit from my Uncle and that's why I am so busy with my education. Sister Clodagh is helping me.'

'I suppose you are a Christian,' she said, 'or you wouldn't be here.'

'I'm not a Christian out loud,' said Dilip. 'My Uncle wouldn't let me change my religion.'

'The religion of this country is a form of Hinduism or else a low form of Buddhism that is, in reality, Animism,' pronounced Sister Adela.

'Is it?' asked Dilip interested. 'How do you spell that? What is it?'

'It's a form of Pantheism,' said Sister Adela contemptuously.

'Pantheism?' he cried, writing it down delightedly. 'And that? How do you spell it and what is it?'

'Saying that God is in everything, animate and inanimate; in the trees and stones and streams.'

'That sounds very beautiful,' he said thoughtfully, 'but it certainly isn't true.'

Sister Adela was surprised. 'Why are you so sure?' she asked.

'Because,' he said, 'we can conquer trees and streams and stones; we can cut down the forest and dam the stream and break up the stones, but we can't conquer God. Now, He,' he said, pointing with his pen, 'might very well be in the mountain. We call it Kanchenjunga and we believe that God is there. No one can conquer that mountain and they never will. Men can't conquer God, they only go mad for the love of Him. We have a legend in this country that among those mountains are strange men, who have gone mad for love of the mountain, and because of being mad, they go naked in the snow with white hair on their necks and chests and arms, and their eyes are like ice. And whoever sees them,' said Dilip, his eyes growing big, 'they kill and devour and we call them the Abominable Men. They have gone too close to the mountain, and they are mad.'

'You have a very vivid imagination, haven't you?' said Sister Adela.

'Well, I got some of that out of a book,' he said modestly, 'but it's all perfectly true. You have to be very strong to live close to God or a mountain, or you'll turn a little mad. The strongest of all,' he said, 'is my Great-Uncle, the Sunnyasi. He makes himself strong inside himself and he can look at the mountain all day.'

She turned sharply. Behind her she had seen a flash of colour by the door, a red sleeve, the end of a veil, and heard a tinkling that might have come from a pair of anklets.

'Who was that?'

'It's only Kanchi,' said Dilip calmly. 'She often passes by here to see me. She is very pretty, isn't she? But she's always bothering me to talk to her.'

Sister Adela started and looked at the clock, and was very annoyed to find that she had been talking to him for a quarter of an hour herself.

26

Just before Easter the knife wind changed to boisterousness, playing round the trees and rattling at the windows, and snatching at skirts and veils; with its roughness it was warm, scented with the orange flowers from the groves in the valley, a languorous scent blown roughly. The snow was melting and the streams were full; their own stream pelted down the hill, swelling up round the bamboos; over the slopes came a green bloom with a blueness in it like a grape and the rhododendrons opened in hundreds, and the magnolia behind the house budded into thick white flowers.

Ayah gathered them and put one in each bathroom.

'What's that for, Ayah?'

'To drive out the fleas.'

'But we haven't any fleas here,' cried Sister Briony indignantly.

'Huh, haven't we? I saw you scratching yourself with my own eyes this morning. If we don't take care, the whole house will be riddled with them. Even the fleas feel wicked in this weather. If I were you,' she added, 'I should keep my eye on Kanchi.'

But Sister Briony was thinking of the fleas. 'As soon as Easter's over,' she said, 'I shall have a good spring cleaning.'

'This place needs spring cleaning in more ways than one,' said Sister Adela. 'That young General has come scented so that one can trail him down the passage and Mr Dean has been very impertinent to me again.'

'I've told you he doesn't really mean to be impertinent,' said Sister Briony. 'It's just his natural way of talking.'

'That's just what I object to,' Sister Adela answered. 'He shouldn't be allowed to talk to me like that, or to any of us. I'm going to complain to Sister Clodagh.'

'Must you bother Sister with complaints just now? I'm worried about her. She's looking so ill.'

'She hasn't enough in her stomach,' said Ayah. 'None of you have with all these days of hen food.'

'Yes, and even when you can see she's ill,' wailed Sister Briony, 'she won't give in and let me make her a nice cup of tea.'

'You should admire her for that,' said Sister Adela. 'That's what I don't understand. She seems so right and just in her discipline, even a little too strict. There's nothing wrong there, but something is wrong. I'm not being critical, Sister, I'm seeing how I can help her.'

'Are you?' said Sister Briony dryly.

'You can't deny it, there is something wrong. Who ever heard of a Convent with a dirty Sunnyasi in its garden, and a man of Mr Dean's reputation going in and out like one of ourselves, and that scented "Black Narcissus" as Sister Ruth calls him, and a very good name for him, too, peacocking about in front of us all; in front of those young girls. I call it asking for trouble.'

Sister Briony told Sister Clodagh what she had said. 'She's probably right,' said Sister Clodagh, wearily.

At morning and evening now, there was an hour of grape-gold light and warmth, that Nima said was to make the plants grow. It made her think of Sister Philippa. *'Isn't it a pity to give in? Not when it's something more important than yourself.'*

One evening she climbed the hill to see the Sunnyasi. She stood between the young firs watching him, her hands folded in her sleeves because the wind was cold up here on the height. She did not know quite why she had come, but she stood there very close to him; if he had seen her, he did not turn his head. He sat staring out across the gulf; if he had looked down, he could have seen the Convent on one side of the hill with the deodars along the drive, and on the other, the village round the walls of Canna Villa, but he did not look down. Faint human sounds came up on the wind but they were lost in the quiet; it was very quiet; only the birds made sounds in the tree over his head, or a shuffling and whispering showed that people had come out from the forest path, and were going down the steps. When they saw the Sunnyasi, they turned to face him with a stare as a salutation, but he did not notice them either.

A woman came up from the village, a little Bhotiya with a monkey face and a plait of hair round her head; she salaamed to Sister Clodagh but passed in front of the old man to fetch his bowl; Sister Clodagh noticed that when her shadow fell across him, he did not blink. She wondered how he could sit and look into the wind, and how he kept so still without trembling; his hands rested comfortably on his knees, his back was straight, his head steady; and he was as still as if he had left his body sitting there on his deerskin, comfortably arranged, while he had gone out of it. Only the beads, moving up and down on his bare chest, showed that he breathed.

She watched him for a little while, and then climbed down the steps behind a party of coolies and walked along the drive to the terrace. Mr Dean was waiting in the porch with his pony.

'Sister,' he said, with dangerous meekness, 'will you tell Sister Adela that if I go into the chapel and look at the statues I won't contaminate them. I only want to measure them for their niches.'

Sister Adela hovered behind the door. 'He didn't take off his hat,' she whispered.

'Oh, it was old Feltie you were objecting to, and not to me?' he said. 'You didn't make that plain before.'

Sister Adela turned her back and went away. 'Do you think she'll ever get used to me?' he asked with a grin, and then looking at her, he said: 'What's the matter with you? What have they been doing to you? You look starved.'

'Thank you,' she said with an hysterical little laugh; at the quick friendly concern in his eyes, she felt suddenly in her sleeve for a handkerchief.

He took off his hat and gave her his, which he kept in the crown. 'It's quite clean,' he said. 'I washed my hair this morning.'

She shook her head and walked quickly to the terrace, where she stood thrumming her hands on the railing, trying to control herself. He followed her and said: 'Don't you think you could tell me what it is?'

'Ever since we came here,' she answered with a laugh that was almost a sob, 'over all our problems it's been "ask Mr Dean"!'

'That was because there wasn't anyone else here you could ask,' he said. 'None of your own people were here, or of course you wouldn't have had anything to do with me. I don't see anything out of the way in that.'

'And I had to have the young General here, in a way, didn't I?' she said. 'And I couldn't turn the Sunnyasi out. Everything

I did I was more or less forced to do, wasn't I?' She appealed
to him.

'Just what are you talking about?' he asked her.

'Ask Mr Dean! It's becoming a positive habit.'

She bit her lip and he waited patiently for her to explain
herself. 'Sister Philippa brought it home to me,' she said,
'and Sister Adela's rubbing it in. Now I don't know how
much is true and how much is my imagination, Mr Dean,'
she said, turning to him and angrily plucking her veil down
as it blew over her shoulder. 'Do you think we've changed
very much? Do you notice a change in us since we came
here?'

'In what way?' he said.

'Father Roberts said we were not as single-hearted. I didn't
take much notice then, but when Sister Philippa came and
asked to be transferred, it gave me a shock.'

'She *asked* to be transferred?' he said.

'Yes, and she gave that as her reason; that she was getting
obsessed with the garden. Now with that, and what Father
Roberts said, I'm watching them all and I can't make up my
mind. Is it imagination or not?' She paused. 'Tell me truthfully, Mr Dean. I have to ask you this, though it's difficult to do
it; has Sister Ruth ever tried to speak to you?'

'I keep out of her way,' he said quickly.

'Have you ever noticed Sister Honey and the children?
And Sister Briony—'

'Sister Briony's always been a bit of a Martha,' he said
cautiously.

'There, you have seen it,' she said bitterly. 'You see you
have. And I? Am I very different?'

'Yes,' he said at once, 'you're much nicer.'

'How?'

'You're human. Before you were inhuman, much too invulnerable. Now you're not. You can feel.'

'I can feel!' she repeated. 'Yes, we're none of us strong enough, are we? We feel.' She looked down and saw that it was getting dark in the valley and the mist was coming up the hill, only the last light was left in the sky. 'When I was a girl,' she said slowly, as if she were not speaking to him, but were telling it out for herself, 'I loved a man. We were children together in Ireland where I come from, a little place called Liniskelly. I thought, everyone thought, we should marry. But he was ambitious and I found out that he was going to America to his uncle, and—he didn't mean to take me too. He didn't think he was doing anything wrong, I don't think he had ever thought of marrying me; but in a little place like that—and I had shown I loved him—I had to get away first. You see, everybody knew. They were waiting for the announcement. They talked about it to me and I was so sure; my godmother had promised me her jewels. It all doesn't sound much, but it was to me; so I did it first.'

She had comforted herself with that. She had done it first, and then later she had come to be ashamed of that very thing; that it had been for that secret unworthy reason, she had entered.

Now she saw again the library at home, the morning she had told them; mother in the armchair had given one small cry, father had said nothing at all.

At last he said: 'But, Clodagh, what about Con? Is this fair on him? You've been going everywhere together. People are waiting, most of 'em take it as a fact. Think of him, having to face them all.'

'Clodagh, think of the poor boy!'

On the bridge that evening she had said: 'I'll miss you, Con, when you've gone.'

'I'll miss you too, Clo. We've had great times together, haven't we? Now I wonder you don't get something to do yourself, a clever girl like you with all your English education.'

'Yes, I did it first,' she said to Mr Dean, holding her veil down. 'At least I've always known that; but afterwards when I'd entered, I knew what I'd done.'

'And being you, I suppose you wouldn't go back.'

'I was right,' she said. 'It was a strange way of bringing me in, but God works in strange ways. He gave me strength to bring me through that time and He gave me my reward. After the first few years I never thought of it. I had work to do and I had the life; no one outside can possibly know what it means. It came to mean everything to me. I had forgotten—until we came here. The first day I came, I thought of him; in the first time for years. I seemed to go back to the beginning, when we were children on the shore. The young General reminds me of him too, I don't know why, they're not alike. I've been drifting and dreaming, and now I seem to have come to the struggle and bitterness again. It's queer how it's repeating itself, isn't it? After all these years I thought I had forgotten, until I came here.'

'Then I think,' he said, 'that you should go away at once.'

'Run away, like Sister Philippa?'

'Yes, if you've got any sense.'

'And leave all this? Abandon all this work, like the Brothers?'

'Yes,' he said. 'Before you ever came I told you not to. It's no place for a nunnery. There's something in it that makes everything exaggerated. I don't know what it is unless it's the very unlikeliness of the place. You should go, and take them all with you, before anything happens.'

'But what could happen now?' she challenged him. 'I'm on my guard.'

'Well, it seems to me,' he said earnestly, 'that you're all in a highly dangerous state; an exaggerated state of mind, or heart, or soul, or whatever you like to call it. Why can't you have the sense to leave? It's not easy to stop people once they let themselves go, and you can't change conditions here however hard you try. What's the good of deliberately running into a stone wall?'

'Is it a stone wall,' she answered, 'or is it mist?' and she said briskly: 'I didn't think you'd advise us to give in. I don't know why I told you, but I'm glad now I did. When it's out, it's nothing at all. Nothing has happened, why should it?' She turned to him and said with a smile: 'Thank you, Mr Dean, you've made me feel much better.'

'Well, I didn't mean to, you daft pig-headed woman,' he cried. 'All right, watch. Be on your guard. Watch yourself first, mind and see what time that gives you for Sister Ruth, and Dilip, and Kanchi, and all the others. Don't forget me. You can't afford to trust me a yard and I'll not help you. All right, try. I give you till the rains break. Where's that confounded pony? Phuba! Phuba! Good-bye.'

27

Father Roberts wrote that he was in bed again with his lumbago; he could not move out of bed. *'It always catches me in the spring,'* he wrote, *'and I shall be worse when the rains break. I really ought not to be sent to a climate like this and I don't know when I'll be able to see you. I've written for a relief, until then do the best you can and write to me if you need help or advice.'*

'In any case he couldn't have come for Easter,' said Sister Clodagh, 'his own people must come first. I wish we could have ridden in for one day at least, but as he says, we must do the best we can.'

All through Easter she had scanned the Sisters' faces and thought about them ceaselessly, and it seemed to her that each of them was normal and well and took her due part in the outer and inner life of the community. It was a quiet time, and on Easter Sunday, in spite of Father Roberts's absence, a feeling of joy and serenity seemed to bind them all together. It was a day of prayer and meditation and after Compline each went silently to her cubicle with a face of blissful peace. Sister Clodagh knelt on in the chapel after they had gone, and she felt that she had been right to stay, and humbly gave thanks for her decision. She thought and prayed for every Sister. Sister Honey had given coloured eggs to the children with no more than a nod and a happy smile, Sister Ruth asked if she might arrange the lilies that Pin Fong brought them for the altar, Sister Adela was almost amiable and reassured. The day was serene, the night dark and quiet; the moon had gone, and the roses had opened on the trees in the garden, bursting into such magnificence that it was easy to look at them and not at the snows.

Then after Easter, Sister Briony started her spring cleaning.

'Ayah, have you seen the small brass vase from the chapel? It was among the other vases. I've counted them over and over again and I can't see it.'

'It was on the shelf,' said Ayah.

'It isn't there now,' said Sister Briony, and unwillingly she said: 'I gave them to Kanchi to clean this morning.'

'Kanchi wouldn't steal,' Ayah flared up; but her eyes sparkled and, as soon as she could, she went unostentatiously away towards the Lace School.

That afternoon the young General Dilip Rai came for his algebra lesson with Sister Clodagh for the first time since the Easter holidays. 'I don't want a holiday,' he had said. 'I want to get better and better and better as quickly as I can. It's my plan to be clever very soon so that my uncle will think again about sending me to Cambridge where I do so want to go. Need I have a holiday, Sister Clodagh?'

She explained that the schools must be closed so that the Sisters might celebrate Easter. 'I hope you understand,' she said gently.

'Yes, of course I understand. It is quite right. It is what I should do myself,' he said. 'First of all I mean to be very clever and then very famous and then very holy. Like my great-uncle. At least,' he added truthfully: 'I should choose a bigger place to be holy in; after all, there are not so very many people here to know how holy he is, are there?'

Now he came down the drive wearing his corded coat that made his white pony look almost grey. He had on new ruby earrings and his shoes were new too, brown and white buckskin from Calcutta. Kanchi opened the door to him before he could ring. She had pleated her skirt so that it fell into graceful folds in front; it was a brighter blue than St Elizabeth's which he had admired. Her bodice was white, straining its pearl buttons over her breasts, and she had braided her plait of hair with red.

She stood stroking her veil into gathers, eyeing him. It was a beautiful veil of net edged with lace, but he did not even glance at it. He went quickly past her to Sister Clodagh's room.

Sister Clodagh was sitting upright at her desk, another table and chair were ready for him and the embroidery frame was pushed against the wall.

'I am to sit here?' he asked, puzzled.

'Yes,' she said, 'and before we begin, General, I have something to say to you.' Without glancing at his work she told him that he must come more suitably dressed for lessons.

'I've wanted to consult you about that,' he said, looking up with eyes as large and lustrous as the antelope's who stood at St Francis's hand in the embroidery frame. 'I've been thinking of it all through the holidays and I wrote for this.' He took a catalogue from his pocket. 'I've been thinking that, as I'm planning to go to England, and when I'm visiting and receiving instruction from European ladies, it would be very polite of me if I wore European clothes. Like this. It was the algebra lesson that reminded me. Sister Clodagh, why are they called plus fours?'

Sister Clodagh frowned at the picture of the young man in plus fours. She did not want to talk. 'We must get on with your lesson, General,' she said.

'One minute, Sister. Perhaps it's a mathematical measurement,' he suggested. 'It looks a kind of knickerbocker suit. That's what my Narayan Babu often talked about, a knickerbocker suit. Perhaps these are plus four inches bigger on every side than the usual kind of knickerbocker. They certainly look very big. This is another that I have thought of.' He flipped over the pages. 'You see what it says. "*A very gentle-manlike suit. Highly recommended. Double-breasted, pin striped, in a choice of colours. A nice quality material that hangs well.*" That sounds nice, doesn't it, Sister Clodagh? But what does it mean?'

'A pin stripe is a very narrow stripe, almost a thread, and a suit is said to hang well when it's well cut.'

'Well cut out, you mean.'

'It looks very nice in the illustration.'

'But is it the thing?' he asked anxiously. 'I do want to go about as fashionably as possible.'

'The catalogue's a new one, so that it's sure to be up to date,' she soothed him. 'And now General—'

'Shall I have to wear braces?' he interrupted her.

'Not if you don't want to, but really, General—'

'But I *do* want to,' he broke in. 'I've always wanted to. And I must have some underclothes. Here are some pictures and you see it says "*Viyella is best for underwear.*" I believe what it says because this is a printed catalogue so it must be true, but what is Viyella, Sister Clodagh?'

'Really, General Rai, you must ask someone else these questions,' said Sister Clodagh. 'In the Convent we can't—'

'Why, have I said anything not right?' he asked in

confusion and distress. 'Is Viyella not a proper subject? Oh I *am* so sorry.'

'No, no,' said Sister Clodagh. 'Viyella is only a kind of flannel, but I meant that we are not suitable people to advise you on your clothes.'

'But who is to help me if you won't? I was depending on you. Why, already I've ordered a box of shirts and ties and socks, and pyjamas to be sent here to you on approval, so that you and all the Sisters could help me to choose them.'

'You ordered them to be sent *here?*' she asked faintly.

'Yes. I thought we should have such fun choosing them. You mustn't say you won't help me. You see, my uncle doesn't care for English clothes, and the only European gentleman I know is Mr Dean and he isn't very tidy, is he? I mean he doesn't look at all like these gentlemen in the pictures. I only know what Narayan Babu taught me and I do want to be charmingly dressed, Sister.'

'You are charmingly dressed,' she said, helplessly. 'You shouldn't change it. You look nicest as you are.'

'But I want to wear English clothes. I want to learn to be just like they are in England. My cousin Pratap lives there in London. He has a valet and a flat and a car. It's a Delage. My uncle would buy me a Delage if there were a road here for it to go on.'

'General,' she said, 'we must start your lesson. You don't come here to talk to me, you know. If you want to continue your lessons you must—'

'One minute,' he said again. 'Sister Clodagh, you know all my ambitions. You know that I want to go away.'

She shut her eyes for a moment, and leaned her head back against her chair, bracing herself against it. She would not think of Con.

'*Please* let me tell you,' he was saying, 'because you help me so much. There are so many things beside the lessons that I need to know.

'There are several other ways,' he said shyly, 'in which I'm trying to improve myself. I have a great many books and records now and I'm learning to play golf. Do you know golf, Sister? The English think it's a very serious game. I was going to learn a much more serious game called cricket, but you need twenty-two people and a perfectly flat place to play that, and as you know there isn't a flat place anywhere here and I always have to play by myself. For golf you only have two, or four, and you can play quite well alone. The only thing is that it's difficult to understand from a book. Have you ever seen golf, Sister?'

'Well, yes,' she said. 'I used to play it—once. But that was a long time ago,' and hastily she added: 'I've forgotten now.'

'You will remember how it went as soon as you see my clubs. I sent for them from the Sports shop at Darjeeling. I'll bring them to-morrow and you can give me a lesson.'

She began to laugh and abruptly broke off. It was Con who had said: 'You're getting so good, Clo, you'll have to give me a lesson.'

To reach the Caragh course you had to drive four miles from Liniskelly over hills and marsh and bog. She had walked it back once after a full round—after a quarrel with Con.

'*Will* you get in the car?'

'No, I will not. I'd rather walk.'

'Walk then, and when you're tired don't sit crying by the road, for I'll not come for you.'

She had walked it quickly and easily, up the hill where the goats raised their heads to look at her, skirting the marsh where the flags were yellow and they were cutting peat for the early spring drying, taking to the road where the bogs were worst. Her legs were free under her short skirt, her hair was tucked under her hat and only a loose curl whipped her face and neck; the wind blew soft and damp on her face and the grass blew round her feet; she walked in angry exhilaration.

Half a mile from home she met Con and the car, come out to look for her. 'Well, are you tired?'

'No, thanks. Not in the least. I liked it.'

She walked on past him with long strides, her cheeks red and her eyes scornful. She heard him call and open the car door.

'Get in. You have me beat, Clo. Get in and I'll say I'm sorry.'

She came back with a jerk to the office where the General was patiently turning over the leaves of his catalogue, waiting for her to speak.

'General,' she said with an effort, 'will you go now, and remember, when you come again, I can't let you talk so much or I must stop your lessons.' He stared, and she cried: 'Really, I don't know how I can go on having you here.'

The dark colour came up under his dark skin; he stood up at once with his books. 'Why are you angry?' he said. 'I try to behave exactly as you want me to. I try to memorize every-thing you say. Don't you like me to come here?'

'You mustn't talk so much,' she cried. 'Now go. Please go. I'll make up your lesson to-morrow.'

'Very well,' he said, but his lips trembled. 'Good-bye, Sister Clodagh. Thank you for helping me, and excuse me for any-thing I may have done wrong.'

He walked down to the stables. He shouted for his pony, but no one came; he had come out early but it should have been waiting on the drive and he thought he would walk

down to the stables and catch his groom playing cards with
the Convent peons.

It was cold and he wanted his coat; as the sun went down,
its rays slanted higher on the hill, and as always there were
shadows under the deodars; not the black winter shadows,
but purple with a spring bloom on them and a crescent
moon was showing in the sky. He was still smarting from
Sister Clodagh's sharpness and he did not see them; then
close to him he heard screams, loud women's screams that
rang in the air. As he came out from the path under the trees,
he saw a crowd of people gathered in the clearing in front of
the stables.

The servants and coolies were laughing at Ayah who was
beating Kanchi with a knotted rope. Her pigtails flew up and
down as she flung up the rope and brought it down with a
thwack on Kanchi's shoulders; she was shrieking abuse with
a great deal of side-talk to the servants, and Kanchi's screams
were the loud ringing screams that Dilip had heard from the
path. She crouched on the ground, her face hidden, her veil
off and her bodice torn open, and when she saw the young
General she doubled her screams and watched him through
her fingers; Ayah saw him out of the corner of her eye and
doubled her antics too.

Then the servants saw him, and with slightly sheepish
faces they moved off up to the house. He knew they were not
really ashamed or they would have stayed where they were
caught, dumb and expressionless; he knew there had been no
malice in their laughter, nor in Ayah's whipping, and that Kanchi's screams were excellent showing off, but it suited him to
smoulder and burn with pity in his present smarting mood,
and though they were quite innocent, the servants quailed
under his look and went quickly up to the house.

Ayah did not move, but smiled at him, as she panted for breath. 'Why, it's the little General Bahadur,' she said.

'What has the girl done?' he asked, sternly.

'She's a thief,' she said between breaths. 'She stole a brass vase from the church room. A brass vase that wasn't worth two annas, mind you, and hid it in her skirt where it goes jangle, jangle, jangle against her keys and of course I discovered it at once. When she cries they let her off, but this is my affair and she can cry all she likes and they won't hear her. I brought her down here and whipped her without asking, once for stealing and twice for the silly way she did it.'

She looked him over again and said: 'You look very doleful. What sort of a beating have you been getting?' and cackled. He flushed, and she came close and put her hand on his arm. 'There, there,' she said, 'you mustn't mind your old Ayah. You'll be a great man, my little General. Not like your uncle, oh, dear no! Like your grandfather. *He* was a man. Isn't it time to put your books away, Dilip Raja, and be a man?' She looked at Kanchi sobbing industriously at their feet, and put the rope in his hand. 'Finish the beating, General Bahadur. I have to take the Sister Sahib's tea. Finish the beating as you like and begin to be a man.' Chuckling gently she went up the hill to the house.

The rope felt like a plait of hair, but hard and hairy in his hand, and his eyes went to Kanchi's plait of hair as straight and soft as silk, tied with its red braid. It was trailing on the ground.

'Get up,' he said, 'your hair is getting dusty.'

She crouched lower, sobbing into the earth, and the echo of her sobs from the ground sounded like the beating of a drum; soft and throbbing like the drums he had heard since he could remember. The sun had gone up to the garden above, the clearing was filled with the peaceful after-glow; the light that was left was strained of colour, clear and cold. Dilip's skin shone and Kanchi's hands and the soles of her upturned feet. He looked down at the soles of her feet and saw that she had stained the heels with red, and he saw the bright colours of her clothes and remembered how she had always tried to attract his attention.

She sobbed more softly, and then she put her hands on his feet over the Calcutta shoes and laid her cheek on them.

From her hands pressing his feet, a warmth stole up his legs and flickered along his thighs. He stood quite still, holding the rope while the warm delightful teasing stole upwards from his feet. Now Kanchi lifted her face and knelt on the ground, her waist swayed inward and her hand slid up to his knee. Now she pressed her face against him and her hands came up, smoothing, gliding, pressing. Her face was lifted to him, her skirt knot hung loosely, the buttons had burst open and he could see her bare breast.

The stable had no door; the smell of the ponies and baled grass met him as he turned, looking for a place. Almost dreamily he drew her up, his hand gently pinched the flesh of her shoulder that was firm and springing and soft.

'Go in,' he said, and followed her from the light to the darkness inside.

28

She must have run away,' said Sister Adela in a pleased voice. 'It's a week since she was here.'

Sister Briony shook her head. 'These people are very strange,' she said. 'It's difficult to fathom them at all. I think she's staying away because she stole the little vase from the chapel.'

'But we haven't said anything about it.'

'I told Ayah. She must know that we know she did it. Yes, I think that's why she's hiding.'

'But isn't it very odd, that from the very same day, the young General hasn't come for his lessons?' asked Sister Adela. 'Isn't that a curious coincidence?'

'Not at all,' said Sister Briony, still obstinate. 'Sister Clodagh said she had occasion to speak to him that day. He's not at all the kind of boy who'd do anything deceitful. Doesn't he talk quite openly to us all?'

'He does indeed,' said Sister Adela, 'but I still maintain that it was asking for mischief to have him and that little minx here together.'

'She isn't half the minx she was when she first came,' retorted Sister Briony. 'She was getting to be quite clean and useful. I wish I had talked to her about that vase myself. It was silly of me. You have to be careful with these people. Mr Dean is always telling us that, and he knows them better than anyone else.'

When the girls were questioned they looked down at their fingers and smiled. Not one of them would say.

'Perhaps she has gone away,' said Maili helpfully.

'Ayah, I think you know.'

'Perhaps I do,' said Ayah, 'perhaps I don't. I'm not going to say anything till I'm sure.'

'But Ayah, don't you understand. We're responsible for her.'

Ayah only smiled. 'I *would* like to know where she is,' said Sister Briony.

One evening Ayah came to her in the Refectory. 'Lemini, a woman has come with a baby.'

'Where, Ayah?'

'She has gone to the e'clinic to see the Smiling Lemini. She sent me to fetch you.'

'Is the baby ill then?'

'Lemini, the baby is ill. Don't let the Sister take off his clothes and put him on the scales or she'll kill him, I'm sure.'

'What is this, Sister?' said Sister Briony, bustling into the clinic. A woman stood by the table, holding a baby under her shawl.

'It's Om's little brother,' said Sister Honey. 'He doesn't seem very well.'

'Put him on the table where I can see him,' said Sister Briony, folding a blanket to make a pad for him to lie on.

'He'll cry,' said Sister Honey, but the baby lay quietly on the blanket without moving, his eyes closed. Now and then he knit his brows and clenched his jaw as if he were worried. 'Do you think he's got a pain,' asked Sister Honey. 'Do you think that's wind?'

Sister Briony took him gently and sat him a little up. He turned his head away from the light but still he made no sound. 'Fetch me my thermometer,' she said. 'How long has he been like this?' she asked the woman.

'Three or four days, Lemini. To-day I couldn't wake him.'

Sister Briony only grunted in reply as she put the thermometer under his arm. 'His eyes seem to hurt and he doesn't like the light, but he's not in the *least* fretful, is he?' said Sister Honey. 'I don't think he's got any fever.' She read the thermometer over Sister Briony's shoulder. 'A hundred and three!' she said. 'But that's not much in a baby, is it? I mean they go up and down so easily, don't they?'

Sister Briony did not answer; she began to question the mother whose eyes flickered from the Sister's face to the baby.

'Has he lain still like this for long?'

'Since this morning. I couldn't wake him. Before that he moved his head like this,' she turned her head sharply from side to side, 'but he isn't asleep, Lemini!'

'Has he vomited lately?'

'He very often vomits a little, Lemini. Yesterday and to-day he wouldn't take any food.'

'She gives him too much,' put in Sister Honey. 'I expect that's what is wrong. He's been a little out of sorts for a long time. I thought it was teeth.'

Sister Briony bent over the table and turned up his coat; the muscles of his stomach seemed very retracted and rigid, and his legs were drawn up.

'It's probably teeth,' said Sister Honey. 'That tummy looks as if he ought to have a good dose. Shall we give him magnesia or some of that paraffin emulsion?'

BLACK NARCISSUS   201

But Sister Briony shook her head, and picked the baby gently up and gave him back to the woman.

'You can't wake him, Lemini?' She looked at the rows of bottles on the shelves. 'Give him something to wake him, Lemini. All yesterday and to-day he's lain asleep like this.'

'Let him sleep,' said Sister Briony quietly and drew the shawl across him. 'Take him home and put him on your bed and let him sleep,' she said.

'But aren't you going to give him *anything*?' cried Sister Honey. 'Sister, aren't you going to do *anything* for him?'

Sister Briony answered: 'There's nothing I can do.'

'What do you mean? He's quite quiet. He hasn't much fever. He can't be very bad.'

'He's very bad. I can't help him. I daren't try.'

'You mean—he might die?'

Sister Briony nodded, her lips pressed together. The woman's eyes went from one of their faces to the other, trying to understand what they said.

'There must be something you can do,' cried Sister Honey. 'At least you could bathe his eyes and relieve his tummy with a little oil. That couldn't hurt him. You can't risk letting that lovely baby die without raising a finger to help him.'

'I've told you I daren't touch him, Sister. I don't think he feels any pain—'

'You've only got to *look* at him to see how it must hurt him,' Sister Honey burst out. 'Look at those spasms in his face. I know what it is; you're thinking of Mr Dean and what he said. That's it. You're afraid of getting into trouble and so you'll let him die. You'll give up his little life without a struggle. You'll stand by and let him die.'

'I've told you,' Sister Briony's voice was high, 'there's nothing I can do.'

The woman still stood, trying to make out what they said, listening intently, holding the baby under her shawl where Sister Briony had laid him. 'Lemini, give him something.' She hardly opened her lips, her eyes were on Sister Briony's face. 'Give him something.'

Sister Briony shook her head. 'Let him sleep,' she said again.

'Then God in Heaven be your judge,' said Sister Honey solemnly. 'God have mercy on you. This little baby—this darling—and you won't even try.'

'That's enough of this, Sister,' Sister Briony's temper snapped. 'I know what I'm doing. I'm as sorry as can be, but she must take him home. The best and kindest thing you can do is to make her go home where she can be with her own people. Ayah can go with her. Tell her to let him sleep and persuade her to go home.'

'But *Sister*!' pleaded Sister Honey in anguish. '*Try*. At least try.'

'Sister!'

Without answering back, Sister Honey went to the woman and put her arm round her shoulders, patting her, drawing her to the steps.

'There, you see, that's the way,' said Sister Briony. 'I'll leave her with you and send Ayah. Try and make her understand that she's to take him home.' She tiptoed away, her face very sorrowful.

She did not see the woman turn and draw the hand that patted her shoulder down to the baby's head, and hear her whisper: 'Give him something, Lemini. Give him something.'

'The children are very late this morning,' said Sister Ruth to Joseph next day.

'Perhaps they think it is a holiday,' he answered almost under his breath.

'How could they think it's a holiday when they've just finished their holidays, you silly little boy? Go up to the path and see if they're coming and tell them to hurry up.'

Joseph stood by the desk and looked thoroughly dismayed. 'I don't want to,' he said.

'You—don't—want—to?' Sister Ruth could hardly believe her ears. This from Joseph whose obedience was his shadow. 'How dare you answer me like that! Go at once.'

'No,' he cried loudly, 'I won't go,' and made a dart for the door, but Sister Ruth had pounced and caught him by the collar and dragged him back to the desk. 'Now you stand still and tell me what you mean.'

'Whatever are you doing to Joseph?' Sister Honey came quickly in. 'Why, Joseph, what's the matter?' But instead of sidling up to her as he always did, he stood where he was and drooped his head.

'Haven't the children come?' asked Sister Honey. She was pale and looked as if she had not slept. 'I came to see because none of the girls are here, and I went to meet Om and none of them were on the path. I wonder why?'

'Joseph knows,' said Sister Ruth. 'Tell us, Joseph.'

'I don't want to,' cried Joseph in a panic. 'Lemini, don't make me tell.'

'Joseph, you must tell us,' said Sister Honey; she was even paler now and her voice shook. 'Please, Joseph dear.'

'Tell us,' said Sister Ruth, shaking him by the collar.

'Om's brother is dead,' cried Joseph. 'He died in the night and they say that the Smiling Lemini killed him.' He burst into terrified tears.

Ayah told Sister Briony. They were in the dispensary. 'There's no one here this morning,' said Sister Briony looking out of the door. 'Now I shall have a nice long time to give to turning out the reception room. What a good thing no one has come.'

'Lemini!' Ayah planted herself beside her. 'No one's likely to come. That baby the woman brought died in the night! It began to twitch, and twitched worse and worse, and then it seemed to die only it was breathing, and then it did die; and they are saying all over the village that the Smiling Lemini killed him.'

'Then you can tell them it isn't true. The Smiling Lemini never touched him.'

'Oh yes, she did,' answered Ayah. 'When you sent me to help her last night, she was washing the baby's eyes.'

'What?' cried Sister Briony. 'What, Ayah?'

'And what's more she told the woman to do it herself at home and gave her a bottle to take away and some of our cotton-wool; and I think,' said Ayah with relish, 'that she must have given some medicine, because a spoon and a bottle were on the table too.'

'Which bottle? Show me.'

'This one,' said Ayah, holding up a long-necked bottle of oil.

'Dear goodness!' breathed Sister Briony. 'Of course. Go and find her, Ayah, and tell her to come to the office at once. Give me that bottle. Where's my report book? Go on, find her and tell her to come at once.'

'She's coming already,' said Ayah, as they hurried down the passage, and there was Sister Honey and Sister Ruth and Joseph all making for the office door. They swept in, without knocking, on Sister Clodagh who was talking to Sister Adela.

'There's only one thing to do now,' said Sister Briony, at the end of the story, 'and that's to send for Mr Dean.' Sister Ruth sat up abruptly.

'Tcha!' said Sister Adela. 'What could he do?'

'He's the only person who could do anything. He knows how

to deal with these people. He may be able to think of something. We don't want this to get to the General's ears, do we, Sister?'

Sister Clodagh did not want it to get to Mr Dean's ears either. 'Let me think,' she said. 'The General is away.'

Sister Honey sat in a chair, her hands rolling her soaking handkerchief into a little ball and unrolling it to wipe her eyes; the bottle of oil and the report book were on the desk and Joseph and Ayah, the witnesses, stood in front of it. Sister Ruth was by the window and Sister Adela had gone to the door and stood with her back against it.

'We've already offended the young General in some way,' went on Sister Briony. 'We don't want anything else to get about, and Ayah says the people are very furious.'

Sister Honey gave a faint moan.

'But Ayah, don't you think they'll get over it?' asked Sister Clodagh. 'Don't you think it will all die down and the children will come back? When you tell them that the baby was dying when the woman brought him? When you tell them that in any case he would have died?'

Ayah shrugged her shoulders. 'If only the Lemini hadn't touched him,' she began.

'What's the use of talking like that when she did touch him? Very well, I suppose we'd better send for Mr Dean.'

Sister Ruth watched her as she wrote the note, trying to see what she said.

'Joseph, can you take this to Mr Dean? Can you find him and ask him to read it at once? Don't let him put it in his hat and forget it.'

'No, Lemini. Yes, Lemini.' He trotted forward. As he took the letter, he slid his handkerchief to Sister Honey under the desk. She burst into fresh sobs.

'Before you all go,' said Sister Clodagh, 'I want to tell you that, much as I blame Sister Blanche, she did not kill the baby. She probably hastened his death by giving him the oil, but he must have died anyhow. Sister Briony diagnosed it as a case of tubercular meningitis, and she's more than ever convinced that this was it, by the way in which he died. It's always fatal. Ayah, do you understand?' She repeated it in Hindustani, and added: 'Go and tell everybody what I've said.'

'I had to do it,' moaned Sister Honey. 'I couldn't let him go without trying to help him. Sister Briony never told me what it was, and he was such a darling. Such—a—darling.'

They all sat waiting for Mr Dean; it seemed hours before he came.

'Do you think it's serious?' Sister Clodagh asked as soon as she had told him. He had already had it from Joseph on the way up. 'Don't you think they'll come back? Is it serious?'

'I think it may be very serious,' he answered.

'Tcha!' said Sister Adela again.

'Sister Clodagh,' he said looking at Sister Adela. 'The Agent here before my day was riding his pony down to the factory one day and he let it kick an umbrella that was open on the path, over the edge. There was a baby asleep under it and it was killed. It was an accident but they murdered him that night.'

Sister Honey gave a shriek and Sister Briony's mouth fell open and they all stared at him, breathing a little quickly. 'I'm not trying to frighten you,' he said, 'I'm trying to make you see that it may be serious. Nothing of the kind's likely to happen to you, but you'll find the servants and the people will be sullen and queer-tempered for a while. I'll go to the village and the lines and talk to everybody. Meanwhile you must none of you go out of the garden, but try to go about as if nothing had happened and as if you weren't at all perturbed.'

That was more easily said than done.

A sinister quiet hung over the Convent. In the class-room there was only Sister Ruth at the teacher's desk and Joseph sitting miserably at the end of the first row of empty benches; at every sound they started and looked at one another. In the Lace School Sister Honey worked with clumsy fingers at a pattern she could hardly see for her swollen eyes; she had her back against the wall facing the door and had shut the windows. Sister Briony turned out the reception room as she had planned to do, and in her nervousness she kept up a stream of orders to the servants; but Sister Adela was the bravest of all; she went up and down the garden as usual, standing over the coolies, turning her back on them, and they, as Sister Briony said, 'with mallets and hoes and I don't know what lying round them'.

'Sister, I shouldn't do that,' she called out of the window.

'Do what?'

'I wouldn't go so close to those coolies, if I were you. Look at that man with the fork. I'm sure he's not safe.'

'Nonsense,' said Sister Adela. 'Do you think I believed all that talk?' But all the same she did not go quite so near the pig-tailed coolie swinging the three-pronged fork.

That was the worst of it, that the servants should have gone suddenly silent and sullen. That Nima and the fat cook Toukay and Jangbir and the smiling house-boys had changed into enemies.

'I'm sure they're perfectly loyal,' said Sister Clodagh. 'It's only because we're afraid that we imagine they're unusual. All the same,' she added: 'I should be careful what you say to them.'

When Mr Dean came back all of them without waiting for permission left their work to see what he had to say. Sister Clodagh made no attempt to send them back.

'I don't think you've anything to be afraid of,' he told them. 'They're perfectly quiet.'

'But what did they say?'

'They didn't say anything. They listened to me and said nothing.'

'Did they believe you?'

'I don't know. They went back to their houses, but I saw the woman, and I drank the bottle of lotion that Sister Honey gave her.'

'*Drank* it?'

'It was only boracic and water. I wanted to show them I wouldn't drop down dead . . . I don't think you need worry yourselves, but if you like I'll send Pin Fong and Phuba up to sleep here with Jangbir to-night.'

'Do you think they'll come back?' asked Sister Briony. 'Do you think they'll come back to us?'

'They may,' he said comforting her. 'Yes, I think they'll come back.'

'We shall look very silly if they don't.' That was Sister Ruth. 'With a dispensary and a clinic and a school with no one in it.'

'Of course they'll come back,' said Sister Clodagh.

'But if they don't?'

'Well, if you want me again, send for me,' said Mr Dean. 'I won't leave the factory and the bungalow. If you ring the bell continuously, I'll know it's for me. I don't think you need be afraid.'

Sister Ruth had put herself close beside him. She could almost have touched the sleeve of his shirt; it only came to his elbow, and she could see the muscles and veins of his arm, thick with chestnut hairs to his fingers as he held his hat, flapping it against his knee. She thought that he deliberately did not look at her, but kept his head turned to Sister Clodagh. She bent across him and picked up the bottle of oil.

'Look,' she cried, flourishing it in front of his face. 'That's what Sister Honey gave the baby. Aren't you glad it wasn't this you had to drink; it's castor oil. Hee! Hee! Hee!' She began to laugh and, seeing their scandalized faces, she could not stop. 'Hai! Hai! Hai!' she laughed.

Still laughing, she pushed him away and stumbled to the window, her handkerchief to her mouth, and stood with her back to them, still shaking. After a while she grew very still, Sister Briony saw tears running down her cheek as she pressed it against the glass.

'Mr Dean will begin to think this is an asylum, not a Convent,' said Sister Clodagh. 'Well, we're all very grateful to him, but I think I'm right in saying that we're not afraid and there's no need to send Pin Fong and Phuba. Am I right?'

'Yes, Sister,' came firmly from Sister Adela, and more subdued from Sister Briony and Sister Honey. Sister Ruth did not move.

After he had gone there was silence except from Sister Honey who had begun to cry again, and occasional small sniffs from Sister Ruth.

'Well, it's no use crying over spilt milk, that's what I say,' said Sister Briony. 'We can only pray that they'll come back, that's all.'

'Yes, we can pray,' said Sister Clodagh. 'It's nearly twelve o'clock. Sister Ruth, if you've recovered yourself, will you ring? I think we'll say the Angelus in chapel to-day.'

29

Two days passed and no one came. That quietness hung over the Convent, there was no one on the path; no voices and running footsteps in the playground, no rings at the dispensary bell. There was no sign of Kanchi. Every day the books were set out, the lace cushions put ready on the table, the General's desk opened for him and his chair dusted, and every day they were put away again.

Sister Briony finished her spring cleaning; Sister Adela started her silent coolies on their work each morning and talked over her plans with the strangely monosyllabic Nima; Sister Ruth taught lesson after lesson to Joseph who did not hear a word that she said, and Sister Honey sat sodden with crying, and worked on a particularly elaborate rose pattern with four small cushions with their spread bobbins sitting useless on the table opposite her.

'Really, for all the good we're doing, we might be the Sunnyasi,' said Sister Ruth.

'Are you so sure he does no good?' asked Sister Clodagh.

'What do you mean?' asked Sister Ruth.

'Think about it,' said Sister Clodagh. 'Sister Briony, we will have extra time for meditation to-night after Evensong. I think we all need it.'

But all through the hour they were listening and straining, even Sister Adela was not as prompt as usual. Sister Honey wept steadily all the way through, and Sister Ruth sat with a smile round her lips, not attempting to pay attention.

The long dragging idle day passed, and the next. There was only a pretence of doing work. It seemed to Sister Clodagh that she sat for hours at her desk, trying to keep her thoughts at bay. There were no report books, no accounts, nothing to inspect, though she went round from Sister to Sister to keep up the pretence that they were busy, and found endless small tasks for them to do; they were so obviously manufactured that it hardly seemed worth while doing them. The silence was unnerving; the servants and coolies and workmen used to shout and talk while they worked, and, though the Sisters had often complained about it, now they missed it. The loud cheerful people were sinister in their silence, and if anyone came down the path, they went quickly and sullenly past the house, turning their faces away.

The weather was fine and warm, the roses filled the garden with hot sweetness, the folds of the hills were blue and the snows shone solidly into the sky. Sister Clodagh declared a holiday all round and organized sewing parties in the garden and thought of small competitions to make them think of something else. But her kindness and the relaxation only seemed to make the trouble worse. She had hoped to make something of it; she had hoped that it would bring them closer together, and had imagined them drawing together as one person. They were not close together, they preferred to sit apart without anything to say to one another, they were not struggling, they were simply waiting, and in chapel she felt that not one of them, not even herself, had prayed.

She dared not think; she sat at her desk and, pretending it was important, she began to translate a carol for next Christmas into the dialect.

It was on the fourth day at dinner-time that Sister Honey burst into tears for the hundredth time. She was cleaning her plate with a piece of bread when she bent her head and began to sob violently. 'I can't bear it. I can't bear it!' she sobbed. 'I couldn't let him die without t-trying to help him. I loved him so.'

They looked wearily at one another. Sister Adela took the piece of bread from her hand and laid it down. Sister Clodagh was beginning: 'Now, Sister, you must really—' when Sister Ruth sprang to her feet and crashed her plate down on the table.

'I've had enough of this,' she cried, in a high-pitched voice. 'I can't stand any more. What's she crying for, I'd like to know? Not for what she's done, but for a little black brat of a baby that's not even her own. That's why she's crying, only she hasn't the courage to say so. Because all the time she's been pining and longing for a baby of her own. Yes,' she sank her voice and leaned towards them and whispered, 'she—wants to—have—a—baby—of—her—own.' She stood up again and cried: 'She won't say so. She's afraid to say it. She's afraid. And you're afraid,' she turned on Sister Clodagh. 'You're more afraid than anyone. You're afraid we'll know why you steal away and walk on the terrace, aren't you? And why you have consultations alone in the office, and why you're always visiting the buildings. You're afraid we'll find out, that's why you hide it. But I know. Yes, I know. And I'll tell you something else. It isn't you he likes, it's me. Yes, me. That's why you bully me, that's why you make *them* watch me. Oh yes, you're clever, very clever, but I'm not afraid of you. Not if you starve me and poison me and shut me up. I'm still not afraid. He'll help me. I'll tell him all about you. I'll tell him what you do to me and he'll be very angry. So take care.'

She put her chair between herself and them. 'I know you're all watching me,' she whispered, 'I know all about you, but take care. Take care. He's stronger than you are.' Her eyes looked at them without any sense in them, strangely terrifying. 'I know you're looking at me, but I'm not afraid. I'm stronger than any of you.'

'She's *mad*,' breathed Sister Briony.

'Don't move,' said Sister Clodagh in an undertone. 'Sit still. Go on eating. Don't look at her.'

She stood behind her chair watching the dip and rise of their heads over their plates, at Sister Clodagh breaking her bread and Sister Honey clattering her fork on her plate. She was shaking now so that the chair legs rattled on the floor; she looked at her own place, at the plate she had broken and the salt cellar she had spilt and her lips began to shake too. She pushed her chair in violently and ran out of the room.

'Let her go. Don't touch her,' said Sister Briony, catching Sister Adela who had jumped up after her. 'It's over now. We must leave her alone for a little, and presently when she's calmer, I'll go out and talk to her. None of you must look as if anything had happened. She must be sent away. Dear, what a week we're having.'

None of them could finish the meal; they could not forget Sister Ruth standing behind the chair talking in that threatening whispering voice. It wiped everything else out of their minds and filled the whole afternoon. The servants went to their quarters, whispering and predicting, the news spread to the village and the coolie lines.

Sister Briony found her sitting on the horse-block. She was perfectly quiet and looked up calmly when Sister Briony came and leant on the railing beside her. Sister Briony looked out across the gulf; she was trying to think of what she could do next. Her lips moved once or twice, but she could find nothing to say.

Sister Ruth pressed her hands together. 'Steady. Steady now,' she was telling herself. 'You've done it once, you mustn't do it again. Be careful. Be steady. Don't think about *Them*.' 'They've been cutting the bamboos,' she said aloud.

'So they have,' said Sister Briony looking at the sharp white and green spikes below them.

'They look like swords,' said Sister Ruth, her eyes on them.

'Yes, don't they.'

Sister Ruth stretched and yawned. 'Why does doing nothing make you feel so tired?'

'Do you feel tired?' asked Sister Briony, carefully. 'You shouldn't do that in this beautiful air.'

'I feel as if I'd been beaten all over,' said Sister Ruth.

'You do look a little tired.' Sister Briony chose her words carefully. 'Would you like me to get permission for you to lie down?'

Sister Ruth did not make her usual protests. 'It's my head that's so bad,' she said. 'It isn't as if there were any work for us to do, is it?'

Sister Briony helped her on to her bed and drew the curtains of her cubicle. 'I'll get Ayah to sit here with her mending,' she thought, 'and tell her to fetch me if she gets restless. I'll give her a strong powder that will put her right under for a little while, and quieten her down.'

'Here's something for your head,' she said, giving her a white paper. 'Tip it into your mouth and drink some water after it.'

Sister Ruth tipped it neatly down between her coverlet and her chin and drank the water. 'Thank you, Sister,' she said.

When Sister Briony looked in half an hour later she was sound asleep.

It was in the evening that Ayah knocked on the office door where Sister Clodagh and Sister Briony had been for two hours talking, and wondering what was the best thing they could do.

'I came to tell you,' said Ayah, licking her lips uneasily, 'that it's a quarter past six and no one has rung l'Angelus.'

'Where's Sister Ruth? Where's the young Lemini? Why have you left her?'

'Well, I came to tell you that too, Lemini. She's gone out.'

'*Gone out*! Ayah, why didn't you stop her?'

'You should never stop mad people from doing what they want,' said Ayah decidedly. 'You should never interfere with them at all.'

'She might hurt herself,' cried Sister Briony.

'If she's really mad, that won't matter,' said Ayah. And if she's not really mad she'll look after herself.'

'And you mean to say you just sat there and let her go?'

'Well—I can't tell you a lie, Lemini. I wasn't there when she went.'

'You left her after all I told you?'

'She was sound asleep. I touched her toe and she didn't move, I gave it a good jerk and still she didn't move, so I went down for some tea.'

'What time was this?'

'It was more than time for my food. I know that, and the Lemini hadn't given me any time to have any. My head was going round and round with hunger.'

'About three o'clock?'

'Perhaps.'

'What time did you go back?'

'Oh, I wasn't away very long. Let me see. I had a little food and I gave a cup of rice to the hens, and then my brother's son came. He had made some good arrangements for the summer; he's bearer in the hotel at Ghoom—'

'And so you stayed talking for most of the afternoon! A long time?'

'Oh, I wasn't very long,' said Ayah. 'I went back and sat down on my stool and everything was quiet and still. Then I thought I'd take a little look, and if you'll believe me, the Lemini wasn't in the bed. I was never so astonished in my life.'

'She may have been gone over three hours!' said Sister Clodagh.

30

Sister Ruth had not been outside the Convent grounds before. As the path went down and she came to the coolie lines, her heart began to beat; the houses were like dark boxes on stilts lining a lane of dusty earth, and the dogs began to bark. She went back a little up the hill but no one came out; only the great red pai dogs stood in the lane and barked at her. She looked at the houses curiously; they had roofs beaten out of kerosene tins and some had broken earthenware pots as a chimney; there were marrows with bright yellow flowers climbing up a trellis, and a broom leant against a wall. They did not seem so frightening after that; there was nothing to be afraid of in cooking fires and sweeping and growing marrows. '*Don't go out of the garden.*' She bit her lip and went on down between the tea.

Presently she saw the River below, streaked with green and white, looping the factory which stood on a foot-hill above it. She looked up, but the terrace cut off the house except for the top line of roof; the buttresses looked like fortifications and the bamboos made a spray of green round them, except for one bare spot.

'That's what Sister Briony and I were looking at,' and remembering dinner-time, she felt the blood surging up into her eyes again. 'Steady, steady. You must go quietly. You're all right if only you can be quiet.'

As she came near the factory, the coolie gong rang out; it was the four o'clock signal for the pluckers to cease working and bring in the leaf. In another two hours she should have been ringing the Convent bell for vespers and the evening Angelus. She looked over her shoulder but the hill was bare of anyone but herself, and, far off, the pluckers with their baskets. Then she turned and saw Mr Dean riding towards her.

She felt breathless, as if she had been running up the hill, instead of walking leisurely down it. The blindness was coming on again and she spread out her hands and swayed. 'Steady. Go quietly.' She drove it away, and she was standing calmly on the sunny path as he came riding towards her. Calmly she noticed everything about him; how his width made his pony look even smaller than it was, and it was so small that he had to hold his feet up off the ground; how his shirt and his hat flapped gently in the wind, and he was whistling a loud gusty tune. When he saw her, he put his feet down and braked the pony.

'Sister,' he said sternly, 'what are you doing down here?'

Sister Ruth was pleased with the way she answered steadily: 'I came to find you,' with her eyes on him.

'Then you can think again,' he said, and kicked his pony's stomach with his heels, but she caught at the reins as he went past, and dragging after him, stopped the pony.

'You're *not* going to leave me like this,' she cried wildly. 'You're not to go away. Stay with me, just while I tell you. Stay with me. Take me where I can talk to you just for a little while. Just for a minute.'

He looked helplessly up the path to the Convent and down to the factory. She was holding his hand and the reins tightly and now she laid her cheek on his hand. The dusty smell of the pony, and the smell of leather and tea and tobacco and sweat and eau-de-Cologne that came from him filled her nostrils. She shut her eyes and humbly kissed the back of his hand among the chestnut hairs.

He snatched his hand away as if a snake had bitten it, almost knocking her down. 'Sister!' he cried in horror. 'Sister! Stop it. How can you! What on earth are you doing? You can't behave like this.'

'I can't help it,' she said. 'I came on purpose to find you. I can't stand it any longer. I love you. I want to be with you always.'

To her surprise he turned a dull hot red. 'Aren't you ashamed of yourself?' he asked. 'Sister, you're a nun. You can't behave in—in this shocking way.'

'It isn't shocking,' she said. 'How could it be? I love you and you'll help me and take me away.'

'Aren't you ashamed of yourself?' he said again.

'No,' said Sister Ruth loudly. Her green eyes shone and her odd thin face was illumined. 'I'm not ashamed because I can't help it. Nothing else matters to me now.'

As she spoke, a file of coolies came round the corner, men and women going up to the lines and the village after weighing in their leaf. They passed so close that they brushed Sister Ruth and she shrank against the pony's neck. Mr Dean called to one of them and the man looked at Sister Ruth and answered tersely. Mr Dean's face darkened but he said nothing.

'What did you say to him?'

'I asked him to go up and tell them in the Convent that you were here,' he said brutally.

She was not dismayed. 'He said he wouldn't. Didn't he?'

He grunted. 'You'd better walk up with me.'

'I won't.'

'Then I shall leave you here by yourself.'

'You can't. You couldn't do that. Did you see the way they looked at us? It wouldn't be safe.'

'Do you think I care what happens to you?' he said, but her eyes did not falter.

'All the same, you wouldn't leave me here.'

He stood up and let the pony escape between his legs, then caught it by the tail and turned it round.

'I can't drag you up the hill by force,' he said. 'You come with me. I'm going to talk to you.'

He went quickly down the path to the factory. In his thonged chapli shoes, he could walk like a native, but the stones rolled from his pony's hooves and Sister Ruth slipped and slid behind him.

'Don't go so fast,' she panted. 'I'm tired and I'm out of breath.'

'It'll do you good to be tired,' he answered over his, shoulder, 'and I'd rather have you out of breath.'

At the factory door he turned his pony loose, slipping its bridle on to its neck. 'Come in,' he said, and she stepped doubtfully inside.

After the brightness outside, the room was dark, but presently she was able to see that it was filled with brown light and the sound of machinery and the clap, clap, clap of wicker trays where the women were sifting tea on the floor; at once she noticed that in the din and clatter some of them were suckling their babies while they worked and she flushed painfully, and the blood sang in her ears. 'Steady. Go quietly. Steady.'

She had a confused sense of the big brown room; brown faces and hands, and the bare legs and thighs of the boys at the furnaces; the paler faces of the babies pressed to the dark breasts; the brown iron of the machinery and the canvas belts, and the wooden tea boxes and glittering tin foil. The room had an overpowering smell, strong and heady, that made it swim in front of her eyes. 'Steady. Steady.'

Mr Dean was showing her over the factory. In a dream she let him walk her round and round, upstairs and down. He stepped among the women and picked a handful of tea for her to break in her hand and sniff; she only saw his hand as he gave it to her, the hand she had kissed. He showed her the rollers and fermenting trays where the leaf looked like spinach, and the withering trays where they were spreading the fresh leaf to die; he explained and instructed, and she looked at him with those eyes that were greener than the new plucked leaf itself and did not hear a single word he said.

He began to be intensely angry with Sister Clodagh. It was she who had put him in this impossible position, she should control Sister Ruth. *'Does she ever try to speak to you?'* she had asked. She knew all about it. *'I'm on my guard,'* she had boasted, and then let the Sister escape from her like this. 'Damn all women!' thought Mr Dean.

The Sister was leaning on the tiers of trays, looking at him. He remembered how she had stolen up to look at him that day in the porch; she was looking at him like that now, and there was something snake-like in her face with its intent eyes that sent a coldness down the back of his legs. He clapped his hand to his back pocket to find his pipe.

'Damn, I've left my pipe in the office.'

'Can we go in there? I'm tired. I want to sit down.' She was leaning on the trays as if she were exhausted.

The long narrow room with its hot damp smell and dirty windows was gloomy and stifling; the corners were dark and it suddenly filled him with a kind of panic. 'Come along then,' he said roughly.

There was only one chair in the office, she dropped into it, and he stood in front of her and said before she could speak: 'Now I understand perfectly why you've come here.'

'Yes. To be with you. I want to be with you.'

'Let's talk it over, Sister,' he said desperately. 'You know this isn't like you. You've forgotten who you are. You're a religious. A nun.'

'What makes you think a nun can't love?' she asked.

'But you can't love me. It's ridiculous. How could you? It's the spring,' he said desperately. 'You must tell yourself that. It brings everything to the surface, like coming out in spots. You must tell yourself that it's the spring.'

'It isn't the spring. You're not really thinking. You say that because you've heard it so often. This isn't the spring. All through the winter it's been the same. I've loved you ever since I saw you. It's not your fault, you've never taken any notice of me. Once or twice you've spoken to me; the first time was about that woman with the cut wrist, her name was Samell and I wrote it down as Samuel. You see, I haven't forgotten. And this is the hand you held when you caught me. I think I was going to hurt Sister Clodagh, but you stopped me, didn't you? You hurt my hand, but I liked it to hurt.' She smiled. Her eyes were soft and she spoke tenderly and gently. 'I've loved you ever since I came to Mopu.'

He had not seen her radiant and softened like this and in spite of himself he was touched. 'Are you sorry you came?' he asked.

'If I went away to-morrow I shouldn't see anything else as long as I lived,' she cried passionately. 'I wouldn't want to live if I went away from here.'

She looked suddenly startled. 'They'll send me away. Of course they will after this. They'll send me away at once.' She sprang up and came close to him, shaking his arm in her hands, and now her face was crafty and narrowed. 'You mustn't let *Them* get me.' She whispered: 'Don't tell *Them* where I am.' She looked back over her shoulder and round the room. 'They'll come after me. They'll send me away. They will unless you stop them.'

'I can't stop them,' he said.

'You must. You must take me away.'

'I can't.'

'You must. You don't know,' she cried violently. 'You don't know what *They* are.' She came still closer and now she whispered again: 'They watch me. She told them to watch me. She gave orders. Do you know why? She thinks I'm mad. I know she does. She and Sister Briony were whispering. They spy. They all spy on me, and *They* whisper, whisper, whisper about me. To-day they set the Ayah to spy on me, but I got away. I don't know how. I'm so strong, you see. I can do anything. Soon they'll come after me. She'll find out where I am. I'll tell you why. She's jealous. She's jealous of you and me, and I'll tell you a secret. She's mad. Quite mad and she knows that I know. That's why she says I'm mad, she's afraid. She wants me to make scenes. Sometimes I do and then she's glad. She wants me to go mad.'

'My dear. My dear, be quiet,' he said, taking her hands. 'It isn't like that. You know it isn't.'

Her hands clenched his. 'It is,' she cried. 'Take me away. Oh, take me away.'

'I can't,' he said, very pitifully.

She said violently: 'You say that because you love Sister Clodagh.'

'Of course I don't,' he said, shaking her hands. 'I don't love anybody. I don't love Sister Clodagh and she doesn't love me. She never would. She never could. I like her—and admire her in a way; she makes me very angry sometimes just as she does you. I like to talk to her. That's all there is to it with either of us.'

'Then why can't you take me away?'

'Because I couldn't think of such a thing, and I don't love you either.'

'Is it because I'm a nun?'

'Of course it is,' he answered. 'But if you weren't a nun I wouldn't love you.'

'Why don't you like me?'

'I do like you. I like you and I'm very sorry for you.'

'Then take me. I won't be any trouble. You needn't love me if only I can be with you.'

'I can't. You know I can't.'

'What's to become of me, then?' she cried. 'What can I do?'

'You must let me take you back.'

'I can never go back. Never!'

'Of course you can, you silly child,' he said carefully. 'No one will know. I'll say I found you wandering on the path—'

'They're all waiting for me, I tell you,' she cried. 'Do you think I can stand it any longer? Do you think I'm made of iron? *They* whisper, whisper, whisper, and the way *They* watch me! She sends Sister Briony after me with those doses of medicine and I'm afraid to touch them. I tell you I daren't take them, because,' she looked round again and tightened her hands, '*they're poisoned.* Do you wonder I'm afraid? I'm afraid all day and all night. At night I can't sleep because she comes and stands by my bed, so do you know what I do?' She laughed. 'I go and stand by hers, right over her while she's asleep, to see if she's afraid. She's trying—'

'Steady, steady, steady!' he said.

She stopped and looked at him wonderingly. 'But that's what I say to myself. That's what I say, isn't it?'

'Of course it is,' he said.

'You understand. You do understand,' she said, holding him. 'I have to say it. Things run away with me, but that's all. You understand?'

'Of course I understand,' he said, heartily, backing a little away from her. 'Now listen. You go back and I'll come up with you and explain everything to Sister Clodagh.'

'You'll take me away? Promise. You'll take me with you?'

'I promise I'll get you away.'

'You *do* understand?'

'I understand.'

She searched his face and turned away. 'You're only saying it,' she said in despair.

He was silent, and then he said: 'I'll come up with you, Sister, and explain.'

She turned her back on him and went to the door, looking at the path that went up in the sunlight and down at the River rolling by the orange trees below.

'No, let me go alone,' she said. For a moment she waited in the doorway and then went out and up the path.

After she had gone he sank into the chair and wiped his head and face with his handkerchief, and with shaking fingers lit his pipe. He bridled his pony and set out by the long River way to avoid passing her. Several times he stopped to watch her black figure with the dot of veil toiling up the path, until he was satisfied that she was going home.

He had meant to go up to the Convent at a gallop to warn Sister Clodagh, but he had to pass his own house first, and he was aching for a drink. He felt shocked with a feeling of repulsion mixed with a pity that he could not forget and he was a little disgusted with himself. He had done the easiest thing; he felt cheap and more than a little false. The more he felt that, the angrier he grew with Sister Clodagh.

His pony stopped by itself at his gate, the monkey chattered a welcome and the dogs stood up wagging and yawning. 'I damned well will have a drink first,' he said, throwing the reins on the pony's neck.

The more he drank the angrier he grew. That was fine. He wanted to be more angry than he had ever been in his life, before he went up and saw Sister Clodagh. He wanted to be so angry that this disgust of himself, that he could not help feeling, would be drowned.

Angrier 'n' angrier 'n' angrier.

By nightfall he was very drunk indeed.

31

'Ayah,' said Sister Clodagh, 'you're not to say a word of this to the other servants.'

'Oh no,' said Ayah. 'I'll keep it absolutely secret, and anyhow they all know.'

'To think this had to happen now,' said Sister Briony. 'Just now, on top of everything else.' She avoided Sister Clodagh's eye and with a burning face she said: 'You remember the things she said. You don't think she could have gone—after Mr Dean?'

'She was in the mood to do anything.'

'We mustn't forget she's mad.' Sister Briony twisted her hands. 'She doesn't know what she's doing. We mustn't lose sight of that.'

'Sister,' said Sister Clodagh, 'you can't ride down these hills as I can. I'm going to take Love and go down to the factory.'

'Go down there! You might meet coolies or anyone.'

'She may be there. Will you, meanwhile, go across to Mr Dean's bungalow?'

'A-alone?'

'You can take Sister Adela if you like, but I'd rather you didn't. For one thing, if we all go we'll be missed, and then there'll be a hubbub, and you know how she reacts to Mr Dean. You can take Ayah.'

'Dear goodness!' Sister Briony twisted her hands more fiercely. 'If she's there, what am I to do? What am I to say?'

'He'll help you, I'm sure. He's got no love for Sister Ruth.'

'He's got a terrible reputation,' wailed Sister Briony. Then she stopped and said: 'He's never shown it to us though, has he, now I come to think of it? He's always been very kind and sensible to me, and if I hadn't known about him, I should have called him a really good man though he's certainly unusual. A regular *Boheemian,* isn't he, Sister?'

'Bohemian,' said Sister Clodagh absently.

'That's what I said.'

'Then you're not afraid to go?'

'I'll go. But I can't get over this. I thought Sister Ruth was neurotic but I never dreamed of this. I blame myself for not having seen, I seem to have been so busy lately. Things have been too easy and pleasant for her here.' She paused and said: 'It's odd I should say that, because lately I thought you were almost too severe with her.'

'I wasn't severe enough.'

'But you were,' cried Sister Briony. 'Sometimes I felt you were driving her—' She broke off distressed. 'Oh, I shouldn't have said that to you now. I only meant that you seemed to have a peculiar effect on her and I think you should be careful when we find her. It's not your fault, they should only have given you tried Sisters for this outlandish place. Sisters whom you could trust in everything.'

'Isn't there always one thing for each of us, when we can't trust even ourselves?' answered Sister Clodagh bitterly. 'Now hurry, Sister. Take care that no one sees you go. I'm going to ring the bell for Vespers and I shall give out that you are in the infirmary with Sister Ruth.'

It was getting dark. There was no sign of anyone on the path as she rang the bell, but there was a light in the factory. After Vespers she went to the stables and ordered Love to be saddled. She walked down the path in the dusk with Jangbir leading the pony after her; every few minutes they stopped and called into the shadows, the pony lifting its head looking this way and that after their voices. When they reached the factory Jangbir went in, while she waited by the door. Love cropped the grass; there was no other sound but an occasional tread or a voice from inside.

'No one's there,' said Jangbir, 'but the watchmen and some women; they say the Young Lemini was here this afternoon with Dean Sahib.'

'Then he has taken her back. We shall find them at the house, I expect.' Sick with relief she mounted Love and cantered back up the hill with Jangbir holding on to the pony's tail. She stopped at the stables and walked up to the house.

There was no one there but Sister Honey and Sister Adela.

'We were wondering where you were,' said Sister Honey. 'Supper's ready. Where's Sister Briony?'

'I don't think she'll like to leave Sister Ruth,' said Sister Clodagh. 'I'll take a tray in to her afterwards. I'll go and see. You can start.'

Sister Briony was waiting in the office, her cloak huddled round her; her face, when she turned it to Sister Clodagh, was shocked and grey.

'Well?'

She shook her head.

'What did he say?'

'Sister, I—I think he was drunk.'

'But what did he say?'

'He was sitting on his verandah. He had whisky, there was a horrible smell of it and he looked so funny. She wasn't there and he wouldn't tell me if he'd seen her. He—he asked me to have a drink,' said Sister Briony with a rush of horror.

'What did you do?'

'I told him we were searching for her, and he—he tipped his chair back and waved his hand and said: "Search away. Don't mind me".'

'And did you?'

'The rooms were open, but I thought I'd better. I told him I didn't want to search but I thought it my duty to, and he laughed. Then I said that if he were a gentleman he'd help me look for her, and I—I can't tell you what he said then.' She drew a hurt shocked breath. 'Never in all my days, Sister!'

'I'll bring you a tray of supper to the infirmary,' said Sister Clodagh. 'You'll feel better when you've eaten and I'll tell them to make you a cup of tea for once. We can say it's for Sister Ruth. After Compline we'll organize a search.'

'Not till after Compline? Sister, suppose she's down by the River; there are bears and leopards there.'

'We have to get men and lights and you must rest. That will give the others time to—get to bed. You'll join us in chapel, Sister.'

'Jangbir, you must get men and lights.'

'If I can get them, Lemini.'

They were talking in the shadows beyond the chapel.

'Of course you can get them.'

'It's not easy,' said Jangbir. 'The Lemini knows,' he said, turning his head aside and speaking into the ground, 'that the people don't like to come here lately.'

'We must get them,' said Sister Clodagh. 'We have Nima and Toukay and the two house boys and the stable boy. Have the garden coolies gone?'

'At sunset, Lemini.'

'That's not enough then. We must get more.'

'We must go to Dean Sahib.'

'I don't—' began Sister Clodagh, then she said 'Go at once, Jangbir. If—if Dean Sahib is out get Phuba and tell him to bring men.'

Just before nine o'clock Jangbir knocked at the office window. 'Did you get anyone?'

'Phuba is here and his brother.' Phuba salaamed from the path. 'Dean Sahib is—'

'The Sahib is ill,' said Phuba in his deep voice. 'He shivers like this, and his head is going round and his stomach is full of pain and he has terrible fever. I have put him flat on the bed and covered him with all his blankets. My brother and I will come with you to search for the Snake-faced Lemini.'

'That makes eight men,' said Sister Clodagh. 'That's not enough. Jangbir, are you sure the men won't come? Not if you offer them double baksheesh?'

They conferred together on the path, then Jangbir came back to the window and said: 'We could ask the young General. He might make them come, but I don't think so.'

'No,' said Sister Clodagh at once, 'that's out of the question. We must go as we are. Ayah and Sister Briony must keep watch from the house and keep the fires in. We'll start after our Church is finished.'

Sister Clodagh attended to the chapel herself that night. She closed the windows and snuffed the candles, cutting off the wax drops that had fallen down their sides and pressing them into the candle head so that nothing would be wasted, and turned up the carpets for to-morrow's sweeping. Then realizing that she was only putting off the moment when she would have to go out into the darkness, she knelt down for a minute, and then picked up her cloak and went out. Sister Briony was waiting outside.

'You and Ayah will watch here. I'll go with the men. If she comes back ring the bell, very softly.'

'Don't you think Sister Adela should go with you?'

'Let's keep it to as few as possible, while we can.'

Sister Briony watched the lights going up the drive; the men carried flaring wood torches and lanterns; they went first above the house to the forest. 'We'll begin here and work downwards,' said Jangbir.

Phuba's young brother went ahead, bending low on the ground looking for signs on the path. On the fringes of the forest by a fire that streamed up into the branches sat the Sunnyasi. Even at the sudden invasion of men and lights he did not move; the men stopped to face him respectfully.

'Ask him if he's seen her?'

'Oh no, Lemini. We couldn't do that.'

'But, Jangbir, the Young Lemini may have hurt herself. Anything may have happened to her.'

Jangbir looked embarrassed, 'That would be a very little thing to him, Lemini. He wouldn't notice it.'

Far into the night the torches went backwards and forwards across the hill, down the short cut to the factory and down the long path to the River. Sister Clodagh had not been that way before; it was the way the procession had gone last autumn with the young General walking behind it. At the thought of him, her face hardened.

She thought then that he was to blame for it all; that if she had never seen him or let him in, this would not have happened. He was the beginning of it all, he had put these fan-tastic ideas into the Sisters' heads and had made them think that anything could happen. 'Look what you did to me,' she thought. 'If it hadn't been for you and your people I should never have thought of Con. You bewitched us all and I wish I had never set eyes on you.'

They were down by the River; they could hear it running in the darkness. The eight days' moon was hidden by clouds and they could not see the water except where the torches shone down the bank. They were deafened by it; they could not hear their own footsteps and their shouts were thrown back to them. It was easy to believe in Sister Briony's bears and leopards creeping up behind under the sound of the rushing water. 'If she went in here,' said Jangbir, 'we shall never get her. The currents would sweep her under and hold her for days.'

In the darkness Sister Clodagh was sick with dread. The River ran close by the factory. They had said that Sister Ruth had been there that afternoon. She would have heard it below her, running quickly to forgetfulness under the orange trees.

Sister Clodagh felt turned to ice as she stood there while the men went down the banks between the trees, casting the light of their torches over the water. Her hands and feet were ice cold, her wimple was pressing its band round her face, and her teeth were chattering.

What was the use of blaming Dilip Rai? Now she saw clearly that no one was to blame but herself. *'You're not the sort of person who'll admit you're wrong. Go before something happens. What can happen now I'm on my guard?'* She had deliberately stayed; and now the men were searching the River for Sister Ruth, the people stayed sullenly away from the Con-vent; Kanchi had gone, Dilip Rai had gone—even Mr Dean had failed them when they most wanted his help.

They went along the bank to the ford and she followed them; then they separated round the factory and turned up the hill. It was dark; the tea and the trees seemed breathing in the darkness, when they stopped to listen they could only hear that breathing, a sighing in the tea and their calls came back to them a dead echo.

Now the men went through the tea, making a cordon across the hill, throwing their torchlight low on the ground. There were cries and a leap of hope when an animal that had hidden there ran out. To the left they shouted that it was a leopard, but Nima saw it and called out that it was only a wild cat.

At the foot of the buttresses they paused, while the men came straggling in. They had seen nothing. It was two o'clock.

'In two or three hours it will be light,' said Jangbir. 'We'll come back then. We can't do any more now. We must wait till daylight.'

She had to agree, though she was appalled by the thought of day, when the light would come and nothing could be hidden. 'In four hours it will be daylight, we have four hours left.'

She told Sister Briony to go to bed. 'I'll keep watch. Someone must watch.'

'Shouldn't you let me stay?' said Sister Briony with an effort. 'Instead of you. I mean if she saw me alone, she might come to me more easily than to you, poor child.' Her voice broke; with a clumsy futile gesture, she turned away. 'It's so terrible when there's nothing we can do.'

From two to four, the hours faded slowly for Sister Clodagh. She could not bear to think of herself picked out on the hill by the lantern's light, and she put it away on the terrace and sat down on the horse-block to wait. Watching and straining her eyes, she was afraid. She was afraid of the dark and the wind that sounded like a voice, and the sense of something lurking and hiding behind her back and watching her. Sometimes she stood up suddenly, her heart beating, ready to fly to Sister Briony or down to the men's quarters, but she forced herself to sit down again and wait.

Towards four o'clock the dew fell, and she smelled a gust of sweetness from the roses and a paleness showed in the sky to the East. It was cold; the wetness was cold on her hands and she felt the skirt of her habit dragging round her ankles, and she had to go into the porch. The light spread, there were long lines of cloud in the sky and presently above them the outline of the snow peaks appeared, cold and hard as if they were made of iron; they turned from black to grey, to white, while the hills were still in darkness.

Then the forest came, mysteriously dark out of darkness, and the light moved down, turning the trees dark blue and green, and the terrace was full of a swimming light that was colourless and confusing. The sky had no colour, the earth was coloured only with dim toneless colour, swimming and indistinct. Then she looked up and saw that the Himalayas were showing in their full range, and were coloured in ash and orange and precious Chinese pink, deeper in the east, paler in the west.

The people called it 'the flowering of the snows'; and she thought that it was true, the mountain looked as if it flowered, stained with brilliant flowery pink; the spring of pink, of hill crocuses and almond trees and girlish cotton clothes. It seemed to come nearer, to spill across the valley and the terrace, to her feet.

It was light. Joseph came up to the house, gingerly skirting the bamboos as if he thought he might be pounced on, his eyes rolling as he passed under the trees as if he thought Sister

Ruth might drop on him there; he jumped nearly out of his skin when he saw Sister Clodagh.

'Put out the lantern,' she said. 'Tell Ayah to wake Sister Briony and tell her I'm in the chapel. It's morning.'

'It's morning, Lemini,' he agreed. 'Auntie's watch says it's nearly five.'

More than ever in the chapel she thought someone was watching her. She looked up sharply, but there was no one. Twice she got up from her knees and went to the door. She felt sincerely now that she could have prayed, but she could not settle. 'I'm tired and jumpy,' she told herself. Then she could have sworn she heard a noise, a drag like a wet skirt on the floor, but the room was empty.

Presently she got up from her knees and went into the side room. At the sink where they filled the vases, she washed her face and bathed her eyes. As she turned off the tap she whipped round at a noise; it was only the towel slithering off the rail; that was all, but as she bent to pick it up she was trembling.

At six o'clock she went out to ring the Angelus.

The light on the drive was blinding after the chapel; her strained eyes blinked, her skirts dragged at her as she went to the bell. The top of the horse-block and the steps were slippery with dew; she had to step up carefully, lifting her skirt, and balance carefully as she reached for the bell.

'Hail Mary, full of grace.' She searched for the River, winding below among the orange trees; the light in the gulf was miraculously clear and blue.

'Blessed art thou—' Her eyes were too tired to see the eagles. The specks of tea swam in the paler green; that sharp white just below was where they had been cutting the bamboos.

'Blessed is the Fruit of thy womb Jesus—' Fear came over her then, the fear of the night and her vigil, and the chapel.

There was someone behind her, holding her skirt on the block. Desperately she rang the bell.

A wet hand came over her shoulder, and an arm with a mad strength. The bell jerked with a clang. Her fingers tore at Sister Ruth's arms and her gripping hands, that were pushing and forcing her to the railings. She hung over them, balanced on the wet block, swaying above the gulf. Then her boot slipped on the stone and she fell heavily sideways, missing the railings and hitting the gravel beside the block.

As she fell she snatched at Sister Ruth.

She had a vision of her mad wet face against the sky, as she rocked on the slippery stone. She tried to catch at her habit to help her, but the stuff was slimy with wet and dirt. Then Sister Ruth seemed to fall into the sky with a scream, as she went over the railings.

Sister Clodagh pulled herself to her knees against the block. She could not stand, the fight was going round her in circles. Painfully, inch by inch, she dragged herself to the edge and forced her eyes to look down.

She had fallen where they had been cutting the bamboos. Her hand and veil were flung out curiously sideways. A spike had driven through her chest, holding her up with her head hanging down.

When they reached her she was dead.

32

The nuns kept watch in the chapel for two days and nights, kneeling two by two by the bier, but as soon as Pin Fong could make the coffin they buried Sister Ruth. The grave was dug at the foot of a tree on the hill above the drive, and every day they found it daubed with whitewash and a pot of milk or marigolds laid beside it.

'The people are afraid of the ghost, the bhût,' said Ayah. 'They say she has gone into the tree and no one will pass under it.'

The servants had been afraid of the body. They said that the bamboo spike had pierced the heart and that Sister Ruth would never rest. They went down from the kitchen to their quarters all together at night, the whites of Joseph's eyes rolling with fear.

Sister Clodagh could not discover who visited the grave; when the servants were questioned they were obstinately silent. It was more than ever strange because the people would not come near the Convent; they were far more afraid of the Sisters than the Sisters had ever been of them, but morning after morning there were offerings on the grave, fresh milk and butter and fresh bright flowers.

'I think it's horrible! Horrible!' sobbed Sister Honey. 'Sister Adela had turfed it so nicely and Pin Fong had made such a beautiful cross. It's horrible!'

That feeling of horror was everywhere. The servants were frightened and sullen, the nuns avoided speaking to them and one another, and yet they kept close together; they could not bear to be alone. The useless heavy days dragged on; the heart had even gone out of Sister Briony, she had not turned out a cupboard for days.

'It would be sheer waste of time,' she said. 'I know Sister Clodagh is only waiting for the letters to come with permission for us to go.'

Father Roberts wrote that he had tried to come to them. '*I managed to get on my pony,*' he wrote, '*but I was too weak to ride. None of you have been out of my thoughts and prayers. Though I cannot come to you, you are in my prayers.*'

He might have written 'I told you so.' Sister Clodagh was ashamed and abashed when she thought of the old sick priest and the things he might have said.

In these long sad days something strange was happening to Sister Clodagh. She thought it was as if she were born again; as if at the end of their time at Mopu had come the birth of a new Clodagh, a birth out of death. First there had been the days when she had dreamed and drifted, her life shaping itself to the old dreams of Con with the little sharpness of reminders from the young General and Mr Dean; then the days had become altogether sharp and she had striven with intensity and agony. Now all that had fallen away; she was defenceless and unencumbered as a new-born child. She had no pretences, no ambitions and no pride; she hardly had an identity.

She was not Sister Clodagh any longer, she was a new, not very certain Clodagh, and it seemed to her that she had new eyes and a new understanding.

She had written to Mother Dorothea; not in an outburst of grief and self-reproach, but telling it as simply as a child would have told it with none of the little bits left out. It began with the rest they had taken that first day in the forest and her thoughts as she turned the wine-cup in her fingers. They were all in it, everything was in it; the things she had thought and said and done, the things they had all thought and said and done; she had written them all out quite simply in her letter to Mother Dorothea and she sent the letter off and waited for Mother Dorothea's answer to come, telling her what to do and what her punishment would be. She had no doubt at all that they would be recalled and she knew what to expect for herself.

Sister Philippa had said it all before her, she was only treading out the path that the wise Sister had made. *'It will be a bad mark against you.' 'It's what I need.'* How well she understood that now.

But when Mother Dorothea's letter came, the colour flooded into her face and for the first time in all those days the tears came into her eyes. Her knees trembled so that she had to sit down.

'Dear, dear, Sister, don't let it upset you so,' cried Sister Briony who was with her. 'How can she judge when she didn't *feel* the circumstances, if you know what I mean? As soon as I see her I'll explain and she'll understand how wonderful you've been in this terrible time. I'm sure you didn't do yourself justice when you wrote. I know you blame yourself. She won't do that when she knows—'

Sister Clodagh shook her head. 'She doesn't—' she tried to say. 'It isn't like that—It's so *unexpected*. It's the surprise that's making me cry.'

It was the surprise. '*This is the first letter I have ever had from you that pleased me,*' wrote Mother Dorothea at the end of her letter. There were two letters; one officially recalling them, and this to Sister Clodagh herself. '*This is the first letter I have ever had from you that pleased me in spite of the terrible news it brought. In it I seem to find a new Clodagh, one whom I had long prayed to meet.*'

After a while she went into the Sisters and at once they looked at her with attention, for there was a subdued but certain happiness about her that seemed to give her wings. It was strange to see happiness again.

'Sisters,' she said, and she said it as if she truly meant them as her sisters, 'you can begin to pack.'

'At once?' asked Sister Honey.

'Why not?' said Sister Adela. 'There's nothing to keep us here.'

There was nothing. Nothing in the disused class-rooms and the empty dispensary and clinic and the house cut off from the outside world. Silently they began to pack.

They could not tell what the servants and people thought. They knew that at once the news had gone up to the village and down to the lines, "They are packing!' and they seemed to be watched by a hundred unseen eyes that counted every box, every little piece of their identity as they took it from the house and folded it away. No one came. Sometimes they thought they heard footsteps, rustlings, but it was only the wind; Sister Honey had a dream that Om escaped from his mother and came toddling up the path to her arms, but he changed into a little girl and ran away from her.

After that she had an idea of asking Joseph to bring Om secretly to say good-bye, but in the sense of that glowering watchfulness she did not dare. In the evenings she used to go up to the gate where the games of hopscotch had been played, and the children's voices seemed still to tremble on the air. There was no one there. It was the wind that tugged at her veil and the wind that stirred the branches of the trees and made them whisper. 'I *hate* this wind,' she said.

Sister Clodagh often came up and joined her there. They did not speak but looked down over the edge of the steps to where the coolie lines showed blank and still and shut away from them. 'It's as if they had built a wall between us,' sighed Sister Clodagh.

'If I went to the market what would they do?' she had asked Mr Dean.

'They wouldn't do anything,' he said, 'but it would be very embarrassing for them.'

'Yes, I suppose it would,' she said.

They thought Ayah was longing to be rid of them. 'You want us to go, don't you, Ayah?'

But Ayah answered, 'Yes and no.' For once she did not seem quite certain what she wanted. 'I thought I would be glad and so I am,' she said. 'I hoped you'd go and quickly too, and now I'm sorry. Yes, in a way I'm sorry. But I'll soon get over that,' she added cheerfully.

'I'm sure you will,' said Sister Clodagh. 'You'll have forgotten all about us, and if anyone speaks of us, you'll wonder who we were. You don't remember things for long here, do you?'

'Why should we?' asked Ayah. 'And yet,' she said, 'I remember my Srimati Devi here. I don't know why that is. You are better to me than she was, but she belongs here and you don't.'

It seemed that even the weather was waiting for them to go, waiting for them to go and for the rains to come. The sky was empty of clouds and the valley in the haze seemed empty below; the hills were curiously vague and pale, the whole panorama was colourless and the clouds were heavy in the north.

Still the rain held off. 'It would be better for us to go before it comes,' said Sister Briony. 'We don't want to travel in the first break of rain.'

'The garden will be ruined when it does come,' said Sister Adela, 'with all these half-built terraces. I can't think why Sister Philippa ever started them. I don't want to be here to see it. I hope it won't come before we go.'

'I don't think it will,' said Sister Clodagh, and she thought with a stab of pain of the deluge coming after they had gone to wipe these small traces of them away.

'It seems a long time to wait just to see the General,' said Sister Adela. 'We could have got safely to Darjeeling by now.'

But Sister Clodagh had told Mother Dorothea that to go without seeing him would be like running away, and now Sister Briony answered Sister Adela and said: 'We have to stay and apologize. It's the very least we can do.'

'It's so sad,' said Sister Honey, 'when you think how eagerly we came here and how hard we worked. It's so sad I can hardly bear it.'

'It's no use thinking of it like that,' said Sister Adela. 'Every Order has its failures. I don't say this couldn't have been avoided, but I expect we've all learnt something from it. Now we must look forward to trying again somewhere else.'

But Sister Honey was thinking of the children again, and their brown rosiness and the feeling of their hands pulling her and twitching her skirt. 'Lemini, Lemini, come.' If she shut her eyes she could hear them still. In spite of the baby, and she was sure she had broken her heart for him, in spite of the baby she could not bear to go.

Sister Briony looked at her store-room and cupboards and the rows of jam and jelly and pickles that she must leave behind, and at her neat dispensary; she had a lump in her throat that made it difficult to tell the servants what to do. She was so sorry to leave the servants that she did not know how to tell them so; she could only give them their orders very sorrowfully and gently; none of them would look at her directly, but hung about her standing first on one foot and then on the other.

'They are so honest and truthful,' she sighed. 'There isn't a single thing missing from the house. Even Kanchi brought that vase back.'

'Only because the young General made her,' said Sister Adela.

There was an uncomfortable silence. They preferred to forget about Kanchi and the young General.

He had come back on the afternoon of Sister Ruth's death. Sister Clodagh, sleepless and haggard, had to come out and see him. 'What do you want?' she asked tersely.

He looked a little dismayed, but he said: 'Sister, I have just heard the news about Sister Ruth. I'm most bitterly sorry.'

'Thank you,' said Sister Clodagh. 'Is there anything else?'

'You're angry with me?' he said in surprise. 'Please don't be angry.'

'General, I'm tired and very distressed. You haven't been near us for days, you haven't even sent us word that you weren't taking your lessons, and then you must choose this day of all days to come.'

'I didn't *choose* it,' he said, more surprised. 'I came at once as soon as I heard the news because it reminded me of you.'

'Did it really?'

'Yes,' he answered gravely. 'Sister, I have done a very wrong thing, but I didn't mean to do it. I don't mean to do anything wrong again, and I'm going to give up being clever and famous. I'm going to be exactly like my ancestors. I've been reading books about them; they were warriors and princes, Sister. They were modest and brave and polite and they never did anything cheating; that's why I came to you as soon as I was reminded, to tell you what I had done.'

'Must you tell me now?'

'Please, Sister.'

'Well, what have you done?' she asked wearily.

'Sister Clodagh, I have had Kanchi for a week. At least,' he corrected himself, 'I have had her for eight days, and as I don't want to do anything cheating, I have brought her back to ask you if I may have her for always.'

'Isn't it rather late to ask when she's been with you for a week, no, eight days, already?'

'Well, yes, it is rather. I know it would have been more polite to ask you first, but I took her before I had time to think of that. As soon as I *did* think of it,' he added virtuously, 'I brought her straight to you.'

'Where is she?'

'She wouldn't come in. I couldn't make her come in. She said she would until we were here, and then she said she wouldn't. She asked me to give you this—' he held out the little brass vase from the chapel. 'But I couldn't make her come in.'

'In that case it seems to be settled already. But you must go and see Mr Dean. He's responsible for her. I have her trunk and some money her uncle gave me as her dowry. If Mr Dean agrees, she had better have it.'

'But I'm not going to *marry* her,' said Dilip. 'You know I can't do that. My uncle would never allow it.'

'What is to become of her then?'

'I want her as a concubine,' he said. 'My ancestors had concubines. You see, my marriage will be arranged, and I shall not see my wife very much. She will not be very sympathetic. I wish you could see my wedding, Sister Clodagh. My ancestors had elephants and horses and a hundred bridesmaids dressed in violet and red. I shall have mine exactly like that.'

'And poor Kanchi is to be a concubine?'

'Yes. They all had concubines and the concubines all committed suttee when they died.'

'And will Kanchi have to commit suttee?'

'Oh no, that's old-fashioned now. I only told you that to show you how faithful and good they were. I'm sure Kanchi will be faithful and good too.'

'I'm sure she will,' said Sister Clodagh. 'But what about you?'

'Me?' he said and flushed. 'You are cross with me, Sister Clodagh.'

'I'm afraid I am. I'm sorry, General. I can't be polite any longer and I must ask you to go. I'm very tired and very sad.'

'Have I made you sad?' he asked quickly.

'A little,' she answered. 'Yes, you've made me sad and very disappointed. And now, General, please excuse me.'

'Then I may have Kanchi?'

'Kanchi doesn't belong to me. You must settle that with her and Mr Dean and your uncle. It can be nothing to do with us now.'

Without speaking he mounted his pony and turned it on the drive. He waved to her and his hand was above the tops of the rose trees: when he moved forward his waist was level with the clouds and over the crest of his pony's head the mountain reared into the sky, blue-white above the sparkling mane. She shut her eyes; when she opened them he was gone.

'What is going to happen here next?' Sister Briony had cried when Sister Clodagh told her. 'What will his uncle say?'

'We shall know soon enough. He must be back before the rains break.' They seemed to talk of nothing else but that, and now Sister Briony said again: 'Well, I hope he is. We don't want to travel in the first outbreak of rain.'

Mother Dorothea's letters came and went, and further letters came from Father Roberts; all the arrangements were made, the packing cases and heavy luggage had gone and still the General did not come. 'We shall get caught in it if we wait much longer,' said Sister Briony.

'It will be much cooler down below if it breaks before we get there,' said Sister Honey. 'Mother Dorothea said the heat had been terrible.'

'Dear Reverend Mother,' said Sister Briony. 'How nice it will be to see her again. She wrote such a kind and understanding letter to Sister Clodagh. She did not write as if she were angry, though of course she must have been very grieved.'

'All the same, I wonder where she'll send Sister Clodagh when we do get down,' said Sister Adela.

That was what Mr Dean asked her. 'What will they do with you?'

'I'll be sent to another Convent with less responsibility. I'll be superseded as Sister-in-Charge.'

'Will you be able to stomach that, a stiff-necked, obstinate creature like you? I'm sorry, I shouldn't have reminded you of that just now.'

'It's what I need,' she answered. 'I expect I'll have to remind myself a hundred times a day. I don't think, like the young General,' she smiled, 'that I'll change in a minute. I'll have my bhûts to remind me.'

'Well, you're leaving me with more than one,' he said.

She remembered how he had broken in on them when they were washing and dressing Sister Ruth's body in the chapel. He had looked so wild that she thought he was still drunk and she had driven him out and shut the doors behind her. 'You can't come in here,' she said. 'Haven't you done enough already?'

He was dirty and unshaved, his face was blotched and his eyes were bloodshot; he must have slept in his clothes, but he was not drunk. He looked haggard and ill, but he was perfectly sober.

'They only told me when they brought my tea this morning,' he said. 'Why didn't the fools wake me?'

'The fools couldn't wake you,' she said crisply.

'I got drunk,' he stared at her. 'I'm not surprised.'

He was shivering. The wind was still cold and he had no coat; he must have come straight out of bed and ridden hard, his pony was steaming on the drive. 'You'll get pneumonia if you stand here,' she said. 'Go and sit in the office and Ayah will bring you some coffee and I'll send the boy up to your pony. I want you to tell me what happened. We know Sister Ruth was with you yesterday. If you can wait, Sister Briony and I will come to you presently.'

Sister Briony did not want to go near him. 'After the way he spoke to me last night!' she said and her very skirts rustled with her perturbation. 'Sister, how *can* we speak to him again?'

'I honestly thought she was going back,' Mr Dean said; his cup and spoon rattled in the saucer. 'I watched her right up the hill and I'd every intention of coming after her to tell you what had happened. I did my best.'

They said nothing and he burst out: 'Why should I have done more? Why should you expect me to? I'm not infallible. You should have kept her under control. I warned you. Damn this coffee, it won't keep still.'

He had come back that afternoon to arrange that Pin Fong should make the coffin. He had arranged everything, and all the time he had scarcely spoken. His hat was laid on the table as he came in, he did not whistle and Sister Clodagh thought that he was as hostile as he had been on the first day she had met him. But each time Phuba saw her, he gave her a significant and reverent salaam. 'He's trying to show me that he, at any rate, is on our side,' she thought. He was not one of their servants, they had done nothing to make him stand apart from his people, and she thought that his courage and approval must have come from Mr Dean. It was Phuba and his salaams that gave her confidence to talk to him with their old friendliness in spite of his hostility.

'Have you any news of the General?' she asked him every day, and he always answered: 'Not yet.'

'You said you'd give us till the rains break,' she said one morning, looking out through the porch door to the hills. 'It looks as if we'll still be here when they do.'

'They haven't broken yet,' he answered.

The sky was blue and smooth as silk with a few shapes of floating clouds and the valley had a dim skein of hills covered with pink from the almond groves, and the honeysuckle was out. Already the roses were almost over; the snowline had shortened on the peaks; their flanks were bare and blue. It was past the middle of June.

'They must break soon,' he said, and Sister Clodagh sighed. It was then that he asked her: 'What will they do to you?'

'I'll be sent to another Convent,' and as she said, 'I'll have my bhûts to remind me,' there was a wistful edge to her voice that he had heard there before.

He bent his head to the case he was nailing and said gruffly: 'Well, you're leaving me with more than one.'

'If only we could go now,' she cried. 'It's this lingering I can't bear. Oh, when will we be able to go?'

He stood up and looked past her. Two grooms in violet puggarees were running down the drive.

'Here's your answer,' he said. 'Here comes the General now.'

Two men with trays had been waiting since the early morning in the porch. They had not explained themselves, but now they stood up and uncovered the presents they carried. They were heavy plated trays of nuts; big and little nuts, roasted, salted and plain, and some of them were tied with tinsel. 'Car-ry them in. Car-ry them in,' said the General as he rode up. 'Car-ry them in and divide them up. But the trays must be given back.'

'Dear goodness, what are we to do with them?' cried Sister Briony. 'There must be bags and bags of them here. How can we take them?'

'We must,' said Sister Honey. 'And we must take them away with us or he might find them in the cupboard after we've gone. I think he brought them to show us that he isn't angry with us. I think it was a very *touching* thing for him to do.'

That was just what the General had tried to tell them, but he was so polite that it was hard to come to the point. His face was a mask over his feelings and Sister Clodagh's heart began to beat nervously. They talked of the weather, and of course of the lateness of the rains. Then there was a silence; Colonel Pratap crossed one leg over the other and uncrossed it again, Sister Clodagh's fingers closed on the knot of her girdle, the General looked at his hat.

'Your Excellency,' said Sister Clodagh, 'I should like to tell you how sorry I am. I feel we have failed you in every way.'

That embarrassed him. 'You must not blame yourself for it. It was too much for you. It is too much for ev-er-y-one, though I don't un-der-stand why.'

'I have always been very bothered over this house,' he said, 'and I have always wanted to put it right. Why is it so important to me, can you tell me that?' Sister Clodagh did not answer, and he did not expect her to, for he went on: 'It is not the waste of money that makes me sad, though that is a pity, it is true, but I cannot bear this house to belong to me and be as worse as it is. Now it will be like that always. It is something that won't come right for me, Sis-ter Clo-dagh. It was right for my Father. He would have chuckled to think that it bothered me.'

He sighed as he sat on the chair looking at the hard gold stars on the walls, his hands with their pointed nails spread on his knees, the skirt of his achkan falling in a dove-grey loop between them. He sighed, and his eyes in their slits seemed to be looking at something he wanted very much. Then he gave it up and turned to her. 'Per-haps it will come right for Dilip,' he said.

'I blame myself for him too, very much,' she said. 'I'm very sorry about the young General, Excellency.'

'You must not mind for it, Sis-ter Clo-dagh. It was only to be ex-pec-ted. No, you must excuse *me* for the trouble he has caused you. He has al-ways been a trouble-some boy. Ev-er-y time I arranged any-thing for him the apple-cart was upset and noth-ing came of it. He is a sick-en-ing boy.'

There was another silence.

'You really have to go?' he pleaded.

'I'm sorry, General.'

He said slowly: 'I was glad when the Brothers came and then they went. I was more glad when you came, and now you are going too. I thought I was wise in trying la-dies, because I thought they might be more—more'—he waved his hand—'and now you are not; no, not at all. I am very sad for it, Sis-ter

Clo-dagh.' After a pause he added: 'I shall al-ways remember you, Sis-ter Clo-dagh.'

Suddenly she said, as she had said to Ayah: 'And I have a feeling that no one will remember. Soon you'll have forgotten our names and who we were. Nothing of us will be left but the empty buildings and the bhût from the grave. You'll have for-gotten whose grave it is, there'll be only a legend and a ghost.'

He was surprised at her vehemence. 'Is it because of the young Sis-ter who died,' he said. 'It is because of her that you can-not bear to stay. Yes. Yes. I un-der-stand.'

'It isn't only that—' she began. He waited for her to speak but she could not go on. Presently he said: 'The Brothers would not tell me ei-ther,' and sighed.

33

Is this the same place that we rested in before, do you think?'
said Sister Briony. 'It looks exactly the same.'

It might have been the very same; they sat on their saddles
resting as they had before, in the green shade of the trees. For
three hours they had ridden uphill, following Jangbir who
showed them the way. They rode in single file up the path with
Sister Clodagh at the back, and soon after they entered the
forest they passed the porters struggling Up the hill with their
loads and left them far behind. Now they rested, the green
light slipping over them, the sulphur butterflies flying past
them through the trees, and the grooms sat round a fire that
they had made and talked in whispers.

The Sisters said nothing. They had started out at eight,
after a silent breakfast. None of them seemed to have anything
to say as they ate; nor had they said much to the servants who
had given them their quiet salaams as they watched them
mount their ponies on the drive. 'Give salaams to the Silent
Lemini for me,' Nima said to Sister Clodagh, but the others
had not spoken.

Joseph had cried so much that his face was a black pulp; he clung to Sister Honey, kissing her foot as she put it in the stirrup, and she was crying too. Ayah watched them from the porch door; she stood there, her eyes watering in the wind, seeing them out; and they had the feeling that the minute they had gone, she would walk in and shut the door. Sister Clodagh thought that the shutting of that door would sound down the valley, up to the village and down to the lines, and that a sigh of relief would go up, and then the quiet would settle over it again and it would be gone for ever.

When they passed Sister Ruth's grave they rode silently by it. They had gone there with Sister Clodagh before breakfast and had thrown away a pot of curds, that they found, into the bushes. 'But there'll be no one to do that when we're gone,' sobbed Sister Honey.

'Mr Dean will see to it,' Sister Briony comforted her.

But he had said to Sister Clodagh: 'It's better for you to go and try and not to remember it. No one can stop them from doing their poojah to the grave.'

He had not come to see them off but had come up to them the night before. He had said an abrupt good-bye, and then turned back reluctantly and asked if there were anything else he could do to help them.

'There is one thing,' said Sister Clodagh. 'It's a thing I know you would rather not do.'

'I'll do it,' he said at once, without asking what it was that she wanted.

'Will you take care of the grave?'

He looked away from her and down at his hat, the old Feltie she knew so well. 'I'll try,' he said, and it was then he added: 'But it's best for you to go and try not to remember it. No one can stop them doing their poojah to the grave. I'll try all the same.' Then he said again: 'Good-bye, Sister Clodagh,' and went out to his pony.

That was the last sight she had of him, as he rode away sitting loosely in his saddle, his legs dangling, his shirt tails and his hat brim flapping against the summer sky, and Phuba running beside him at a steady jog trot, his pig-tail slapping his thighs as he ran.

There was no sign of Mr Dean that morning, but at the turn of the path was Phuba, and he had in his hand five compressed little buttonholes of flowers. The smell of them mingled with the smell of his dirty coat-sleeve as he gave one to each of them, but they were touched and smiled as they took them. 'Goodbye, Phuba. Salaam. Salaam,' they called, but he only grunted and stood back from the path to let them go by.

They did not take the short cut because Sister Briony was nervous of the ponies falling on the steps; they rode out through the gate posts and turned back to join the path again. As they turned they saw the house and terrace, the tea slopes and the valley and the River spread out below them. In the haze they looked already far away and the gulf seemed wide and spaceless, separating them from the hills.

'I wish we could have seen the snows,' said Sister Honey. 'They should have shown themselves for us this last time.'

There was no hint of them in the heavy line of clouds. Sister Clodagh's eyes went from one to another where the peaks were hidden, saying their names; when she came to the mountain Kanchenjunga she hesitated and stopped. Abruptly she turned her pony on the path.

At the top of the hill the Sunnyasi was sitting under his deodar tree.

'I don't believe he's moved since we were here,' said Sister Honey. 'I don't believe he's stirred. It's hardly human, is it?'

But they noticed that his disciples had spread sacks on the branches over his head, and someone had ingeniously tied an umbrella to a tripod of bamboos above his fire.

'He's all ready for the rain,' sniffed Sister Briony. 'It's wonderful how they can bother with him. What good is he to them?'

They rode past him into the forest. 'Seeing him like that,' said Sister Honey, 'makes you feel that it's not a moment since we all rode down the hill.' She sighed. 'And it's nearly a year.'

Now Jangbir came to them from the fire and said: 'The General Bahadur said you were to have some tea. He sends the tea with many many salaams.'

One of the grooms carried the tray and put it down on the ground in front of them. 'It's exactly the same as we had before,' cried Sister Honey. 'I've never forgotten those cups. Do you remember, Sister Ruth told us they were jade? She was always so clever about everything.'

She began to cry again. 'Sister, you're not to cry again.' But the sight of the cups was too much for her. It was not for Sister Ruth that she cried. She had only to shut her eyes and she could feel the little hands pulling her and the voices that cried, 'Come, Lemini. Come.'

They did not talk. Each one of them was closed in her thoughts. Sister Adela's face was intent and avid, as if she were picking over her impressions of the last few days, examining them and holding them up to the light; and from time to time she looked from one to another of the Sisters as if she were holding an examination of them too. Sister Briony's face wore a look of regretful sadness; then her lips moved and presently she took out her keys and counted them. 'Sister,' she said. 'Do you remember if I took out the key of the little black box? The one with the packets of tea for

Reverend Mother. It was under that roll of blankets. I can't think I *could* have been so careless—Ah, here it is. I thought I couldn't have been so forgetful.'

The groom brought round a plate of cakes; he handed one to each of them between his finger and thumb which he had wiped on a leaf, and put the plate down beside the tray. 'Have your tea,' he said kindly, and held the cups out to them.

Sister Adela said: 'What a ridiculous idea to have cups with no handles. You do nothing but burn your fingers.'

'They are meant for wine,' said Sister Clodagh, and Sister Adela sniffed.

'Well, the tea is quite good,' Sister Briony answered her. 'It was kind of the General to send it, particularly when you think of all the money he's wasted on us.'

Sister Clodagh sat with her tea in her hand, crumbling her cake. She was thinking of the road that went back and back the way they had come; through the forest and past the Sunnyasi, down the steps where the women had sat chattering and smoking their cigarettes and the coolies rested their baskets on the stones. There was Sister Ruth's grave under the tree; the people were afraid to pass under it down the empty drive to the porch. She thought of how the General had come there yesterday with his trays of tinselled nuts. Afterwards, as he mounted his pony to ride back to Canna Villa he had said: 'I shall not come here any more, Sis-ter Clo-dagh. It is good-bye for me too. I shall not come back again.'

The house was empty now; the corridors and rooms empty and silent except for the creaking and straining in the wind. Ayah could bawl as loudly as she wanted from the kitchen, and let her cooking smell in the rooms and bounce in at any door without knocking. The servants would have gone back to their homes and soon they would forget the Leminis except in tales to tell their children. In the village they would be glad and their lives would close over them, and this time they would be undisturbed to sleep and eat and work a little in the tea and orange groves, to drink on feast days and laugh and quarrel and go to market, to marry and get children and, when their time came, to die. The children would forget that they had ever been to school, except in some dark dream at the bottom of their minds; Samya and Maili and Jokiephul might remember that they had once made lace, but that was a long time ago; Sister Honey had packed the small red pillows in the work-box with their patterns still spread out unfinished between the bobbins.

She thought how Kanchi had been brought to them by Mr Dean. Little ripe sly Kanchi; last night her box and umbrella had been sent up to the General's house, but the money bag had gone to her uncle who had come and demanded it back.

Those yellow butterflies were the colour of the feathers in Mr Dean's hat. 'Are they from birds you've shot yourself?'

She turned the cup in her fingers. He was sitting on his verandah and with him were his dogs, his cockatoos, a mongoose, three cats and a monkey. All the trite phrases fitted him; blue eyes, chestnut dark hair, charming face; his skin was brown and smooth and his lips red like the Irish children she used to play with long ago.

That was when the first thought of Ireland had come to her; from Mr Dean. The road went on down below the terrace to the River where the young General Dilip Rai had gone, where she had dreamed of him and Con. Con was so white for a man, Dilip was dusky black, yet she had dreamed of them in one.

They were all startled by a sudden clap of thunder that went roaring down the hill.

'Dear goodness, we must hurry! That's the rain.'

The grooms sprang up, stamping the fire out. The Sisters rose stiffly, brushing leaves and moss from their habits.

Sister Clodagh put the cup back on the tray.

ABOUT THE AUTHOR

Rumer Godden (1907–1998) was the acclaimed author of over sixty works of fiction and nonfiction for adults and children. Born in England, she and her siblings grew up in Narayanganj, India, and she later spent many years living in Calcutta and Kashmir. Nine of her novels were made into films, including *Black Narcissus*; *The Greengage Summer*; and *The River*, which was filmed by Jean Renoir. Godden won the Whitbread Literary Award for children's literature in 1972, and in 1993 she was named an Officer of the Most Excellent Order of the British Empire. She died at the age of ninety in Dumfriesshire, UK.

RUMER GODDEN

FROM OPEN ROAD MEDIA

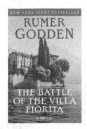

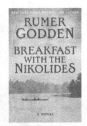

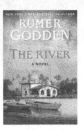

OPEN ROAD

INTEGRATED MEDIA

CPSIA information can be obtained
at www.ICGtesting.com
Printed in the USA
JSHW031353021220
9947JS00001B/2